NO PLACE TO HIDE

A Philippines Thriller
featuring Ash Carter

Murray Bailey

Three Daggers
An imprint of
Heritage Books, Cornwall

Chapter 1

The heat of Manila's old town was oppressive enough to make Satan himself call for ice. But it hadn't deterred the protesters. There were hundreds of them milling around and gathering in Roxas Park.

I was staying at the luxurious Manila Hotel, courtesy of the British-India steamship company. Long story, short: my boat from Singapore to Hong Kong had run into engine trouble. We'd diverted to the Philippines, limped into harbour and been told repairs would take three days.

While we waited, a group of first-class passengers did the tourist thing. We visited all the sites and spent most of a day around the old town with its war-damaged baroque cathedral, churches and fort.

American soldiers and sailors were ever present. Their base was at Subic Bay, around the coast, but Manila was where they came to wind down. They weren't interested in the architecture though. Manila had too many distractions for a young man with a pocket full of dollars.

The protesters carried hand-painted signs in Spanish and Tagalog, and I needed to ask what the trouble was about. Our guide wasn't sympathetic to their plight. With disdain, he called them villagers and ruffians; people-of-the-fields. He said they were moaning about the land reforms.

"But to prosper, we need bigger farms," he said. "Subsistence isn't the future."

That sounded like government propaganda. It was January 1954 and a few months earlier, a new president had been sworn in. He'd promised sweeping political changes and prosperity. He'd talked of anti-corruption, defeat of the rebels and self-reliance. By that, I was informed, he meant moving further away from their American financial heritage.

I was strolling on my own in the late afternoon when things started to happen. The police presence grew rapidly with new arrivals carrying long batons. Protestors began forming up into rough lines. I figured they would marching on City Hall. I heard that there had been protests outside the presidential palace earlier, but since he wasn't in residence, they'd reconvened here.

A skinny old man with leathery skin started shouting through a megaphone. His voice crackled with passion despite his frail appearance.

I didn't understand his words, but the throng rumbled its agreement. The march began.

I watched with going concern.

I'd served in British Palestine, at the end, during the troubles. More than six years in the Royal Military Police had taught me how to read a crowd. This one was upset more than angry. I saw frustration rather than aggression.

But the potential is always there in these circumstances, simmering beneath the surface. And the police looked nervous.

The front of the protestors passed me, the old man with the megaphone leading them. I should have moved away, but something made me watch. Before I knew it, I was on the edge of the crowd.

The police closed in. They blocked the road and everyone stopped. The shouting intensified, the placards thrust up and down.

Something in the air told me this situation was balanced on a knife edge. The protesters were passionate but peaceful. The police response seemed disproportionate—too many officers, too heavily equipped for what was essentially a gathering of aging farmers and their families.

And then the police line advanced, batons at the ready. Standard crowd control tactics but executed with an eagerness that raised the hairs on the back of my neck.

The two lines met.

A police officer grabbed the old man's arm, yanked away the megaphone.

That was the spark.

The crowd surged forward. I didn't see who struck first—a protester or police officer—but suddenly the street erupted. Batons rose and fell. People screamed. The disciplined police line fractured as officers pursued individuals. It wasn't crowd control anymore. It was a beating.

Training and instinct made me back away. I had no dog in this fight, no reason to get involved. I was an ex-pat, an ex-military cop with no standing here. Just another foreigner who should mind his own bloody business.

Then I saw her fall.

A woman in her fifties, gray-streaked hair coming loose from its bun as she stumbled to the ground yards in front of me. Nothing distinguished her from dozens of others except the police officer bearing down on her, baton raised high, his face contorted in a rictus of authorized violence.

She raised her arms in a futile gesture of protection. The baton began its downward arc.

I moved without thinking. Three quick strides and I was between them, my left arm raised to block the strike, my right hand extended toward the officer.

"Easy!" I shouted. "She's down! No threat!"

The baton connected with my forearm—a white-hot spike of pain followed by numbness. The officer looked shocked for a split second, then furious. His eyes narrowed, taking in my Western features, my obvious foreignness. That seemed to make him angrier.

He barked something at me. I ignored him.

Bending, I started to help the defenceless woman to her feet. The second blow caught me across the shoulders. The third might have cracked my skull if I hadn't dodged.

Then rough hands seized my arms. Someone kicked the back of my knees, driving me to the ground. My chin hit the ground hard enough to make my teeth clack together. The taste of blood filled my mouth.

"I'm not resisting," I managed to say before a knee pressed into my back, driving the air from my lungs.

Cuffs snapped onto my wrists. They yanked me upright with no regard for the natural movement range of human shoulders.

As two officers dragged me toward a waiting police van, I caught a glimpse of the woman. She'd scrambled away during the confusion. At least there was that.

She bowed her head in thanks.

Then I was pushed inside, standing, crammed with a dozen others.

The man who'd been forced in behind me said, "You know Luisa?" His voice was heavily accented. He had a weathered face and simple clothes. His lip was split. I could see others with worse injuries, blood pouring from head wounds, facial gashes and broken noses. "You saved her."

"I couldn't just stand by," I said.

The van doors slammed shut. No windows, no ventilation. The temperature instantly rose ten degrees. Someone retched in the corner. The smell of sweat, blood, and fear intensified.

"What brings an Englishman to interfere in Filipino politics?" the man asked.

The van lurched forward, throwing us against each other. People swore. Someone prayed. I concentrated on breathing through my mouth and taking inventory of my injuries. Bruised forearm. Bruised shoulders. Nothing broken, nothing permanent. I'd had worse.

"I wasn't interfering in politics. I was trying to stop an old woman from getting her skull cracked."

"Here, that *is* politics. They are stealing our land, our livelihood. Stand up to them and you are the enemy. As bad as the Huks."

The journey was short and we were herded into police cells; cattle pushed through a series of holding pens, each one more crowded and fetid than the last. No water. No toilet access. Questions were met with silence or casual backhand slaps from bored-looking officers.

At six foot two, I was a head taller than most. Perhaps that was the reason I was processed last in my group. Or maybe it was the colour of my skin.

It was two hours before I was pushed into a small office where a desk sergeant eyed me with undisguised contempt.

"Name," he demanded in accented English, not bothering to look up from his form.

"Ash Carter."

"Occupation."

"Tourist."

That made him look up and shake his head. He took in my appearance, the way I held myself. His eyes narrowed.

"Military?"

"Former. Royal Military Police. Special Investigations Branch."

"Military police." He said the words like they tasted bad. "You are not the first British MP here. Rank?"

"Captain."

I told him my old units and that I'd come from Singapore but served in British Palestine then Israel. For my address, I provided the Manila Hotel and explained I was enroute to Hong Kong.

Something shifted in his expression. Not respect, exactly. Recognition, perhaps. Or confirmation of a suspicion.

"You will leave tomorrow?"

"On the SS Empress of India."

"Be on that ship, Captain Carter. Do not stay. We have had enough trouble from that other *Special*

Investigations Branch MP." His voice was full of derision as he mentioned the division.

I said, "Who?"

He scribbled something on his form, ignoring my question. "Do you think Filipino police need British MPs telling us how to do our job?"

"No."

"You interfere with an arrest. You obstruct justice. You think because you are white, because you are former military police, that the rules are different for you?"

"No."

Each accusation was punctuated by stabbing his pen at the paper. I didn't elaborate. Experience had taught me that self-justification rarely improves these situations.

He continued the booking process, deliberately taking his time, making me stand there with my cuffed hands going numb while he filled out forms with exaggerated care.

"You are lucky," he said eventually. "No formal charges. Just make sure you are on that ship tomorrow."

I nodded.

Despite no charge, I was given a fine. It probably went straight into someone's pocket. But it wasn't much, and I was glad to be released. Hot, thirsty and in desperate need of a shower and clean clothes.

Outside, the night air never tasted so sweet. Too late for dinner at the hotel, so I picked up street food and water as I walked back.

After freshening up at the hotel and feeling human again, I sought the manager. Had he heard of a British MP in Manila?

"Of course. He is a famous bounty hunter—owns a bar now though."

"Do you know this man's name?"

"Of course."

He told me and I slapped my thigh. I never imagined I'd see Bill Wolfe again. And here he was in Manila.

Chapter 2

A taxi ride took me past Roxas Park, now eerily quiet, no sign of the earlier protest. We crossed the Pasig River and turned towards North Port. Before we got as far as the bay, the driver stopped outside a lower-end bar called the Crazy Bear. There was a green awning out front that had seen better days. Bars on Dewey Boulevard always had people spilling onto the street. This one didn't. Despite the rock and roll I could hear playing on a Juke Box, the whole thing looked sad and sorry for itself.

As I entered the bar, I heard a rowdy exchange—the kind of thing military police know all too well. I may have been an investigator, but I'd still been involved in plenty of incidents requiring the control, and sometimes arrest, of troublesome squaddies.

The bar area was dingy. There were twenty or so men inside, plus a couple of pretty girls perched on stools. In the corner to my right, next to the Juke Box, was an ugly stuffed grizzly bear wearing a hat. And toward the rear, there seemed to be the start of a squabble. It wasn't a full-scale fight. Just a bunch of men pushing and shoving. No one was rushing to join in, which was good. These things could quickly get out of hand.

I met the eye of the bartender. A young Filipino. He seemed relaxed, like this was an everyday occurrence. Part of the cost of doing business.

Then he shook his head, as though warning me not to get involved.

I wasn't planning to. All I wanted was information.

I closed in on the bartender.

"Bill Wolfe?" I shouted over the rising ruckus.

The man nodded at me and then at the scuffling group in the rear.

And that's when I spotted him. Wolfe was in the middle of it, tussling with three other men.

I closed in fast, just as the nearest one grabbed a barstool. As I intercepted his improvised weapon, he swivelled and glared at me. Then he took a swing with his free hand. I ducked the telegraphed punch and hit him with a combination that turned his legs to jelly.

I grabbed for the second man, but as he responded, Wolfe took the opportunity and threw a pile-driver of a punch into the guy's gut. Wolfe swivelled, caught the remaining man around the neck and pulled him into a headlock.

The next second, Wolfe had the last standing man under his other arm. Pounding toward the entrance, he pushed them out, one at a time, with a boot up the backside for luck.

The man I'd punched was dazed and compliant. I lugged him to the door. Wolfe met us and together we launched him into the street.

"I didn't need help," Wolfe growled. He walked away, and I figured he hadn't properly looked at me.

"Bill, it's me!"

Wolfe turned his bulk around slowly and eyed me. "I said, don't interfere or next time, I'll knock your block off as well!"

His words were slurred, and his bulging bloodshot eyes looked like fractured car taillights. He didn't recognize me.

My ex-colleague swung back and stomped away, leaving me staring after him in surprise. A pretty Filipina peeled away from the bar and trotted after him. He disappeared through a door at the back, and she closed it behind them.

Over the intervening years, I hadn't given Wolfe a great deal of thought. We weren't best mates, but I expected some recognition. I hadn't seen him for over three years. He looked rough, in need of a good barber, whereas I hadn't changed at all.

"Don't feel bad," the barman said as I approached him. "You know—or knew—him, right?"

I nodded.

"Friend?"

"Yes."

He shook his head. "Don't feel too bad. He's not been good with friends for a while now." He indicated the array of spirit bottles behind him. "So, what's your poison?"

"Coca Cola, please."

The young barman raised a critical brow before ducking below the counter and returning with a cold Coke bottle.

Based on the small number of clients, I figured the price would be high, but it wasn't. In fact, the drink was cheaper than I would have paid in Singapore.

"I don't drink," I explained, handing over the cash.

"And the boss drinks too much," he said.

I liked the young man. He looked under twenty and local. His accent was American, which was to be expected since most Filipinos spoke English because of the US presence. The tour guide had told us that the US acquired the islands after the Spanish-American War. Astounding how the trouble in Cuba had had major consequences halfway around the globe.

Changes had happened after the Second World War. The Philippines had been independent for close to eight years now. But the Americans were still here and playing an influential role.

The barman and I were nearly eye to eye, but based on the raised platform beneath his feet, I guessed he was five eight or nine. His shock of black hair, raised on one side, glinting blue eyes and ready smile, gave him a friendly, if quirky, air. Perfect for a salesman, I guessed, or someone who could manipulate others. Maybe that was just the cynic in me, but I figured I'd need to be careful around him. Trust had to be earned.

"Bill Wolfe's girlfriend?" I asked, nodding toward the door.

"One of many," he said.

"Is he often… drunk?"

"His opinion or mine?"

"Yours."

"Most of the time. But don't tell him I said so. We've had that argument once too often."

"And the fighting?" I asked.

"A few times a week. Especially US soldiers—arrogant ones. That's what sets him off. He chucked one out yesterday and today"—the bartender pointed to where they'd been fighting—"the man came back with a couple of buddies."

I said, "It'll take more than three grunts to beat Bill Wolfe."

"Never seen him lose—and I've worked here from the early days. Saw him man handle five of them once… although to be fair, they were pretty drunk as well."

I reached over the bar. "Ash Carter."

"Quick." He shook my hand.

"Your name? Or is that some kind of joke?"

He laughed. "Short for Quicksilver, although I confess it's not the name I was born with."

He served a couple of customers, then came back and asked how I knew the boss. I told him about being a military policeman in the Middle East. He was the sort of career soldier you can't see quitting. It was in his blood, and he was an exceptional investigator.

Wolfe had had a long-term, long-suffering girlfriend in Jerusalem. Long-suffering because Wolfe wasn't the marrying kind, but I got the impression she was. I think she not only wanted him to make an honest girl of her but also leave the country. Rosa had been a Christian— religious bystanders in the Arab-Israeli struggle. She'd survived through the last troubled years of the British Mandate, but things hadn't improved after we'd left. With his new role supporting British Intelligence, Rosa saw less of Wolfe. I think that's why he finally proposed. It had been early 1950 and, at first, all went well. But Rosa started to complain of intestinal trouble and within four months she was dead.

At the end, I wasn't seeing much of Wolfe, either. I was based in Tel Aviv, officially assigned to the embassy, whereas Wolfe travelled. And when he wasn't on the road, he was in Jerusalem with Rosa. One day he found me in Tel Aviv and said he'd had enough. He was off 'to find himself', which meant travelling rather than going back home.

We'd shaken hands. He'd patted me on the back and said, "Don't make a fuckin' mess without me, lad," then left. That was the last time I'd seen him.

Quick served another customer, then returned to chat again.

I said, "I heard he was a bounty hunter."

Quick laughed. "Once. Not really. Set up a private detective agency first."

"Did he?" I said, thinking of the one I'd briefly operated in Singapore.

Quick nodded. "He did that and hired me first as an assistant and then to run this—although he also doubled as the bouncer." He smiled. "The early days were good. This"—he waved a hand—"was a good investment for him. And he got some detective work, so he wasn't breathing down my neck the whole time—or upsetting the customers."

"So, has he stopped the detective work?"

"More's the shame."

Another customer came in. A regular who called out to Quick and got a beer.

The barman came back to me.

I said, "What went wrong? This is the quietest bar I've seen since arriving in Manila."

"It didn't use to be, but now… well you saw how the boss gets. Had some good friends here, but he drove them away. Drink and self-pity."

I shook my head. Bill Wolfe sounded like the shadow of the man I used to know. Yes, he was a tough guy, but he was also resilient. Rosa's death had knocked him for six, but he'd restarted his life. He'd bought a bar, employed staff, and set up a detective agency.

What the hell had gone wrong?

"How long has he been like this?"

"Over a year."

"I need to talk to him," I said.

"Not now. He'll be sleeping it off. A good fight usually does that to him."

"When?"

"Come back tomorrow morning. I'll keep him off the booze until then."

Chapter 3

Three days after limping into Manila harbour, the Empress of India set sail in the morning, but I wasn't on it. By 9 o'clock, I was outside Wolfe's bar. It was locked up tighter than a clamshell. I should have guessed I would be too early. Quick, the barman, arrived thirty minutes later and let me in.

He put on a pot of coffee. I'd intended to drink only water, but thought I'd better pay for something, so had a cup of the coffee when brewed.

Wolfe appeared almost an hour later, and I was relieved that I didn't have to listen to any more of Quick's life history or have him try and wheedle information out of me about past investigations.

"Carter!" Wolfe's voice bombed. "Well, bugger me sideways with a broomstick. I thought I'd dreamt you last night."

"I was here," I said, getting off my stool to meet him.

He pumped my hand, and I was reminded how large and meaty his fists were. If he had any technique, he could have given me a run for my money in the ring. As it was, Wolfe remained a brawler. We'd tussled once in confined conditions that suited his bulk.

I imagined most rowdy bar customers didn't need much encouragement to calm down or leave.

"What are you doing here?" he asked, pouring coffee into a pint mug and then gulping it down.

Quick left with a bucket and I heard him slopping down the stones outside the building. The bar didn't have a public toilet—few did. Each morning, the side streets were filled with the pungent smell of piss. "US Army water," the tour guide had called it.

The call of shopkeepers reached my ears, and I could smell freshly baked bread.

Wolfe asked, and I told him about leaving the army and Middle East and arriving in Singapore two years ago.

I concluded with: "Briefly worked for the government and liaison with the Army then set up a detective agency."

"I hope you were more successful than me," he said. "Why'd you leave Singapore?"

I wasn't ready to go into details. It was complicated.

"I thought you were more of a bounty hunter."

Wolfe grunted and shook his head. It seemed I'd get nothing more for now.

Quick returned with the empty bucket and a bag of pastries. He took one for himself and set the rest between us before topping up our coffee.

Wolfe devoured a pastry, sending flakes everywhere. Then he gulped at his coffee, belched and grinned.

"So, why *did* you leave Singapore, Carter? It sounded grand."

"Time to move on," I said laconically. "Was heading to Hong Kong, but fate brought me here. What about you? Why quit your detective agency? Despite your implication, Quick told me you'd been successful."

Wolfe shot a glance at the young man, and I read displeasure in his expression.

"Decided I wasn't cut out for it," my ex-colleague said after a pause.

Quick chimed in, "I was one of his first jobs."

I picked up on the unusual expression. The barman didn't say he'd been Wolfe's client, which didn't surprise me since I'd figured three years ago would have made Quick about sixteen at the time. A bit young for appointing a private detective, I would have thought.

Wolfe shook his head. "It wasn't a job. He's called Quicksilver because of his ability to pick pockets. And he chose the wrong pocket to pick."

Quick grinned. "And yet here I am. Seems to me it was precisely the right pocket to pick. The big guy fell for my charms."

"I felt sorry for you," Wolfe corrected. He looked at me. "What was I to do? I couldn't shoot the kid. The police would have just given him a flogging. And he'd have continued with his life of crime."

"Because I had to eat!" Quick added.

"He had to eat," Wolfe agreed. "So we came to an arrangement. He'd teach me Tagalog, and if he kept out of trouble, then I'd give him a job."

"I was his assistant detective," Quick said, grinning.

"He was my dogsbody," Wolfe corrected. "Until I realized he was also good behind the bar."

"Although you still can't speak Tagalog," Quick said with a cheeky grin. "Which is not down to my efforts."

The door at the back opened and the young woman from last night appeared, her hair dishevelled. She walked toward us but Wolfe waved her off. She left with a disappointed expression on her face.

I looked at Wolfe with a raised eyebrow. He glanced at her, back at me and shrugged.

Customers started to drift in, and I recognized faces from the night before.

Over the next few hours, Wolfe and I exchanged stories and he gave me a tour of his place—which only took a couple of minutes. He had a storeroom for the alcohol, a kitchen that he used personally and for washing the bar glasses. There was a large bedroom, and a smaller room used for storage and junk.

I also learned something he'd never told me before about almost getting killed in the King David Hotel bombing in Jerusalem. I wasn't surprised that he hadn't told me this before. He wasn't prone to sharing.

Despite working together in the past, we were very different. Sometimes the differences complimented each other. Other times, we weren't much of a team. Wolfe enjoyed working alone. He didn't like being responsible for others, and he had trouble communicating.

But he was exceptional at chasing down a lead and at interrogating suspects. Whereas I pieced puzzles together and could read people pretty well.

Wolfe was a go-get-em' kind of guy. He'd bulldoze in while I tended to analyse. Except for when women and children were involved, then… Well, I viewed myself as a risk-taker when necessary. Wolfe called me reckless.

By the end of the first evening together, he'd had six pints of beer. Wolfe was two years older than me but hadn't aged well, and I put this down to the booze. It had also added twenty pounds in weight to his belly, and he now tipped the scales at around fifteen stone.

The conversation waxed and waned as it does when you're comfortable in a friend's presence. However, he deflected every time I probed. He'd started the detective agency first and then the bar. They'd both been doing well, according to Quick, but something had happened. Something had killed his detective business and turned him into the alcoholic before me. And his subsequent actions were driving customers away. He was also killing his pub business. It had all the hallmarks of self-destructive behaviour.

He drank during the day and, as the booze took effect, he became less amiable. Quick put on the Juke Box and the evening crowd started to build. Wolfe made himself busy and I decided it was time to return to the Manila Hotel.

But then a striking woman entered the bar and from then everything changed.

Chapter 4

The Filipina, well-dressed in a suit and nice heels, entered the bar and looked around. Her eyes alighted on me and then Wolfe. She was tall, about five ten before the heels. I placed her to be mid-thirties. Too old to be one of Wolfe's girls, maybe not too old to be one of their mothers.

She approached me. "Are you Major William Wolfe?"

"Bill," I called, and he came over.

"I'm looking for the private detective. You are him— the Major?" She peered closely at Wolfe.

"Not anymore, love," Wolfe said.

"Please," she said, "I need your help."

"How did you find me?" Wolfe asked.

"My husband, Martin Gillie—the reporter for *the Times*. You remember?"

Wolfe nodded slowly. "Gillie... the *Manila Times*. Did that piece on me."

I looked a question at Wolfe.

He shook his head dismissively. "Bloody bounty hunting success."

Ah, the policeman had said bounty hunter. So far, Wolfe had avoided discussing it.

He raised a hand to stop me, in case I was about to question him now.

Mrs Gillie maintained an urgent expression on her face. "My husband is missing."

"All right," Wolfe said, sounding less than interested. He took a pull of the pint in his hand. "And?"

"Please, Mr Wolfe. I need you to find my husband."

Wolfe shook his head and walked away.

Her mouth opened in shock. After a second, she took a pace in his direction. I touched her arm and shook my head.

"He's not a private detective anymore."

She collapsed in a chair as though her leg muscles were suddenly jelly. Her head went into her hands.

I took a breath. A woman in distress. I can't help it. "I'm a private investigator," I said. "Tell me about your husband."

She looked up, her critical gaze set on me. The next few minutes were like a formal interview. She asked, and I gave her a summary of my experience, which seemed to satisfy her need.

"Good." She shook my hand as though we were meeting for the first time. "I am Rena Gillie. My husband, Martin, has gone missing," she said. "Two days ago. I know he's been working a case. He's an investigative journalist and sometimes—well, I'm sure you understand that it can be fraught with danger. I knew he was onto something because he was getting excited and making lots of enquires. Then he became irritable, and I think he was anxious. I've seen him like that before—when he's been warned off. But I know Martin. He won't give up. He won't back off." She stopped suddenly and asked for water. I think it was to buy time as she composed herself.

I left her while I got a glass from the bar. Returning, while she sipped her water, I clarified: "So, Martin's gone missing? Two days ago?"

She sighed. "Either in hiding or… or… worse."

I said, "You want me to find him? And if… something's happened?"

"If they've hurt him, you make them hang for it."

I couldn't promise that. My knowledge of the law in the Philippines was limited to something about land reforms. Even if it had been more extensive, all I could do was bring a culprit to justice.

"I can't guarantee that, Mrs Gillie," I said. "I can find your husband. What happens next is beyond my control."

She nodded and opened her purse. "Is a four hundred pesos a fair fee?"

I didn't know, but it sounded reasonable. I'd have done it for less.

She counted out two hundred. "Half now and half when you're successful. Isn't that how it works?"

"We can do that," I agreed. Normally, I would take a retainer to cover costs, but Mrs Gillie seemed comfortably off and keen to part with the cash. I guess she thought it would increase the likelihood of success. I'd be more motivated. I'd already been paid a chunk, so I'd better earn it.

It wasn't how I thought or operated, but who was I to complain? And I had a plan for the cash.

Then I took her to a table at the rear and gathered as much information from her as possible.

Wolfe shook his head at me after Mrs Gillie left.

She'd given me a small passport-sized photograph of her husband. He was forty-three, with short brown hair and brown eyes behind round glasses. He had the face of a schoolteacher with no outstanding features: average nose, average ears, no scars, no angular bone structure. Kindly, was the term that sprang to mind.

I held it out. "Recognize him?" I asked.

Wolfe ignored me. "Don't think I'm stupid. You're trying to involve me. There's no *we*, Ash. I'm out of this business for good. If you want to play private dick, then that's fine, but don't try pulling me down with you."

"I wasn't trying to," I lied.

The bar filled up. A US Navy frigate had docked at the port that afternoon and fifteen sailors came in. Then another twenty.

Wolfe tensed, and I exchanged concerned glances with Quick as my ex-colleague drank more.

I decided to stay.

We ejected a handful of rowdy army and navy kids, but nothing got out of hand and when Wolfe got too plastered, I helped him to bed. He'd not thrown a punch.

Quick was happy, and after I helped him clean up, we sat and talked. There was a put-you-up bed in the storerooms and I said, I'd kip there for the night.

Quick wouldn't tell me about Wolfe's last investigation, except that it had gone badly wrong. It had resulted in his downward spiral.

However, I did hear about Wolfe's money troubles and foray into bounty hunting.

Chapter 5

Quick said, "There's big money offered for information leading to the capture of wanted men. The problem is, very few bounty hunters are successful. It was early on, before I'd met him." Then Quick told me what he knew of the story.

The fugitive had been a collaborator during the war but had turned to the black market and gunrunning to the rebels—the Huks. Wolfe had used contacts in the British and American military. A radio message had been intercepted and Wolfe tracked the man by following money trails—bribes and supplies purchased from unreliable middlemen.

He finally cornered the fugitive in the north—a town called Dagupan—by posing as a buyer. "There was a chase and when he had him cornered, Wolfe let the man know that everyone he trusts is about to betray him, making it clear that escape is impossible. The fugitive just surrendered quietly."

I was impressed. Wolfe had applied psychological pressure rather than go in guns-blazing.

Then Quick couldn't restrain himself any longer. After he laughed, he said, "Of course not! The boss went up against four of them, all ex-military and heavily armed. He came out without a scratch and hogtied the fugitive."

Now that sounded more like the Bill Wolfe I knew.

"He needed him alive… for the reward," I said.

Quick shook his head. "Rewards are Dead or Alive."

Quick had a pile of newspaper clippings, he showed me.

"I cut these out hoping to get the boss interested again."

There were eight sheets. The banner of each showed a figure in pesos. An eye-wateringly large figure. The Reward. The police promised this in return for the capture or information leading to the capture of the criminal pictured below. As Quick had said, the money would be paid whether dead or alive.

"It's like something out of the Wild West," I said, bemused, reading another sentence referring to the 'price on a head'.

Flicking through the pile I saw most were rewards of 50 thousand. The highest was 130 thousand pesos.

"It's a lot of money for information," Quick said. "For 50 thousand you can buy a nice house in the Philippines plus a brand-new car."

"What's catch," I asked.

"According to Wolfe, two things." Quick used his fingers to count them off. "One, there's *no way* they'll pay for information alone. It's impossible to prove that your information led to the capture. That's what Wolfe says. And two, look at the descriptions of these guys. There's a photograph, but the biggest prize is for a man called Jesus."

I looked. Jesus was wanted for sedition, rebellion and murder. My mind flashed back to Israel, but this wasn't referring to the one who'd upset the Romans.

Quick said, "This Jesus is also known as Jessy, Holy, Payat and Pacig... and the description... it could be almost anyone."

Again, I checked. The paper provided Jesus's height and age. It said he had a light complexion and slender build. He had black hair and was well-groomed. The final nugget of information was that he smoked a pipe.

Quick laughed. "If I was him, I'd mess up my image— hair at least—and give up smoking, pronto!"

I looked at the other pages and shook my head. All the descriptions included a comment on their smoking habits. One, called Kidlat, even dared smoke cigars. The devil!

I realized that the cuttings came from two papers: *the Times* and *the Chronicle*: the big English-language newspapers. I wondered if the same adverts were placed in Tagalog and Spanish papers. Or maybe they just expected the English speakers to be bounty hunters. It was a very different approach in Malaya where flyers offering rewards were dropped in their millions from the skies. They were aimed at the general population because they were most likely in contact with the criminals and the lure of a reward would be considerable.

Quick said, "The boss bought the bar with the reward. The publicity—the interview with the Herald—also brought detective business."

"Until the case that went wrong," I said hoping it would lead to information about it. But Quick wasn't sharing.

"Afterwards, Wolfe not only stopped the private detective work, but started drinking more." Quick went on to say, that the more Wolfe drank, the less tolerant he became with his customers. It had been a vicious cycle because, as the bar's clientele shrank, so did the revenue. Money became tighter. He owed instalments for the property and had turned to a moneylender. Which then piled on the interest—at a substantial rate.

"I thought he'd made big money from the bounty hunting reward."

Quick shook his head. "They didn't pay it all. Made excuses and left the boss short."

The last thing Quick told me before I retired to my uncomfortable bed was that Wolfe probably had a month left before he'd go bust.

Tomorrow, I'd visit the *Manila Times* where Martin Gillie worked. I hoped they'd have answers they hadn't shared with his wife. She'd told me Gillie kept work and home life very separate. Never talked about his

23

investigations or interviews. But as I lay awake, listening to the distant sounds from the docks, I thought about Wolfe's situation and how I could help.

Chapter 6

"No," he groused. "I'm not taking fuckin' charity from you, Carter."

In the morning, I made Wolfe talk about his debt then offered to pay it off. "It's not charity," I said. "You can pay it back with interest… a fair rate of interest."

He softened, but still refused.

After he'd had two mugs of coffee, I tried a different approach.

"My client, Mrs Gillie, is paying four hundred pesos. Half upfront. Is that a reasonable fee? I have no idea…"

"A little generous, depending on your expenses," he said. "You sure you're doing this, Carter? Staying in the Philippines? Being a private detective here?"

"Yes, I'm sure."

He shook his head and sighed, unimpressed.

I said I'd rent his spare room. It needed a proper bed, but would save me money. The steamer company had covered the pricey Manila Hotel. I said I couldn't stay there.

He pointed out that it was a storeroom. I pointed out that there would be nothing to store if he went bust. He thought about it then accepted.

One step at a time.

"I'll also need an office—well, more of a base." In Singapore, I'd had a smart office and a grumpy secretary. Most of the time, it was a waste of money. I wasn't there much, and I seemed to spend a lot of effort either keeping

Madam Chau busy or in check. No, I didn't need anything swanky. I was happy with somewhere simple. Somewhere messages could be left for me and reliably passed on.

"Here," I concluded. "If you and Quick could take messages... and since I'm riding on your coattails, I'll pay you commission... if that's all right, rather than paying more rent?"

"There's no need—" he started to say before I cut him off.

"There's every need and I won't take no for an answer."

I dealt out a hundred pesos.

"Fifty per cent?" he scoffed. "That's too much."

"I was thinking it was twenty-five of the total," I said with a chuckle. "I'd keep the rest. You shouldn't lose out if I don't succeed."

"Ten."

"Twenty."

We settled on fifteen per cent of my total earnings, and I was happy.

Softly, softly, catchy monkey. I still needed him to talk about the last case that had gone wrong. Then my plan was to draw Wolfe back into the investigation business. Give him more challenge than how much he could drink in a night or how many GI Joes he could handle.

I showed him the photo again, because he probably couldn't remember it from last night. Wolfe confirmed it was the journalist who'd interviewed him. He didn't offer to tell me the story, and I didn't tell him I already knew about his bounty hunting success.

Yesterday evening, Mrs Gillie had told me she had no clue what her husband was working on or where he might be. I said, the starting point for finding people was always gathering the facts and getting a sense of the person from places like home and work.

I asked for her address to visit there. She'd dissuaded me. She insisted that the clues to his whereabouts would be in his research. He never brought work home, she assured me. The work would be at the *Manila Times* office.

For now, there was another reason for not wanting me in her home, she confessed. She had young children and didn't want to alarm them. They thought Daddy was away because of work. Someone turning up, looking like they were from the police—and she assured me I had the look—would both worry and scare them.

So, my first visit would be to the newspaper's offices, although I couldn't rule out a visit to the family home in the future.

As I travelled to the *Manila Times* building, I thought about Wolfe's problems. He'd slept alone last night, but Quick told me he had many casual women friends.

I'm no psychologist, but I suspected his relationship with women was another sign of his self-destructive behaviour.

Quick said Wolfe wouldn't talk about it with me, which was fine. I wasn't ready to talk about my own disastrous liaison and femme fatale.

Chapter 7

The *Manila Times* office was based in the business district adjacent to the old town. The elegant building had classic, Spanish-influenced architecture but had probably been reconstructed after the war. As I approached, I noticed large windows and a grand, welcoming entranceway. An impressive facade had the newspaper's name prominently displayed across it.

In the naturally lit foyer, there were two signs. One for staff to the left and, on the right, a sign read: Visitors. This took me to a reception desk and smiling faces.

Mrs Gillie hadn't known the name of her husband's boss, so I simply asked for the editor. It turned out that there were eleven editors and so I had to explain I wanted to speak to the one who employed Martin Gillie.

This caused the smiling faces to morph into expressions of doubt. They didn't explain why. A call was placed, and a few minutes later, a young man came down the stairs behind the reception desk.

He seemed friendly enough as he asked for my details. I followed my answers by showing my old SIB credentials. He studied them before handing my wallet back. I could see a hundred questions in his eyes, but instead of asking them, he told me to follow.

We left the calm of the reception and mounted curving stairs to the first floor. Once through the double doors, a barrage of noise assaulted me. The air was thick with the scent of ink and smoke accompanied by the constant clatter of typewriter keys. This was the heart of the operation, buzzing with activity. Desks were arranged in rows, with typewriters and telephones scattered across them. Cables hung down from the smoke-shrouded ceiling. People called out and darted between desks and the hum of conversation filled the air.

"This way," the young man said, leading me into the furthest office. Behind a cluttered desk was a white man in a crumpled suit. He set aside a pipe and looked at me through squinting eyes. I felt like asking if he was the notorious pipe-smoking Huk named Jesus. I suspect he wouldn't have appreciated the joke.

The panel on his door said he was G Edwards, the political editor.

"So, you're an investigator?" His accent was Australian, his voice thick from abuse. From the smell of the room, it was whisky as well as pipe tobacco.

"Ash Carter, formally captain with the Royal Military Police, Special Investigations Branch."

"Quite a mouthful!" The editor held out his hand, and I passed across my wallet.

Unlike the young man who'd brought me here, Edwards didn't scrutinize my credentials.

"So, what can I do for you Ash Carter, formally captain? What's this to do with the Royal Military Police?"

"Nothing to do with them," I said, showing my palms. "I've been asked to look into the disappearance of Martin Gillie."

"Hmm," the editor said. He picked up his pipe, put it to his lips and lit it.

"Can you help me?" I prompted when he didn't look like he'd respond.

The political editor removed the pipe and pointed the end at me.

"The police have beaten you to it."

I placed both hands on his desk and leaned forward. It drew a frown from the man. Maybe the papers on his desk were more organized than I first thought.

"The police have been here? Tell me what happened."

"They raided yesterday evening," he said. "Came bursting in looking for any information on Gillie. They boxed up all his things and went away again."

I cursed my decision last night. Wolfe didn't need a babysitter. If I'd come here straight away, I might have arrived before the police.

The editor took a long draw on his pipe before speaking again. "Suspected of sedition, they said. But it's all nonsense. I didn't see a warrant for his arrest, but they weren't answering questions. All they wanted was information about where he was hiding and evidence of his guilt."

"Do you know where he's hiding?"

"If I did, why would I tell you, Ash Carter, formerly Captain?"

"Because I might be able to help him."

"You try and help him, and you'll get yourself killed—imprisoned at least. That's the way justice works around here. Isn't it?" He shouted this, aiming at the expansive room behind me.

I doubted many heard him above the general hubbub of the newsroom, but a Filipina—about twenty, I guessed—poked her head in. His secretary, I presumed.

"Mr Edwards, sir, do you want something?" The exterior sound appeared to lessen. A few men turned to look our way.

"Just telling the private dick here that helping Gillie will get him banged up."

I saw a couple of nearby heads bob in agreement.

The editor continued: "They probably want to arrest Gillie because he was on to them." He took a swig from a mug on his desk, which I suspected contained whisky rather than tea.

I said, "So, there's not a chance that Martin Gillie is involved with the rebels?" I'd read newspaper articles. I'd learned about the Huk (short for Hukbalahap) Insurgency. They'd been the resistance against the Japanese during the occupation and now they rebelled against the Philippine government.

"I didn't say that," he said.

I decided to repeat my earlier question: "Do you know where Gillie might be hiding?"

The editor shook his head, then shouted a name. A man appeared, and I hoped he was about to give me some information. But he didn't. The editor fired some demands at him about columns and inches before looking back at me.

"Good day, Mr Carter."

I didn't move, which caused a flash of irritation to cross the editor's narrowed eyes.

Before he could speak, I asked, "Can you at least tell me what Gillie was working on?"

Edwards stood and glared. "No, I cannot!"

I wasn't intimidated.

He looked past me, then down and picked up some of his papers.

I still didn't budge.

"Look, Carter, I'm busy. Some of us have real work to do!"

I said, "Tell me something useful and then I'm gone."

He bristled. "I could have you bloody—" then he seemed to reconsider and sighed. He returned to his seat, all the fight gone out of him. "Look, Martin Gillie is an excellent investigative journalist. He's onto a number of things, but he keeps his cards close to his chest. But if the police suspect involvement with the communists... well, who knows? Maybe he's crossed over. But I doubt it. Sounds more like the sort of excuse the police would use." After a swig from the mug, the editor said more. "Gillie has missed deadlines, which isn't a good thing and is causing me grief. If he's dead already, then I'm sorry."

31

I thanked the editor for his time and let the young man, who'd brought me upstairs, take me back. I felt a hundred eyes watch me go, as though everyone in the room had overheard the conversation. Hardly any of them could have. Most had been too busy with their chatter and clatter.

As I left the building, I knew I'd not gained the concrete lead I'd hoped for. But I had learned something. Martin Gillie might be involved with the rebels. The police were looking for him, which meant he wasn't being held by them. That was something.

The police thought he was hiding. He might not be in hiding. He might be dead.

Chapter 8

The sun beat down relentlessly as I made my way to Manila's bustling southern port. If Martin Gillie was alive and had fled the country, then I might find evidence there.

The salty tang of the sea mingling with the scent of diesel fuel and fish. Towering cranes loomed overhead, their metal arms swaying and creaking in the breeze as cargo ships unloaded their precious freight onto the docks below.

I approached the shipping offices with determination, Martin Gillie's photo in my hand. The receptionist eyed me warily as I entered the offices of Compania Maritima. According to a poster behind her, it was the largest and oldest shipping company in the Philippines and operated passenger and cargo services across the archipelago as well as internationally.

"I'm looking for information about a man named Martin Gillie," I explained, my voice steady and authoritative. I held out his photograph. "He may have left Manila aboard one of your ships in the past three days. I need to see your manifests to confirm his passage."

The receptionist hesitated for a moment, clearly unsure of how to proceed. But as I fixed her with a steely gaze, she relented, directing me to speak with the shipping manager.

The manager had a weather-beaten face etched with lines of experience, and he wasn't as gullible as the receptionist. He asked about my authority. I showed him my credentials and explained I was acting privately for the man's wife.

"No warrant?" he asked.

"No, sir. He's missing and may be in trouble."

The manager gave me a watery glare for a few beats before nodding.

"Fine. Write the man's name down and I'll check for you."

I printed out Gillie's name and he disappeared with the paper.

Five minutes later, he returned, shaking his head.

I thanked him and continued along the quay. I stopped and spun round. A sixth sense. Was someone following me?

I saw plenty of people busy with their lives. The police interested me the most. One civil police officer crossing the street, looking natural. I also spotted two harbour policemen chatting to a dockhand. None of them seemed remotely interested in me—or appeared to have reacted to my turn.

A stranger in a strange land; I was just paranoid.

The next office I came to was the Philippine Steam Navigation Company. PSNC weren't as big as their giant neighbour, but they went further afield, according to the posters on their reception wall. As well as Asia, they had ships going to and from Australia and the US.

This time I immediately explained my urgency in this private matter and got an assistant manager who didn't ask for any credentials.

He listened intently, his brow furrowing with concern as he studied the photo. "We don't get to see faces, but I'll need to check our manifests," he said, his voice gruff but earnest. "It'll take some time, but I'll see what I can find."

I waited anxiously as the manager disappeared into his office, the minutes ticking by like hours.

When he returned, I again got a negative response.

"Who've you tried?" he asked.

"Just Compania Maritima, so far."

He nodded. "Do you know where Madrigal's office is?"

When I said I didn't, he told me who to ask for and directed me to a grimy old building on the fringe of the port.

Despite the appearance, this was another large passenger and cargo shipping company. An elderly Filipina answered to the name I'd been given and was concerned to help.

Rather than disappear to check manifests, she picked up the telephone and started calling people. She talked urgently and vigorously, and I sensed that she'd taken this task to heart, although I had no idea what she was saying.

"Bingo," she finally announced to me as she slammed the phone down with satisfaction.

"You've found him?"

"I've been calling all the others—I thought the international steamship companies the most likely: American President Lines, Nippon Yusen…" She proudly rattled off a list that would have been useful to know before I'd started my quest. Then she ended with: "Holland America Line. That's who you should talk to."

HAL's office looked more like a shop than the other buildings I'd been in. They had a bench-desk with three local members of staff and a white-skinned manager who had his own desk. They handled ticket sales, reservations and other passenger services, including concierge, luggage and accommodation booking.

I introduced myself and at the mention of Gillie's name, the manager said, "Hallo." He had a strong Dutch accent and firm handshake. "We had a call from Ligaya."

That was the helpful woman at Madrigal.

I held out the photograph. "You have information on Martin Gillie?"

The Dutchman took it and then passed it over to one of the girls at the bench.

She nodded. "Yes, that's him."

The Dutchman said, "He came in here two days ago asking about a ticket to Hong Kong. He seemed nervous, yes?" He addressed this question to the girl.

"Yes," she confirmed. "And when he said his name, I thought I recognized it. 'Martin Gillie the reporter?' I said." She paused.

"Go on," the manager prompted.

"Well, that's when it got peculiar. Mr Gillie shook his head, looked panicked, mumbled something and then hurried away."

My heart leaped at the revelation, a surge of adrenaline coursing through my veins. Gillie had been here looking for passage off the island.

Thanking the staff profusely, I left the office. Gillie was out there somewhere. The simple confirmation that he'd been sighted, gave me encouragement. I tracked many people in the past, and all I needed was a start. A would lead to B which would eventually lead me to my quarry.

As I stood on the street, wondering where this lead took me, I again sensed someone watching.

I set out once again into the bustling streets of Manila, determined to identify who was following me.

Chapter 9

Before midday, I returned to the Crazy Bear bar, sheltering from the relentless sun.

I told Wolfe about my morning, and he only paid attention when I told him I had a constant sense of being followed.

"You're being jumpy," he said. "Took me a while to get used to the culture here. They're more open, less inhibited. The girls in particular. I'm sure you've noticed."

Yes, I had, especially the number of girls Wolfe bedded. No benefit in raising the issue now. One thing at a time.

"The eye-contact and the following," he continued. "It's something you get used to. Tall good-looking white man—and I'm referring to myself here—gets you a lot of attention."

We were interrupted by Mrs Gillie entering the bar. She marched over to my table.

"Have you made progress?" she asked urgently.

Ordinarily, I might have been irritated by this. She'd only just commissioned my services and a day later was here pressing for an update. However, I understood. She was anxious about her missing husband.

"I've learned the police raided his place of work and took everything."

"The police?" Her face froze.

"Have they visited your home yet, Rena?" After what she'd said about not worrying her children, I was concerned about heavy-handed police ransacking her home.

"No. Oh my goodness. The police!" She panted and sucked in air. "What do they…?"

"He's suspected of sedition, apparently."

Mrs Gillie shook her head. "Not a chance! Not a chance!"

"I'm sure you're right. I—"

"You'll clear his name? Please, Captain Carter, say you'll clear his name."

"I'll do my best." I'd decided that I wouldn't mention the possibility that he was already dead. Yesterday, when I was thinking I'd find him dead or alive, I'd hesitated. She'd assumed I was going to say someone might have hurt him. From her expression, I didn't think the idea that he was dead had even crossed her mind.

She took a calming breath and nodded. "Good. Thank you. I'm sure what he was working on has the answer. You must find out!"

"The police took everything from the office." I'd already effectively said this, but suspected it hadn't all sunk in.

"No. He'll have…" she paused, thinking. "He's in hiding, so he must have known. He'll have either hidden the important stuff or have it with him."

It made sense. Again, providing he wasn't dead.

I said, "Does your husband know anyone in Hong Kong?"

"Hong Kong?"

"Two days ago, he called in at the Holland America Line ticket office."

"Two days ago?" She leaned forward, a flash of eagerness in her dark eyes. "And bought a ticket for Hong Kong?"

"Tried to buy a ticket," I explained. "He left in a hurry when the clerk recognized his name."

"Really two days?"

"Yes. That's what they told me."

"Then it's since I saw him." She hadn't needed to explain this, but I could see she was struggling with everything, and the good news took time to register.

"Did he give you any indication he was considering Hong Kong?"

"No." She frowned. "Do you think he's there?"

"It's a possibility," I said. But I thought the odds were long. He was trying to leave in a hurry, it seemed. He'd been recognized and changed his plans. Why hadn't he told his wife what he was doing? He was anxious and possibly in hiding. Which told me he was concerned for her safety. Maybe the safety of the whole family. Better that they didn't know anything.

"Do you have somewhere *you* can go?" I asked gently. I didn't want to cause alarm, but Rena Gillie could be in danger.

"We don't know anyone in Hong Kong," she said. "No one I can think of, anyway. You think he's gone to Hong Kong?"

She was focused more on my original question than her situation.

I beckoned Quick over and ordered us both tea. A break would reset the conversation. While we waited, I asked about her family, about the two children. She seemed less keen to talk about them than to tell me she'd met Martin a week after he'd arrived in the Philippines. She'd been working for a construction company. He'd come into the office, writing an article about the reconstruction of the city following the war. They'd hit it off immediately and been married within a year.

From his photograph and her good looks, I'd say they were a mismatch, but love is blind. Allegedly.

I brought her back to the subject: "Yesterday you said he'd never been missing before."

"He's always told me where he's going," she said. "Would never leave the islands without telling me." She shook her head at the thought. "Never."

"He's worried," I said. "Has he ever told you of his fears?"

"No. As I said yesterday, he doesn't mix work with family. At home, he is the perfect husband and father. He's not the reporter. He doesn't talk work. He never mentions worries."

"But a wife knows?" I prompted.

She narrowed her eyes and wobbled her head, lost in her thoughts for a moment.

"Yes, he has been preoccupied. But if he's been scared enough to run away, why not tell me?"

"He didn't say, because you're better off not knowing."

"What does that mean, Captain?"

"It means you might be in danger. He was protecting you and the children by leaving. No one can force you to tell them what you don't know."

She studied me hard, took a sip of tea, then nodded. "That makes sense. I can go—"

I interrupted. "Don't tell me your plans either. Don't tell anyone. Just pack your things and leave."

"Has Martin gone abroad?"

"I'll keep enquiring," I said. "Does he have a passport in another name?"

She frowned. "No, why would he?"

Gillie had been recognized once. If he did leave the country, then he'd change his name and appearance. That's what I would have done. But getting an alternative passport wasn't easy. Not a convincing one in a hurry— and my sense was that Martin Gillie had disappeared in a haste. Without papers, I would have taken a short hop somewhere. Then used my real name and passport for the long-haul.

She asked if I'd considered someone might be hiding him. I had.

"Do you have any suggestions… any names for me?" I asked.

She shrugged. "Someone from *the Times*? He wouldn't tell me…" She paused for thought. "He mentioned a name a few times… Let me see… Tappo or Topo. Although I couldn't tell you anything about them. Perhaps you could look for that person?"

I wrote the possible name in my notebook, to demonstrate I'd taken the suggestion seriously.

She asked what my next move would be. Again, I could have been irritated by the pressure, but I had an answer. I'd continue my investigation into whether he'd caught a boat off the island. I'd also go back to the newspaper's offices. They had archives that would include the articles Martin Gillie had written. I had a sense that his abrupt disappearance had been triggered by something he was working on.

What I didn't tell her was the reason why I'd come back to the bar. It wasn't just because of the heat. I wanted to talk to Wolfe. He had contacts, and I was sure he could help. I was missing a piece of the puzzle.

Chapter 10

"I'm not getting involved," Wolfe announced when I approached him.

"Don't then," I said. "Just give me some guidance."

He looked at me quizzically, probably suspecting I was about to trick him somehow. Maybe I would, but that could come later.

I told him about the police raid on the newspaper's offices.

When I finished Wolfe said, "Sedition doesn't sound good, Ash. If he's involved with the Huk—"

"I don't think he is."

"Is that conclusion formed on the back of a fact-based analysis?"

I shook my head. He knew it wasn't. There wasn't enough information. A man was missing, and his wife and family were worried.

"His editor thought it was nonsense."

"Your man wouldn't be the first newspaper reporter supporting terrorism," Wolfe said. Of course, he was right. We'd seen it in Mandatory Palestine and, later, in Israel. Newspaper reporters had to get close to the action. Sometimes they outright sympathized with the cause, sometimes they were converted by what they saw, sometimes they just wanted to present a more balanced view.

I said, "You're right, I should keep an open mind."

"You should."

"But I still need your help. The police took Gillie's files—what he was working on. Whether he's guilty or not, I'm committed to finding him."

"And you believe those files might contain a clue?"

"His wife does and… it could be my biggest lead."

Wolfe took a long, weary breath. "So, what's this help you want from me?"

"A contact."

His eyes narrowed.

I said, "You were a private detective here. You must have had liaison with the police in the Philippines."

He laughed.

"What's so funny?"

"You are. You had police liaison officers in Singapore, didn't you?" He didn't wait for a response. Of course, I had a liaison. I'd been working for the government and supporting the military police. I'd been official, and I'd had excellent lines of communication with all sectors. If I needed information, I'd get it. Later, I wasn't official, but I could still count on my contacts: my friends in the military police and my old liaison officer, Inspector Singh, in the civil force. It worked well for me in private practice, and I often got the inside track on information.

When Wolfe and I had worked together in Mandatory Palestine we'd been part of the establishment. After the British had left and the new state of Israel formed, we still got support. Wolfe had a wide network of contacts, and I was with the embassy and had friends in the police. If we needed information, we got it.

Eventually, he said, "Here, the police tolerate private detectives but don't support them. They like us to do the dirty work, like bounty hunting, but they'll happily shoot us given an excuse."

"Is that what you found during your last case."

He swallowed. "I'm not talking about that."

"No, you aren't," I said pointedly. "But it would be another reason to quit."

"It's tough out here," Wolfe mused, his voice tinged with resignation. "Without the right connections, it's like swimming against the tide. As you'll soon discover."

"What about the other private detectives?"

He forced a smile. "Aren't any. At least none who we'd recognize as experienced investigators. Lots of unsuccessful bounty hunters, though."

I said, "Quick mentioned there were others."

Wolfe shook his head. "They're basically bodyguards and henchmen."

"Surely, there's someone you can approach."

He scratched at his beard. "I can try. No promises, but there is someone. What do you want to know?"

"Whether the police have any evidence against Martin Gillie, for starters. But most importantly, I'm keen to know what they found at *the Times*. Perfect world—"

"Perfect world, you'd want his files," Wolfe scoffed. "There's zero chance of that. Like I say, I'll try. The police force is large, and it could well be that my boy knows nothing at all. One obvious question: Who did the raid? Was it the civil police or the National Bureau of Investigation?"

"Who? The newspaper editor just said police."

"The NBI are responsible for handling major criminal investigations, but it might not have been them either." His voice lacked enthusiasm, and I figured he was telling me this was no easy task. "Then there's the Constabulary, but we're talking about an operation in the city, so it won't have been them. And there's the CIS—the Criminal Investigation Service. They also focus on criminal investigations including organized crime and smuggling. But since you mentioned sedition, then it could have been the Military Intelligence Service. They have a unit specifically dedicated to matters of national security and counter-insurgency."

I briefly flashed back to my near-death clash with a man from Shebak, the newly formed military intelligence group in Israel.

Wolfe saw my concern. "Let's hope not, eh?"

"The editor said 'police', so we should be all right." He nodded, and I pressed on: "I have a second request."

"Oh God!"

I raised a placatory hand. "This one's easier. I could do with some help on the legwork."

He shook his head angrily. "No! I said—"

"Your man, Quick," I interrupted. "Could I borrow him for a few hours?"

Wolfe shot his barman a glance. "You know his background?"

"He told me."

"Really?" Wolfe raised an eyebrow. "He told you about his criminal past?"

"A pickpocket. You obviously trust him, and I'm hardly asking him to guard the treasury."

Wolfe shook his head.

"I'm paying you fifteen per cent," I reminded him.

"To take messages, not pound the streets. He's my barman and—"

"I'll pay by the hour and only use him at quiet times. He'll always be back before seven. It's never busy until then."

Wolfe sighed. "You're a bloody pain in the backside, you know that, Carter?"

After agreeing the rate, I spoke with Quick, who was keen to be involved. We went out for a couple of hours, working the docks. Then came back in time for his shift behind the bar. Business was picking up because Wolfe wasn't driving customers away.

Most evenings, I planned to roll up my sleeves and help at the bar.

But not tonight.

Tonight, I had an appointment at the boxing club.

Chapter 11

I'd already found the YMCA gymnasium, which was good for morning exercise. But I'd also been directed to the Olympic Boxing Club and an unsmiling coach called Happy Jose.

My first time there, I spent two hours working out. I had no idea boxing was so popular in the Philippines and found it harder than expected. I'd planned general exercise, time with the bags and maybe a little practise in the ring. Instead, I found myself encouraged into the ring. It should have just been basic sparring, but my opponents were definitely point-scoring. They were good and impressively fit, but my superior reach was too much for the five challengers I'd faced. Luckily for me, they'd all been smaller guys. More had wanted to spar with me, but I gracefully retired before exhaustion resulted in a defeat.

Afterwards, Happy Jose said he'd put me on the card for Fight Night. I agreed.

Quick nodded appreciatively as we tidied the bar at the end of the evening. He told me about the illustrious history of Filipino boxers and I decided I'd had a lucky escape. I was a mere amateur, whereas the Olympic Boxing Club counted world champions in its roll of honours. I regretted not checking with Happy Jose that I wouldn't be up against professionals on Fight Night.

★

In the morning, I was awoken by Wolfe cursing and thrashing about in his room.

The skin below my left eye stung and I took a look. A little scratch and swelling, which looked worse than it was. Probably caused by a glove's laces rather than a punch itself. I stretched a few aching muscles, and was just in time to see Wolfe run naked through the bar and out of the door.

"Fuckin' bitch!" he shouted when he came back.

"Who?"

"Chastity."

"Who?" I asked again.

"The fuckin' girl I had in my bed last night. Took all my fuckin' money!" He thumped the nearest table causing it to collapse.

Quick walked in and raised his eyebrows presumably because Wolfe was standing naked in the middle of the bar. Despite the volume of beer he put away each night, he still cut a good figure.

He raised his chin to the young barman.

"Where does she live?"

"Who?"

"The fuckin' girl I was with. Said her name was Chastity."

Quick laughed then abruptly stopped. "Sorry, boss. But the name…"

"Ironic," I said.

Wolfe ignored me. "So, where does she live? She's stolen a few hundred quid."

Quick shook his head. "Sorry, never seen her before last night. Thought you knew her."

Wolfe dashed another table across the floor. "Damn!" He stomped back to his room.

I righted the tossed table and Quick tried to fix the broken one.

"What happened to you?" he asked me. I tentatively touched the scratch below my left eye.

"Helped a granny cross the road. Turns out her shopping bags were a lot tougher than they looked."

"Right," he said, in no mood for humour. "Let's hope you're better at investigative work than you are carrying shopping then."

I got dressed and joined Quick in cleaning up the bar, preparing for the day.

"What happened last night?" I asked.

"What? You don't know?" Then he understood. "Ah, you're not talking about your eye. You mean with Wolfe."

"Yes." Wolfe had returned to his room, and I could hear him snoring.

"You weren't around. He was back to his old ways, drinking too much. Luckily, there wasn't a brawl, but looks like he picked the wrong girl to sleep with."

"Has it happened before?"

"A few times. He doesn't have much..." Quick struggled to find the right word.

"He's not fussy?"

"That's it! Some of the girls are too easy. Some of them expect payment. Some just take payment—or maybe in Chastity's..." he laughed at the name again. "Maybe in this girl's case, she saw an opportunity and took it. Can't blame her for that."

We got into a debate about the rights and wrongs. Quick had a lot of sympathy for the girls since he'd been a pickpocket. He knew how tough it was without a regular income.

In the end, we agreed on having different perspectives but found common ground in agreeing to watch out for Wolfe. Quick would be wary of any new girls looking to bed him.

He said he'd also keep a lookout for me too.

"Why?" I wondered.

He chuckled. "In case of grannies with shopping bags."

Chapter 12

I wasn't making much progress on finding Martin Gillie. I knew the police wanted him for sedition and he'd considered catching a steamer to Hong Kong.

I had a reasonable record when it came to finding people, but in truth, most people missing for more than a week were never found. And we were getting close to a week since Gillie had disappeared.

In the army, I'd tracked down AWOL soldiers. The majority didn't plan on disappearing. They left in a hurry to deal with a personal issue. The true deserters—the men who didn't want to be found—were much less likely to be located. At the end of the British Mandate for Palestine, there had been two hundred deserters. Less than ten per cent had been subsequently located. Low numbers, but they were unusual times and exceptional circumstances.

What I gathered from the Wanted posters in the Philippines, criminals were hard to locate as well. If someone wanted to stay hidden, they could.

And if they were already dead...

Well, I wasn't ready to assume the worse although I knew the likelihood of finding a body wasn't helped by the amount of surrounding water. The country was comprised of thousands of islands. Easier to dump a body in the sea or river than bury it.

And once out to sea, I figured chances of recovery were poor.

I'd recall that much later, but for now, I was assuming Martin Gillie was alive and hiding. It didn't look like he'd taken a boat from Manila. My working assumption was that he'd intended to flee to Hong Kong then changed his mind after being recognized. He could be traced. It didn't mean he hadn't left though. I couldn't rule out a ferry to one of the islands in the archipelago. Mindoro was directly south and the smaller, Polillo Island was east. No passport needed for those.

I'd asked Mrs Gillie about other locations. When people run away, they tend to stick with places they know. She hadn't mentioned any islands, so for now, travelling to remote ferries, was low on my list of priorities.

However, that's what I had Quick doing for me. I sent Wolfe's barman out, armed with Gillie's photograph. He'd ask at all the places a man could catch a small boat without ID. I also figured Quick's local knowledge and language would yield better results than I could.

To hasten his job, Wolfe volunteered his transport. It was the first time I'd heard about his wheels. Maybe his reluctance was because he had a Jeep—ex-US Army, no less. The irony wasn't lost on me.

High on my list of priorities was understanding Gillie's motivation. I felt sure the clues lay in his work. Wolfe's contact at the police might come up trumps with the files taken from the *Manila Times*. But I had another option.

It might not be what he was working on, but an investigation from the past. And that information was readily available.

I returned to the *Manila Times* office and entered the foyer. I took the right fork and spoke to the smiling receptionist. The same young woman I'd seen upstairs last time.

"Good morning," I said, confused. "I thought you worked for Mr Edwards, the political editor."

"Hello again," she said. "I do, and I'm just covering this desk for an hour."

"Then I have a request. I'd like to visit the Reading Room."

"Your face..." she said, ignoring my request.

Ah, my swollen eye from last night's bout with Cezar. "I got into a pillow fight with my bed."

"Really?"

"It might look bad, but the bed looks worse."

She giggled and I regretted using the 'bed' excuse. After Wolfe's experience with Chastity, I needed to be careful with misleading signals and suggestions.

Still smiling, the young Filipina pointed to the corridor behind. "Go right ahead. Take as long as you need... but avoid the troublesome chairs... those cushions can be deadly!"

I thanked her.

After the stairs, and behind a panel that split the foyer into front reception and rear, was a corridor with doors. The first went to the basement. The printing press was down there, and I could smell acrid ink and machinery. It was quiet during the afternoon, but I guessed, by early evening, tomorrow's first editions would be typeset and the printing would commence. I could imagine the whirl and whoosh of paper running fast through rollers. The newspaper business was a tough one. Twenty-four hours. Non-stop. Although I realized that different jobs required different shifts, it was still all about pressure and deadlines.

I didn't envy Martin Gillie or anyone in the building, for that matter.

The Reading Rooms had two doors, like an airlock, and there was relative peace and quiet once I was through into the large room with comfortable chairs as well as desks with reading lights. It reminded me of a library reading area, although the aroma was undoubtedly of newspapers rather than the warmer smell of books.

Beyond this library-like section was a massive vault with a thousand leather-bound binders, each containing so many papers, I figured each would give me a week's reading.

I located the ten most recent binders and carried them, one at a time, to a desk.

With care, I began to sift through the pages, my fingers tracing the columns as I searched for articles written by Martin Gillie. My eyes scanned the headlines, looking for any clues that might shed light on his sudden disappearance.

After three hours, I'd read almost a hundred articles by the journalist. He contributed every day, sometimes more than once, although many of the pieces weren't investigative. It seemed that Martin Gillie was required to write his column inches each day, covering mundane news events. However, every few days, there was a longer article that demonstrated his talent.

He wrote exposes on government corruption, revealing the sordid underbelly of Manila's political landscape. There were stories of human rights abuses, shining a light on the plight of the oppressed and marginalized. And there were tales of triumph and resilience, celebrating the indomitable spirit of the Filipino people in the face of adversity.

I decided to go back another month and then another.

Gillie didn't shy away from criticizing the government. He also wrote a few pieces on corruption in the police. I took a note of all of this and underlined the name, Emilio Santos, Chief of Police.

Many of the papers covered military and Huk activities and Gillie didn't seem to write more column inches on this than other journalists. However, I picked up on the name, Colonel Ricardo Valdez a few times in Gillie's pieces, and underlined his name too.

I went back further in time and wrote more notes and other interesting names. Over the past year, Martin Gillie had written three pieces on the Catholic church. The vast majority of Filipinos were Catholic, so articles about the Church didn't surprise me.

Because of Gillie's style, I expected him to be critical of the Church or expose some atrocity, however he tended to write positive things and the piece I found most fascinating chronicled the actions of Catholic priests during the Japanese occupation. The articles recounted stories of bravery and sacrifice, detailing how priests had risked their lives to protect their congregations and subtly resist the oppression of the invaders.

I suspected the positive stories Gillie wrote were fillers, since they were neither news nor current. Except for one in the oldest paper I'd selected. I'd read the others about the Church, so I found myself reading this one too.

Unusually, the priest—Father Reyes—was outspoken about the impact of political turmoil on addressing the issues of poverty and hunger.

I wondered whether any action had been taken against him. The government he was riling against had been replaced three months later and yet I'd witnessed the public unrest firsthand. Nothing changes in politics, just the faces.

As I read, I was also noting locations in case they pointed to places Gillie might know well enough to seek refuge there. He was a good writer using vivid descriptions that made words leap off the page and create atmosphere. This was particularly evocative when he was describing the military and rebel impact on small communities. I took a note of eight towns and could believe he'd had first-hand experience of them all.

It may just have been his talent, or he may have had been fed information from a source who could provide those details. I went back over all the investigative ones and picked up on something I hadn't during my first read.

There was undoubtedly a source, maybe more than one, but in four seemingly unrelated pieces he used the name Topo. The name Rena Gillie had heard. It could be more than one person, but it seemed to be a name Gillie chose when he didn't want to use the informant's real name.

Was it someone Gillie might turn to when he needed help?

I searched for clues. Who was Topo?

My eyes were swimming when I finally decided I'd done enough for now. Maybe it was because I'd missed lunch or maybe it was the concentration over many hours.

The receptionist had changed, so no need to comment on an attack of the cushions. I walked out of the newspaper's offices into the dazzling sunlight and stretched. Then I found a street vendor and devoured grilled skewers of meat that they covered in a sweet sauce that was somewhere between British brown sauce and marmalade. Again, I sensed I was being watched, but saw no familiar faces or unusual behaviour.

My route back to Wolfe's bar took me through the old town and, as I continued to check for a tail, I realized the Manila Cathedral was close by.

When Gillie had interviewed Father Reyes about the political problems, it had been here at the cathedral.

On a whim, I paid a visit to the Catholic priest.

Chapter 13

The Cathedral of the Immaculate Conception was a ruin and hadn't been restored since the war. Despite the broken walls and destroyed tower, there was a service in full swing.

I waited in the square outside and watched a wizened old lady feed the pigeons. They were undoubtedly the most common birds in the old town, perching on ledges, statues and rooftops.

The service ended. People flooded out, and the pigeons took flight.

Sunlight filtered through the single stained-glass window that remained, casting colourful patterns on the stone floor as I stepped through the shell of the cathedral. The air seemed cooler and quieter than outside, despite a lack of roof. The soft murmur of prayers echoed around me.

I checked my notes and confirmed I was looking for the priest called Reyes before I asked for him.

He was in the south transept—at least that's what it would have been—and smiled beatifically as I approached. He wore a long white cassock with a pattern down the middle and on his sleeves that looked like a series of gold flowers.

"I don't believe we've met," the priest said.

"No. I've only been in the Philippines for a few days."

"From England?"

I laughed. "A long time ago. Singapore recently, before that the Middle East."

"Army?"

I was impressed at his guess. "Ex. Military police."

"An officer?"

"Captain."

"But you're not a Catholic." He must have read my surprise at his correct assumption because he chuckled. "You'd have been more deferential," he said. "Not that I mind in the least. You're here for another purpose… other than religious guidance, I believe."

"Can we talk in private?"

Reyes walked me to a vestry and offered me a seat.

I handed him my credentials.

"Captain Carter, Special Investigations Branch." A smile. "Are you on some type of investigation?"

"I want to help a friend."

He nodded, watching my eyes. "Someone I might know?"

"Martin Gillie."

For the briefest of moments, I saw a flicker in his eyes although I couldn't interpret it other than know that Reyes recognized the name. But that was to be expected.

"The reporter," he said, nodding again after a couple of beats. "The reporter."

"I've read all of his articles—over the past year, at least."

"Ah, so that's why you are here. You read the ones he wrote about me. I can… Well, as you could tell from the articles, I don't believe in remaining silent. Morality requires action. If we see wrong and do not act, then who are we to preach?"

I flashed back to my childhood, remembering a conversation with my mother about morality. I couldn't recall the details but knew she had used similar words.

Reyes said, "You're a good man. I can see it in your eyes."

"I try my best, Father."

He smiled and nodded knowingly. I thought he'd speak next, possibly ask why I was just standing there looking at him, but he didn't. Perhaps priests were used to unasked and unanswered questions.

Eventually I said, "I'm looking for him—the reporter."

"You said you want to help."

"I think he's in trouble."

The priest's eyes narrowed. "What sort of trouble?"

"Perhaps it's to do with his silence. Perhaps he knows something."

Reyes said nothing.

I said, "I read his other articles. His work can be… provocative at times, but it's always truthful. He's worried about poverty and workers' rights, just like you."

Reyes inclined his head, his expression grave. "Some people get fat at the expense of others' suffering," he said solemnly. "It's a truth that needs to be spoken, even if it makes some uncomfortable."

"Or afraid."

"Yes. Sometimes lying low is best for a period."

"He came to church," I prompted. "He was devout?"

Reyes nodded then waved an arm. "People still come here."

"I saw."

He looked contrite. "It's not consecrated anymore, but we have a new archbishop. Officially, he doesn't encourage me, but unofficially…"

I understood. "Did you talk to Gillie about that?"

"Yes, although he wouldn't publish anything that unsettles the delicate tightrope I walk."

"Did you talk about other things?"

"We've talked a great deal in the past."

"Did he mention a source… an informer?"

Reyes said nothing for a beat then shook his head.

I pressed: "Did he mention the name Topo?"

Again, I saw a flicker of recognition in Reyes's eyes. I thought he was going to deny knowledge, but touched his lips before speaking. "I've heard the name, Captain

Carter, but if... well, I can't see how exposing Gillie's source will help him. You called yourself a friend, and I believe you. And, as a friend, you should tread very carefully."

"You're right," I said, handing Reyes my contact details at Wolfe's bar. Then I urged him to get in touch if he learned anything about Gillie's whereabouts.

Reyes hesitated for a moment before nodding in agreement.

"Just remember," the priest said, his voice tinged with concern, "if Gillie is in hiding, finding him may not help his cause. Sometimes, the greatest act of rebellion is simply to survive."

Chapter 14

The pigeons had returned and ignored me as I walked away from the shattered cathedral. My thoughts were on Father Reyes. I sensed he knew much more than he was saying but realized it would be nigh impossible to get him to speak. If only the confessional worked the other way around!

My footsteps echoed off the cobblestones, and somewhere in the back of my mind, a thought returned: I was being followed.

I couldn't shake the feeling. It had begun at the harbour as I'd shown Martin Gillie's photograph and asked about him. Then again, today as I'd left the newspaper offices.

Yesterday, Mrs Gillie had come into the bar shortly after I'd returned. Could it have been her?

My previous response had been to turn, look and hope my tail would appear guilty. They'd stop suddenly and look away. Or become intensely interested in something banal.

Today, I thought I'd try another tried and tested approach.

Leaving the old town, I crossed the river and veered east. Passing beneath the Chinatown arch, I entered a world of its own within the city. The air here smelled different—sweet and savoury, with hints of incense. People bustled past, carrying baskets, pushing carts, their voices rising and falling in a mix of Tagalog, Cantonese, and Hokkien.

Like parts of the old town, these streets were narrower and confined. Another attraction was the number of people. If I had a tail, they would need to get closer, or they'd easily lose me.

I kept my pace steady, my eyes scanning the reflection in shop windows, looking for suspicious movement. Nothing, just the usual chaos of the streets.

I slowed and stopped at a street vendor selling warm, steaming *lumpia* rolls. I wasn't hungry but bought two then loitered, letting my eyes wander, trying to look casual.

The rolls were good—crispy, a touch of garlic and sweet sauce. But the food didn't distract me from the growing sense that I wasn't alone.

I ate my snack and walked deeper into Chinatown. I'd been here a few times, feeling transported back to my time in Singapore. Despite the pull I felt towards the special little island at the foot of the Malayan peninsula, I couldn't imagine returning. Not unless something dramatic happened. Su Ling would need to be free of the Chinese secret societies. She'd need to want me back.

Bill Wolfe seemed to have forgotten his Rosa, but I hadn't let go of what Su Ling meant to me. I'd left Singapore believing she'd tricked me. Let down by her unwillingness to escape. Yes, it was complicated. She was bound to the criminal underworld; she had a young son I hadn't known about. But I would have accepted him too, given the chance.

I'd boarded the steamer, thinking she didn't care. And later I found something in my luggage. She'd written a letter confessing all and telling me that I would remain in her heart—from now until we met again. *When the magpies link their wings.*

I knew what she meant. We'd sat on Mount Faber and stared up at the night sky. We'd talked about science and mythology… and romance. And she'd told me the

Chinese story of star-crossed lovers, a herdsman and a princess. They were stars on either side of the Milky Way and once a year, all the magpies were summoned to link wings and form a bridge so that the lovers might be together.

Su Ling didn't expect me to return, but she wanted me to be safe. She had enclosed a special coin. It was the symbol of the largest secret criminal gang in Singapore and she said it would protect me.

I touched the coin in my pocket. How it would protect me, I wasn't sure, but if I'd learned one thing from my time in Singapore, it was that science didn't hold all the answers.

I took more turns, certain I wasn't alone. Whoever it was, he was good. He knew how to keep distance, how to stay just out of sight.

The coin in my pocket... was it someone from the secret society after me? Had Andrew Yipp sent someone to kill me?

I rounded another corner, quickened my pace, and cut down an even narrower alley. The walls closed in, almost suffocating. I stopped at the next corner, pressed myself against the cool brick, and waited.

Footsteps hurried along the cobbles. They slowed.

I clenched my fists, steadying my breath.

A figure rounded the corner. I grabbed them, spun and pinned them against the wall.

"All right, who the hell are you?" I growled, ready for a fight. But then I stopped. It wasn't a man I had in my grip. It was a young woman, slender, her dark hair framing wide, startled eyes.

"What the—? I—" She stammered, her face a mix of fear and apology.

I let go, stepping back. "Sorry," I muttered. "I thought—"

"No, no," she interrupted, breathless. "I should be the one apologizing. I've been following you."

I blinked. That wasn't what I expected to hear. A brazen admission. "You… you've been following me?"

"Yes," she said, adjusting her coat and catching her breath. "I know you're looking for Martin Gillie." She breathed again. "So am I."

I studied her for a moment, watching her fidget nervously under my gaze. She wasn't lying, but she wasn't telling me everything either. "So, who are you?" I asked.

"Hilary. Hilary Wigglesworth. I'm a reporter too. Martin was supposed to meet me four days ago. He was going to share something big, a scandal. But he disappeared."

I crossed my arms, still not entirely trusting her. "And you think I know where he is?"

"No," she said, shaking her head. "But I heard you asking about him. I'm worried. If something happened to him… If it's because of what he was investigating…"

Her voice trailed off, and for the first time, I saw the fear in her eyes. She was afraid Gillie was dead. Hell, maybe she was right.

"But why follow me?" I asked, softening my tone just a little. "Why not just talk to me?"

"I didn't know if I could trust you," she said, biting her lip. "And then I didn't know how to approach you. But now that we're here… I… I need your help. I think something terrible's happened to him."

I stood there, staring at her. The street was quiet now, the noise of Chinatown fading into the distance. Hilary Wigglesworth. Another reporter with too many questions. Just like Gillie. This thing was getting messier by the minute.

"You're right, I don't know where he is," I said, my voice low. "But I *am* looking. And if he was on to something big, then it might be dangerous."

She nodded, her eyes locked on mine. "I know," she whispered. "That's what scares me."

For a moment, neither of us moved. The city hummed around us, but the alley felt like a different world—a place where people vanished without a trace, where secrets were buried deep.

"Come on," I said finally. "Let's get out of here."

I took her back to Wolfe's bar. We sat at the rear corner table that I'd claimed. My back to the wall, I could watch the whole bar and entrance. I called it my office, much to Quick's amusement.

He served us and Hilary drank three brandies while I told her what I knew, which wasn't a lot. She didn't know Rena Gillie, explaining that Martin never discussed his home life. That tallied with what Mrs Gillie had told me. He kept home and work-life separate, and I wondered whether he'd known this day would come. Had he always intended his family would have the protection of ignorance?

Hilary didn't like that Gillie had either left or tried to leave the island. It confirmed her fears that he was in danger.

I probed her experience, and it sounded similar to Gillie's. An investigative reporter, finding corruption and injustice. She swore she wasn't a communist but understood their concerns. The workers of the Philippines weren't treated fairly. There was the rich minority who exploited the working class.

I mentioned my experience at the protest march. She said she'd seen it too. The land reforms were being sold as beneficial to the country, and maybe in the long term, modernization was a good thing. In the short term, subsistence farmers would suffer.

I asked whether Gillie might have been working on that.

"Possible," she said, "but it would need to be a bigger story, I think. Otherwise, he wouldn't have needed to discuss it. If there was a scandal linked to merging the small farms—for the benefit of the big landowners—then it would make sense. I keep thinking about it. Why contact me? Why my help? All I can think is that I've recently had access to senior government officials. Maybe he thought they'd talk to me."

"Or maybe they told you something crucial?"

She shook her head, disappointed. "I don't know."

We ended our meeting with a promise that we'd stay in touch. I gave her the phone number of the bar and she provided a number where she could be reached.

I was using Quick for minor legwork, but having someone like Hilary was more useful. She not only had experience of the country, but also the background to Gillie's industry.

I had a new partner.

Chapter 15

Wolfe had been watching but waited five minutes before coming to my table. He was carrying a pint of beer. Quick signalled that it was his first of the evening.

"Love interest?" he asked.

"Another journalist," I said. "Hilary Wigglesworth. Know the name?"

"No. I'm thinking I drew the short straw. Would have preferred her over that Gillie chap." He raised an eyebrow. "Pretty."

I'd noticed Hilary was striking in a subtle way. I placed her at about five-seven and mid-twenties. A good jawline and high cheekbones were complemented by expressive brown eyes. Eyebrows were thick, well-defined and slightly arched, giving her a thoughtful expression. Her nose was thin and turned up at the end. Short, dark hair and tanned skin, made me think she had Spanish blood, and yet that very British surname…

"What are you thinking?" Wolfe said, eyeing me critically.

"That she may be an asset to the job."

"Right," he said. "Well, I spoke to my contact in the Manila police. Asked what they'd found in the raid on *the Times*"

I'd hoped to speak with the police officer, but Wolfe had done it without me. No point in complaining. And I wasn't surprised. If the day came when he told me what he was planning, or including me, I'd be suspicious of his motives.

Officially, Wolfe had been my partner in Israel after the British authorities had left. Just the two of us supporting British military intelligence. We'd tracked down the Killing Crew together but, even then, we'd spent most of the investigation working independently. I got the sense that Hilary Wigglesworth was much more collaborative. At least I hoped so, for both our sakes.

"And?" I prompted, expecting nothing good based on his grim expression. "What did you find out?"

"Not much."

I knew there was more coming, so I bided my time. There was a good balance of customers in this evening: regulars and sailors who weren't out to get plastered in as short a time as possible. A clutch of attractive young ladies was also being well-behaved. I wondered which of them would find herself in Wolfe's bed tonight.

I watched Quick working the bar, the clink of glasses and murmur of conversation fading into the background as I waited.

Finally, Wolfe said, "You're angry."

"Disappointed but not surprised."

He knocked back his pint and grimaced. "Without official sanction it's tough to get information. And official sanction almost never happens." He waved to Quick and got another pint. I exchanged eye contact with the young barman. This was Wolfe's second of the evening and the night was still young.

Wolfe said, "The police had little incentive to help—unless there's a benefit to them."

I didn't ask, but suspected Wolfe had paid for his information—cash or more likely a meal—whether it was useful or not. If I decided to continue in this profession, I knew that working with the police could be like navigating a minefield, each step fraught with uncertainty and risk.

He continued: "But it's more than that. If my man was seen talking to a private detective, he'd possibly lose his job. They hire and fire fast in Manila. No second chances. No proper investigation. It's badged under 'cleaning up'. Cutting out the old corruption. The people will trust the police more if they fire any transgressors. Proven or otherwise. That's the argument."

"So, your man told you nothing?"

Wolfe took a long draft of his beer. "My contact isn't very senior, so it could be he doesn't know everything." Wolfe shrugged. "But—"

I waited.

"Saying nothing means something, right?"

"A null result," I said. It was an expression I used, picked up from my scientific background. It wasn't one of Wolfe's.

My old colleague pulled a sour face at me. "Whatever. Look, what he said was he wasn't aware of the order. Which means no warrant."

I arched an eyebrow. Interesting. "The raid wasn't officially sanctioned?"

"Seems that way."

"That's something, at least," I said.

"My man thought they found nothing useful. No evidence of the supposed sedition. But remember what I said, he isn't senior, and you never know with these things… he might have been spinning me a yarn. Might know nothing, really."

"Just want a free meal."

"It cost me a bottle of rum. The good stuff."

We sat in silence for a while.

"I wish you had let me talk to him."

He shook his head. "He wouldn't have said anything. Too nervous. I explained that."

"I'd have asked if the police thought Gillie was alive."

Wolfe's eyes narrowed as he considered. "They think he's alive. This wasn't about getting his work, this was about proving he was a criminal and bringing him to justice. He's alive, all right."

"That's something," I said.

"I'll take that as a thank-you."

He got himself another beer, came back and told me I'd be less uptight if I drank now and again.

I said, "Thank you for asking your police contact."

He grunted and glugged his beer.

I said, "I'd benefit from your skills in the investigation."

"Not going to happen." He shook his head firmly. "I'm out of the business."

"Drinking too much and sleeping with anyone willing." Sometimes things that have been building up in your mind, just come out unbidden. I regretted mentioning the girls so soon. Quick and I were keeping an eye on them, not lecturing Wolfe on his morals.

He laughed. Which surprised me.

I said, "It's not about the girl who stole your cash."

"No," he said matter-of-factly. "It's because you have issues."

I have issues?

I said, "It's about Rosa."

"Don't mention Rosa!"

"Why not?"

"You've no right, that's why not."

"Your behaviour is self-destructive," I said. I'd opened the can and now the worms were truly out and crawling. No putting them back. "The drinking, the girls… You're avoiding a proper relationship."

His face coloured. We'd brawled five years ago in Israel. He had a quick temper and I tensed, wondering if he was about to fly off the handle.

I held up a placatory hand. "I'm sorry. I went too far."

His jaw muscles worked before he got the words out. "Yes, you did. And you're in no position to lecture me on women."

"I'm not?"

"All these easy, hot women around and you're not batting an eyelid. Why is that?"

And so, I confessed. I told him about my ill-fated relationship with the most amazing woman I'd ever known.

We talked for a long time. I shared my feelings about Su Ling and he relived the last months with his fiancé Rosa before she died. I knew most of it, but this wasn't about information, it was about sharing pain.

At one point, he told me to get over my ex-girlfriend. In his inimitable way, he told me, "Move on. Don't be so fuckin' soft."

I steered the conversation away from my problem and back to his. Because men do that.

At the end, I said, "So you'll be more selective in your bedroom partners from now on, Bill?"

"Heck, no!" he said. "I'm a red-blooded male. I thought this was all about getting you to ease up. You might not have my looks, but I'm sure you can find plenty of girls who aren't too fussy."

I sighed.

Chapter 16

We weren't open yet. Wolfe was sleeping off the excess of the night before. For once, he'd rejected the advances of the girls. Score one for me?

Quick was outside sloshing water on the stones, removing most of the smell.

The smiling Filipina I'd seen in the newspaper's offices stepped inside, clutching her shoulder bag across her chest as though it could protect her from the demons of drink.

When her eyes swept over me, she breathed and nodded. "Remember me… from *the Manila Times*?" she asked. "I'm Mr Edwards's assistant, Jasmine, although—" she'd been speaking rapidly and took a long breath. "Sorry."

"Of course I remember. You were also covering the reception desk." However, I hadn't paid attention to her name.

Jasmine breathed. Relaxed. Smiled. "Your eye looks better. Anymore pillow fights?"

"I'm keeping well away from pillows and cushions for now," I said, although tonight would be Fight Night at the boxing club.

She kept smiling. For a fleeting moment, I wondered whether she'd hunted me down for personal reasons. She was nice and friendly, but I didn't feel any attraction. However, as I studied her, I sensed she wasn't here about a relationship. She was nervous about something she needed to tell me.

"Come and sit down," I said, beckoning her to my table at the back.

She walked swiftly with short, hurried steps. As soon as we sat, she started speaking again.

"Martin is a man of integrity," Jasmine said earnestly. "No way is he involved with the rebels."

"Okay," I said.

"Martin is an excellent investigative journalist. He may have been investigating the rebels Not supporting them. The two are very different."

"Yes, they are."

I was playing along. The young woman had something to say and what she'd said so far wasn't it. She hadn't found me just to insist that her colleague was an honourable man who was good at his job. And I could tell this wasn't a continuation of the flirting at the office reception.

Jasmine smiled awkwardly. "I've done a bit of investigating myself. I... I have checked you out."

I raised an eyebrow. "Okay."

"You've only been in Manila a few days and came from Singapore. You had a good reputation as a private detective there."

I figured she'd been in touch with someone at *the Straits Times*. They knew me. They'd have given a better reference than if she'd spoken to anyone from the government—especially the department responsible for security.

She said, "You were a special investigator for the British Army and served with the 225 provost company in Israel."

"I did." Although it had been British Palestine at the time.

"But no one could tell me why you left. You were doing well in Israel as far as I can tell. But—"

"Personal matters," I said ambiguously.

She accepted it without question, although when her eyes met mine, I thought she might cry.

"I'm impressed by your research," I said, buying time.

"I needed to be sure... sure I can trust you." She paused and her eyes looked even slicker. "I'm not sure who can be trusted with this."

I waited, intrigued. What did she have?

"The police boxed up all of Martin's things," she said, speaking faster now. "But not everything. They didn't know where Martin hid copies of his most important work. He was worried in case his work got lost. Sometimes the cleaners get over-zealous and newspaper folk aren't the most organized and tidy. I think he was also worried that someone might steal his work—or maybe get a jump on his scoop. It can be a cut-throat world."

"Could he be hiding with someone, Jasmin?"

"I don't know."

"Who could he turn to?"

"I don't know."

"What about the identity of someone called Topo."

She shook her head. "He didn't share anything with me." Then she glanced around as though someone might be watching from the door. Quick had come back in and was cleaning behind the bar, paying us no attention. Wolfe was still in his room. There was no one else.

"This is why I'm here," she said. Her hands shook as she opened her bag and pulled out a thick envelope. It was torn and tied with string.

She made me promise that I would guard it with my life, then handed me the envelope. Tears brimmed in her eyes as she stood and took a step away. I sensed that she'd felt immense responsibility holding onto the file. Now that she'd passed the baton to me, she could breathe once more.

I thanked her and a tear drop ran down her cheek.

"Help him," Jasmine whispered, and was then gone.

I sat in a secluded corner of the bar and spread the papers out before me. My brow furrowed in concentration as I studied each sheet, searching for any clues that might shed light on Martin Gillie's disappearance.

The first sheet was a map of Quezon Province with plantations marked on it. Then the next page caught my attention—a list of five names. I traced my finger over the names before writing them in my notebook alongside the ones I'd taken from the old articles.

Silva
Monasse
Flores
Rodriguez
De la Torre

How could I decipher their significance? Who were these people, and what connection did they have to Gillie's investigation?

A second map was of the island of Palawan. This one didn't have plantations marked but did have annotations. Deaths and injuries. I counted three injured police officers, twenty injured civilians and five fatalities. There was also a date: July last year. The question written at the top of the page echoed in my mind: *What happened?*

I rummaged through and found a third map. This one was of the northeastern tip of Luzon: Cagayan Province. There was no annotation, just question marks. Eight of them, peppered about, with none at a named town.

I returned to the Quezon map and studied it intently, hoping for inspiration, seeing nothing. Then the island map with deaths and injuries marked. Flipping through the file, I hoped for an explanation or accompanying article. There was none.

The next set of papers revealed minutes from government meetings discussing funding and spending for the army and remote police outposts. Some were in English and others Spanish. I figured they were the same meetings transcribed in both languages.

I sifted through the dense jargon, scanning the pages for any relevant details that might provide insight. Nothing jumped out at me. There was no big arrow pointing to the important clue.

The final page had a list of dates and locations. Thirty-three of them.

Wolfe emerged and I called him over.

"What's this?" He asked, looking at the papers.

"A file of Gillie's—one the police didn't find."

He looked impressed. "How in the—?"

"Another colleague brought it in." I showed him my lists. "Do any of these names ring a bell?"

"Emilio Santos, of course." He pointed to my notebook, reading the wrong page. "Was your man investigating the Chief of Police?"

"He's been in old reports," I said. "Mainly for his role in supporting the new government clean up the corruption."

"Yeah, that'll be right."

I indicated the other list: the five names from Gillie's papers.

Wolfe leaned in closer, his eyes narrowing as he studied the names.

I read something in his face. "You recognize them?"

"One… maybe."

I waited.

"De la Torre. I had a run in with him. If it is him." He shook his head. "Let me warn you now. Avoid him and certainly don't do any jobs for him." I didn't ask about his experience, guessing he'd explain his reaction when he was ready.

After a moment of silence, his expression shifted, a glimmer of recognition crossing his features.

"I think I recognize this one too," Wolfe said slowly, pointing to the list. "Flores. Although I can't place it. And I'm sure there are hundreds of people with that name."

"But not De la Torre?"

"No. He's a businessman. Diverse businesses including farms. He's one hundred per cent dodgy. Wealth originally based on ill-gotten gains. He's not a mobster, but only just on the right side of the line."

"You're telling me to avoid him?"

"I am."

I filed that away, deciding he'd be the last one I contacted, if at all.

I showed Wolfe the deaths and injuries marked on the map of Palawan island. "Could this be about rebel attacks?"

He shook his head and asked for a date. I told him July last year and he shook his head again. "Not rebel attacks. Not there. These, on the other hand,"—he lifted out the page with thirty-three dates and names—"are locations in Central Luzon. I'd bet they're a summary of Huk attacks."

Interesting.

I showed him the map of Quezon Province.

"Farmland," he said.

"Do you know of the trouble there?"

"Not specifically."

"What about government funding for the police outposts?" I asked. "There are minutes here from meetings…"

Wolfe shook his head. "Sounds, to me, like dull political stuff."

Chapter 17

"It's politics," Hilary said.

I'd called her, and within half an hour, she was with me at the bar.

"These tally with Huk attacks," she said scanning the list of thirty-three entries. "Is that what this is about?"

I showed her the names and she pointed to the same one Wolfe had considered. "Flores. Alberto Flores. If it's him, he's a wealthy individual who owns a lot of farmland."

Interesting. Land reform benefited the large landowners.

"So, this could be about the forced acquisition of smallholdings and farms?"

"Possible," she said frowning as she looked at the map of Quezon Province.

"What?"

"I don't know. Although the land reforms apply nationally, the majority are in Central Luzon, not here. I think Flores owns plantations in Quezon province but... well, historically, it's just not been particularly newsworthy."

"Things change."

"Of course. But not land acquisition or rebel incidents."

"What about Palawan?" I showed her the map with the marked deaths and injuries. "What do you know about Huk attacks there?"

"Really?" She frowned. "On the island? I've never heard of any trouble there. And it's not on the list," she said tapping the page with thirty-three events.

I left to get something for lunch whole she read through the government meeting minutes.

When I returned with ham, cheese and rolls, she had all the papers spread out on the table, trying to make sense of them. Her fingers traced lines between different documents, as though searching for connections that weren't immediately apparent.

"I can't tell what Gillie was working on. Are you sure these were his special notes?"

I explained how I'd received them, that they'd been kept separate from the other work. Police had taken everything else and my intel from Wolfe's contact was that the police hadn't found anything seditious.

"The minutes are about police funding. You'll be aware of the tension between the police and army?"

"No."

"That's what I'm thinking this is about. You have the heads of the police and defence: Emilio Santos and Colonel Ricardo Valdez and minutes about police funding... Both departments argue that they need more money to fight the rebels. The army say the Huks are a military issue, but the police point to attacks on towns, cities and businesses. They say it is a police matter."

"It's both," I said. "In Malaya there is a War Executive Committee. Both areas report to a common head and special police forces are military trained."

She cocked her head. "Did it work?"

"It's ongoing," I said, and realized that the strategy hadn't been working. Five and a half years and the Emergency continued.

"And the Korean conflict wasn't a good role model," she said. "It may be over, but at what cost? We don't want to lose half the country to the communists. So here we have the perpetual struggle between army and police: Valdez and Santos."

She was going through the papers again and pulled out a handwritten note that I'd ignored because it was just scribble.

"Shorthand. A draft article, I think," she said as she quickly worked on a translation.

As the standoff between the army and police intensifies, government officials are under increasing pressure to find a solution that addresses the needs of both agencies while ensuring the safety and well-being of the Filipino people. Failure to resolve the funding dispute threatens to undermine the government's ability to effectively confront the rebel threat and risks further destabilizing an already volatile situation.

"Seems to confirm the theory," I said.

She nodded but was back, flicking through the pile. "Look at this," she said, spreading out the third map I hadn't paid much attention to before. "Cagayan Province. Northeastern coast. Gillie's marked several locations, but why? It's mostly mountainous up there."

She pulled out the second map, the one with the plantations drawn on it. Holding it up, she said, "Yes it's a dot!"

I looked and saw the mark, barely visible beside the black dot of a town.

"Tayabas in Quezon Province," she said. "Why? What's the connection?"

I studied both maps. "Could it be rebel activity?"

"Gillie's list looks complete," she said, tapping the list thirty-three entries again. "Now these are *reported* Huk attacks."

"Could some have gone unreported?"

"I don't know. I'd be surprised. And why would Gillie keep maps of these particular regions? What made them special enough to hide away with his private notes?"

We sat in silence for a moment, staring at the documents spread before us. I pulled out the government meeting minutes again, scanning them with fresh eyes.

"Look at these funding requests," she said. "Heavy police presence requested in both areas."

"Why?" I said.

"What's so important about these places? Palawan's northern coast is mostly uninhabited jungle, and In Cagayan apart from the mountains, you have Cagayan Valley..." Hilary's tone was full of frustration. "Which is just farmland, most of it struggling."

"There has to be something we're missing," I said. "Gillie wouldn't have kept these unless they meant something."

She began sorting through the papers again, then the maps, her movements more urgent now. "The Xs bother me. Why mark them? Why these specific locations?"

"Could they be the location of rebel meetings or camps? Or places where something happened?"

"Maybe. But then why include the funding dispute minutes with them? How does that connect?"

I rubbed my eyes, feeling the strain of staring at documents all morning. "We're looking at puzzle pieces without knowing what picture we're trying to build."

Hilary sat back, running a hand through her short hair. "We need to see these places for ourselves. Maybe there's something that doesn't show up on paper."

"Which one first?"

"Palawan," she said after a moment's thought. "That the one with a date and marked deaths. Whatever Gillie was investigating, maybe that's where it started."

I nodded, but something was nagging at me. "Okay," I said. "So why include the minutes in his notes?"

"I don't know." She gathered the papers, stacking them carefully. "But I have a feeling it's all connected somehow..."

"We just can't see how yet," I agreed.

She sighed. "Something I feel awkward asking you..."

I waited for the question.

"Have you made any progress in finding him?"

I shook my head. Since the information about him being sighted at the harbour, I'd found nothing. I'd spoken to Father Reyes and learned nothing useful. Wolfe had gained scant information from his contact about the raid.

Quick had spent at least five hours over the past two days, checking the other boats off the island. He'd got nowhere. Not even a whiff of Gillie's presence. We'd agreed Quick would go out again today, but I was beginning to think it was pointless. If Gillie had got off the island, then we wouldn't trace him. I wasn't one to give up, but my gut was telling me he had changed his plan. He'd been recognized and gone to ground. Plenty of remote places to get lost in. Plenty of places to hide. Or someone was harbouring him.

"Do you know who Gillie's informant is?" I asked.

"He'll have a few."

"His wife mentioned Topo."

She shook her head. "Not someone I know."

It was a potential lead we should look for, but for now, the only progress was this pile of paper.

And it didn't tell me where Gillie was hiding.

I told Hilary about Wolfe's police contact. "No warrant, but they think he's alive."

"Having no warrant doesn't surprise me," she said. "But maybe, this shouldn't be about finding him."

"It shouldn't?" I was intrigued.

"If he is hiding, he's afraid." She waited for my nod before continuing. "So, we uncover what he's afraid of. We find out what he was working on and expose it. Starting with whatever he discovered in Palawan."

I studied her face, saw the determination there. She was right—whatever Gillie had discovered in these locations was probably important enough to make him disappear.

"When do we leave?"

"First light tomorrow," she said, already gathering her things. "I'll arrange a boat."

"Isn't there a public ferry?"

She rolled her eyes. "Yes, if you want it to take two days. I'll find a fast boat. We should go by foot, get a taxi on the island. Are you okay to..." she paused and appeared awkward.

"I have a good retainer," I said. "I'll cover the cost."

She breathed out, stood and grinned. "Thank goodness. A journalist... well, let's say, I'll never be rich."

"You write because you're compelled to," I said, flashing back to the other journalist I'd worked with.

"Something like that," she said. "Although the compulsion often comes from the editor rather than the urge to put pen to paper. One day... one day there may be a book or two in me."

She nodded, walked to the door, then paused and waved farewell.

"Six o'clock tomorrow at Pier 3."

I watched her go, then turned back to the scattered papers on the table. Tomorrow, we'd start unravelling whatever mystery Gillie had uncovered in Palawan.

It felt like we were moving forward. Momentum, at last, to solve this mystery.

Later, before the evening rush at the bar, Wolfe sat with me and started talking about *the* case—the one that had made him quit as a private detective.

Chapter 18

Wolfe's client had worked for him at the bar. A young woman called Margarita Galizina. She cleaned for a number of businesses and for a few hours each day, she cleaned Wolfe's place—doing a much better job than Quick, according to Wolfe. The young man didn't disagree.

Margarita had been pregnant, giving birth to a healthy baby girl called Isa a few weeks after starting the job. Within days, Margarita was back at work, the grandmother caring for Isa when needed.

Kidnapping wasn't common and had come as both a terrible shock and surprise when Isa was taken six months later. Margarita didn't have much money, and so a ransom of ten thousand pesos was unfathomable.

Maybe the kidnappers thought Margarita's parents were rich. They'd once owned a successful franchise and lived well, but most of the money had gone. They didn't have a spare ten thousand pesos.

I asked about Margarita's husband and Wolfe told me they'd separated shortly after she'd had the baby. She'd described him as a good-for-nothing layabout waster.

She thought highly of him then!

As expected, the ransom letter had been written in Tagalog. It had also included the usual warning about not telling the police. If she did, the baby would die.

Margarita was sobbing and shaking when she told Wolfe. She feared that she couldn't tell anyone, but she had no other option. She couldn't raise the money. Her parents offered to sell everything, but it would still fall woefully short.

"At least, if I don't pay and don't tell the police, Isa will live." She told him.

Not likely, Wolfe told me. They wanted money, not a baby.

Wolfe had approached the police without mentioning names. They'd responded with scepticism and questions. They'd wanted the mother's details. They'd wanted to know what she'd done with the baby's body. They weren't interested in looking for the kidnappers.

So, Bill Wolfe had told her he'd take the job. He agreed to act pro bono, and he'd provide the ransom money.

But he'd also catch the kidnappers. So, despite it being a large chunk of his savings, Wolfe rationalized that he'd get the money back.

"It'll be a criminal gang," Margarita said, although she couldn't suggest who they might be. "You cannot go up against them, Major Wolfe!"

"Let's just get Isa back." That was his prime objective, but he knew he couldn't let the kidnappers get away with it. Least of all because it was *his* money.

When his story paused, I said, "You wanted the baby *and* the money."

"Of course."

He resumed and provided details of the arranged drop. The money went in a bag under a car, opposite the Lyric Theatre on Escolta Street. It was an interesting choice of location, being an upmarket and broad boulevard. Cars were permanently parked all the way along.

Would the money be taken by a driver or be on foot? Would he run along the street, possibly toward Jones Bridge, or dart away using labyrinthine streets and alleys to get away? If he was Chinese, he'd likely head for Chinatown.

Wolfe positioned himself outside a café on a side street. He had a good line of sight to the target car, a maroon-coloured Chrysler. Probably the nicest vehicle on the strip.

Margarita arrived twenty minutes earlier than planned. Wolfe had warned against this since the longer the money was there, the higher the risk of a total stranger picking it up. He didn't mention this to her later. There wasn't any point.

As instructed, she stuck the bag under the front wheels and then hurried away.

No one approached the car.

Wolfe watched. Traffic went past, briefly obscuring the target. Each time he held his breath, hoping he'd not missed the collection. Then, with five minutes before the deadline, something unexpected happened.

A gunshot.

Then another. Men burst out of a shop called California Jewellery. Wolfe flicked his gaze to them and back to the Chrysler. He couldn't afford to be distracted.

"Were they the kidnappers?" I asked as Wolfe paused again. He breathed slow and loud, and I could see the memory was still raw.

"Huks. That's what the newspapers said the next day." He shook his head. "Suddenly, there was a bloody policeman and a gun battle ensued. It was chaos. The kidnappers would get the money and get away. That's what I thought. So, I left my post and closed in on the car."

"What happened?"

"The money was still there. The kidnappers hadn't used the distraction, but I'd blatantly checked under the car. I walked away and went into the theatre. I watched from inside, then walked up the road and bought a paper. But they never came. I think… I think they must have seen me. I think…"

I'd not seen Wolfe so emotional before, even after Rosa died. I had him down as a stoic. He was made of stern Yorkshire grit. But this had broken him.

I knew there was more to come, but the bar had become busier and Wolfe was needed. The rest of the story would have to wait.

As I sat in a taxi, I felt even more positive than gaining momentum on Gillie's case. Getting Wolfe talking was a major breakthrough. Possibly the first step on his road to recovery.

Hopefully he'd be sober enough to carry on the conversation later. Tell me what happened next.

However, before that, I had a date: the boxing ring at the Olympic Boxing Club.

Chapter 19

I'd been told that Fight Night drew a big crowd even though it wasn't all serious stuff. In early bouts, fighters still got to wear sparring helmets. But there were proper rules, three judges and benches for spectators. It was a chance for the coaches to see how their lads performed—who had the skill and natural instincts. You couldn't always tell in a training situation. Some guys looked great when there was no pressure but took a beating when faced with real competition. I'd seen the same happen out of the ring: a good Queensbury-rules boxer who lost confidence when attacked by a martial arts kicker.

The early fights were out of the way and after a break, the proper bouts would begin. I checked the schedule and saw I was up against someone called Cezar. Most contenders had first initial followed by second name. Cezar was a great name, and I wondered if my opponent didn't have another name. Or perhaps he thought it sounded more intimidating that way.

My bout was last on the fight card, so I joined a few others in light training before settling to watch the remaining matches.

The buzz of the crowd was a mix of Tagalog and broken English. Most of it concerned odds, although there was no official betting.

Then my turn approached. I wasn't the favourite—that much was clear. I had the height and reach advantage. Cezar was shorter and looked meaner. His muscles stretched taut under the harsh lights, his shaved head glistening with sweat. Tattoos covered his arms and chest; symbols of his life on the streets of Manila.

One of the junior coaches handed me my gloves and headgear. "Ingat ka, kaibigan," he said quietly. *Be careful, friend.* "He's nasty. Keep him at a distance. Use your reach."

I gave him a nod. It was advice I'd give myself, however I liked that the man was on my side.

The familiar coppery tang of adrenaline was on my tongue. I waited for the announcement, then climbed over the ropes.

I met Cezar in the centre of the ring and touched his gloves. His eyes were cold and predatory, never leaving mine. The referee rattled off the usual rules, but neither of us listened. We were too focused, my heart pounding too heavily in my ears.

The bell rang. Cezar wasted no time, coming at me with a wild right hook. I stepped back, letting it sail past my ear, and jabbed him hard on the cheek. He barely flinched. I followed with a quick one-two combination, trying to keep him on the defensive. But for every punch I threw, he slipped, bobbing and weaving like he'd done this a thousand times.

The round passed in a blur of punches and sweat. I kept him at bay with my long reach, but he was faster than I'd expected. The bell rang, ending the round with me ahead on points, though I knew Cezar wasn't beaten yet.

Round two started with a fury. Cezar came out like a bull, his fists pounding me with sledgehammer force. Blocking each punch felt like trying to stop a train. A minute in, I was already breathing hard when he suddenly dropped low, like he was going for a body shot. I moved to block, but his foot tangled with mine, and before I knew it, I was on the canvas.

We went down hard, Cezar on top of me. His weight drove through an elbow into my chest. The impact knocked the wind out of me, a sharp, stabbing pain blooming where his elbow had landed. He made the move look accidental, but I knew it was deliberate. The ref stopped the fight. Had he seen it?

I gasped for air, my lungs burning as I tried to suck in oxygen. Cezar was already up, bouncing on his toes, grinning like a predator circling his prey. I pulled myself up by the ropes, still fighting to get my breath back.

The ref told us to continue. No warning to Cezar.

As soon as we restarted, Cezar moved in, landing two quick shots to my chest, each punch digging deep into the sore spot he'd just created.

I became more aware of the crowd. Their baying pummelled my ears almost as much as his Cezar's blows sent bursts of pain through my ribs.

I clinched, trying to buy time, but the referee was quick to separate us. I stumbled back, barely keeping my guard up as Cezar pressed forward. His hooks found their mark, each punch rattling my head and sending shockwaves through my body. My left eye was swelling shut. I could feel the round slipping away.

The bell rang, and I staggered back to my corner, desperate for air. Across the ring, Cezar sat on his stool, grinning like a man who knew he was winning.

As I gulped down water, I thought about that elbow. He'd done it on purpose, no question. He wasn't just here to win. He was here to make a point.

The bell for round three came too soon. My legs felt like lead as I stood, forcing myself to bounce lightly, trying to look fresher than I felt. Cezar charged forward, fists flying. I blocked, dodged, and absorbed the blows as best I could. He was all power and no finesse now, like he was desperate to finish me off.

I kept him at distance, jabbing. It bought me time. The pain in my chest hurt like hell, but I wasn't going to let him know.

We exchanged blows and moved around the ring. Despite my shortened breath, I kept light on my toes.

Confusion knotted his brow. He thought he'd cowed me, but he hadn't.

Testing his guard, I followed with a right-left combo that sent him reeling. He tried to recover, but I kept the pressure on, landing a sharp cross to his ribs and a hook to his jaw. His feet stumbled, his legs wobbling beneath him.

Thirty seconds left.

Keep going, you have this.

And then he tricked me. Poor footwork made him seem vulnerable and so I attacked. But he was feinting, faking a stumble that took my legs.

We went down again, and I twisted just in time. His elbow missed my solar plexus and drove into my ribs. Then his weight winded me.

The referee stepped in, halting the fight. Cezar was up and ready.

"Get up!" my opponent snarled. "Quit falling to get the fight called off."

"Can you continue?" the ref asked me above the din in the hall.

I pushed myself up. *Don't fight angry*, a voice in my head told me. I knew that rule, but the anger got me to my feet.

We restarted, and he unleashed a fierce barrage that culminated in a right cross that caught my ribs where he'd elbowed me. I crumpled, and he saw me to the canvas with a left that caught me behind the ear.

The referee started counting.

I had nothing left. I could see Cezar grinning, sensing his victory. Sensing the knockout.

I got up at eight. My legs were gone.

Nine seconds left.

The fight resumed, and he unleashed a flurry of punches. A hook, a jab, a right cross. He had me on the ropes.

But I was staying on my feet.

The final bell must have sounded, but I didn't hear it. The ref stepped in, separating us, waving his arms. Fight over.

I slumped against the ropes, still refusing to collapse. I'd lost a boxing match for the first time since I was nineteen. Cezar strutted, arms aloft.

I could have complained about his tactics, the illegal trips and elbows, but what was the point?

I may have lost the bout, but I left the gym with pride. At least he hadn't got his knockout.

Chapter 20

After the fight, I wasn't capable of anything.

Wolfe wasn't too inebriated when I returned but we didn't talk about his last case. He was angry for me. He wanted to find 'Cheatin' Cezar', as he called him, and teach him a lesson. I liked that he was looking out for me and that it wasn't booze talking. However, I convinced him it didn't matter and took to my bed.

In the morning, my ribs were bruised and my chest hurt when I sucked in air.

My face was swollen too—far worse than the mark I'd received before.

Hilary commented straight away, alarmed by my swollen face.

"I don't understand why men have to hurt one another," she said showing no sympathy.

I didn't try to justify it. Boxing for me was about fitness and discipline. The competitive element provided a measure—admittedly against another man. It was in my blood and I craved the adrenal rush. That was the truth.

The pain I felt in my ribs and chest were motivation to train harder and improve, even though Cezar had cheated.

The vessel Hilary had chartered was an ex-US naval patrol boat. It was angular and ugly, but the captain—a crusty seadog called Sam—assured us we would reach the island in under ten hours.

We powered southwest across relatively smooth seas. It could have been pleasurable if not for the drone of the engine and sea spray. Hilary and I exchanged a few words but resorted to watching the sea life and coastline. Based on her dismissive attitude towards the art of pugilism, I thought silence was best.

We left the main island behind and rounded Mindoro. I got excited when we sighted land directly ahead, but it turned out to be one of the many smaller islands of the archipelago. Sam called out the names of islands and other details, but his voice was lost in the fast-flowing air.

Finally, Hilary grabbed my arm and pointed. Palawan, the Philippines' last frontier, as people called it. The coastline was a dramatic mix of limestone cliffs and dense jungle, occasionally broken by pristine beaches.

We followed the coast south to the main port of Puerto Princesa.

As we disembarked, I confirmed that Sam would wait for us, no matter how long it took. I could see the dollar signs rolling in his eyes like slot machine wheels.

We stretched boat-weary muscles and got directions to the main police station. I showed people Martin Gillie's photograph and got no positive responses.

"Want to try some fresh mangosteen?" Hilary asked as we passed small dockside vendors selling fruits I'd never seen before.

"Mangosteen?"

"Sweet and tangy. Nothing like regular mangoes," she explained. "It's what Palawan's known for, along with cashews… and it's good for your skin."

It tasted good but didn't do anything for my bruises.

Two police officers sat outside the waterfront police station smoking. The building was single storey and purely functional, built to withstand the coastal weather.

The officers had khaki uniforms almost identical to the ones worn in Malaya. A smart Volkswagen, marked in black and white, pulled up next to a row of three more. A police officer climbed out and joined the other two.

They tracked us with obvious suspicion as we walked toward them.

"How's the car?" I asked, pointing to the Volkswagen.

After I received blank stares, Hilary repeated my question in Tagalog.

The one who'd just arrived turned down the corners of his mouth and replied.

"He said it's better than walking," Hilary translated.

I'd hoped to break the ice, but either these men weren't friendly, or they were naturally suspicious of strangers asking questions.

I nodded toward the building. "Officer in charge?"

Again, Hilary translated and got a response.

I heard the name: Captain Mendoza.

Hilary took the photograph of Gillie and showed the men. They didn't recognize him.

Leaving them, we hustled through the public entrance into a humid reception area and after more negative responses to Gillie's photo, asked the desk clerk for a meeting with Captain Mendoza.

A short wait and a glass of warm water later, we were shown into a small office and introduced to a Lieutenant Zante. He apologized that the captain wasn't available.

Zante's room was sparsely furnished, with a few faded photographs on the walls. Behind his desk was a life-size photograph of the new president, Ramon Magsaysay. A small electric fan fought a losing battle against the heat.

Zante spoke decent English, and I introduced us.

"A private detective and a reporter," he said warily, noticing but not commenting on my face. "To what do I owe the honour?"

"We're looking for an investigative journalist," I said. "His name is Martin Gillie."

Zante's face showed no recognition. "Is he from Palawan?"

I showed him the photo and explained that Gillie was from Manila and missing. We believed it was because of a piece he was researching. His notes had included a map of northern Palawan and a report of numerous deaths.

"Deaths?"

"At the hands of the Huk."

Now I saw something in Zante's eyes. He said, "There has never been rebel activity this far from Luzon."

I said, "Mr Gillie's notes suggest multiple injuries, including police officers, and twenty civilian deaths."

"I can't comment on that," Zante said.

Hilary glanced at me. We both understood his meaning.

She said, "When did this thing that might not have happened... happen?"

He looked uncomfortable.

I said, "July last year?"

"If something did happen... yes, it would have been in July last year."

Hilary said, "It wasn't in the newspapers."

Zante closed his eyes and breathed. "It is better that you don't ask."

"We are asking."

On impulse, I showed him the list of five names and saw his discomfort.

"Do you recognize any of these?"

Zante looked uncomfortable then sharply up.

Footsteps behind us. I turned to see a big officer stride into the lieutenant's office. Captain Mendoza, no doubt.

He had a wide face, thin moustache and faux smile.

"I apologize," he said, pumping my hand and nodding to Hilary. "We are very busy. Thank you, Lieutenant. I'll take it from here."

I thought the lieutenant looked conflicted, but he nodded curtly and turned away.

"Please." The captain guided us out of the lieutenant's office and into the reception area. "Now, how may I help you?" he said, the smile seemingly permanent.

We repeated our story and Mendoza shook his head.

"Rumour and nonsense, I'm afraid."

"So, no one died?" I pressed. "Last July?"

"No." He put his arm out again, this time guiding us to the exit. "Please. I'm afraid we are very busy and do not have time for nonsense." Although still smiling, he fixed Hilary with a glare. "Do not publish anything regarding this matter because it is not true. It could be... unfortunate."

She bristled. "Is that what happened to Martin Gillie? Something *unfortunate*?"

The captain stopped. "I do not know the name Martin Gillie."

I said, "How about—" and proceeded to run through the five names from Gillie's list.

Captain Mendoza nodded. "Señor Albert Rodriguez. Of course I know him."

I waited, thinking these were the first honest words out of the captain's mouth.

"He's one of the wealthiest people in the region." Mendoza's eyes narrowed. "Don't you go causing him any trouble."

Chapter 21

We walked back to the port and looked for a taxi. Since no ferry was due, the sole taxi driver was asleep. When Hilary told him the destination was Señor Albert Rodriguez's estate, he excitedly beckoned us onboard.

The brightly painted, modified Jeep bounced and rattled as we travelled north on rough roads. Hilary braced herself against the seat in front and door, turning ghost white.

"Terrible passenger," she said when I expressed concern. Through gritted teeth she added: "And this is particularly bad."

"We could—"

She shook her head with determination. "Whatever you're going to say… No! We're doing this. And I've been through worse."

The Jeep taxi was ideal for the terrain. Unlike the Volkswagen we'd seen at the police station. No wonder the officer had said it was better than walking. I thought the German-made car would look absurdly out of place on these rugged roads.

We passed through small fishing villages, each with its own character. The air was heavy with salt and something else—a wild, green smell that seemed to seep from the ground.

The jungle pressed in, close to the road, occasionally opening up to reveal breathtaking views of the South China Sea.

The driver had told us that Rodriguez owned most of the plantation land between Roxas and Taytay, thirty miles north. As we'd travelled from Puerto Princesa, I'd noted the coconut palms everywhere. I flashed back to my time in Selangor state in Malaya which had large plantations. Although they were dedicated to rubber production rather than coconuts.

I shook myself from my reverie. "How much further?" Hilary asked the driver, then translated his reply: "Not much. We're nearly at Roxas."

Señor Rodriguez had a large estate just outside of the town. Based on my flashback to Malayan plantations, I expected something like a British colonial mansion. But it was nothing of the sort. His main property was more like a Mexican ranch, low-level and stucco. There were fancy wooden shutters around windows and a long decking with a sloping titled roof supported by numerous columns.

From a distance, it looked nothing special, but close up it was imposing. Much bigger than it appeared and with fine patterns painted into the terracotta walls.

I knocked on an imposing dark wooden entrance. The weight deadened the sound and, without commenting on my foolish expectation, Hilary yanked on a door pull.

We were greeted by a man who might have been Señor Rodriguez but turned out to be his assistant, or butler, or somebody with equivalent self-importance. Rodriguez was out riding, he informed us, and wouldn't be available for approximately two hours.

This wasn't a problem. Due to the lengthy journey, we'd expected to stay overnight on the island.

The sun was low in the sky, casting long shadows as we returned to Roxas. There were no hotels, just pensions. The one we chose was fine except for the bathroom facilities, which were shared by all residents.

There were no taxis available in the town, so Hilary negotiated with our driver. We'd need him until returning to the port tomorrow. The man made a big thing about losing business from the incoming ferries and needing compensation for lost trade. Since our only alternative would have been public transport, we reluctantly agreed to his inflated price.

After a relaxed wash and change of clothes, we ventured out again. The same cold butler-type chap met us at the door and apologised for misleading us. Señor Rodriguez still hadn't returned. He would be available at ten in the morning if we'd like to make a formal appointment.

We said we would.

This time the butler noted our details and wished us a good evening. A semblance of warmth from him, probably because Hilary looked so disappointed.

Our taxi took us back to town but rather than eat at the pension, Hilary directed the driver to a quiet eatery overlooking the sea.

"You've been here before," I guessed since she'd not doubted her destination.

"Once as a child. I wasn't sure it was still here."

"So that was before the war?" I said.

She nodded and I noticed her throat tighten. The war brought back bad memories for most people, and I guessed Hilary was no different.

"You don't drink alcohol," she said, changing the subject.

"No," I said although in truth I'd had the odd glass.

"Your body's a temple?"

I shook my head. "In that I worship myself, you mean?"

"No... I..."

"I try and take care of myself," I said, possibly a touch defensively. "Health and fitness are important. That's why I box. It's not about the combat."

"I see."

I changed the subject. "You impressed me in Manila."

"I did?"

"You followed me for a couple of days. I sensed it, but didn't spot you until the ambush in Chinatown."

She grinned. "I'm sneaky, you mean? Well, I admit it. A talent I learned as a child and something that serves me well in my job."

She said she'd tell me more, but the food arrived and then she started asking questions about my past. As a competent journalist, she appeared fascinated by my answers and had immediate follow-up questions.

I told her about joining the military police despite gaining a science degree from Cambridge. My initial posting had been to Mandatory Palestine and she was interested to hear about the problems we'd faced with the terrorists on both sides. I gave her a few snippets of information about cases. When it came to talking about my assignment post-Palestine, I was more circumspect. It got very messy at the end, but I didn't tell her that. In fact, I couldn't share anything specific about my tasks in Israel. Instead, I managed to steer her away from the job and discussed the country.

She'd never been to Cyprus or Israel, so it was easy to describe the beautiful countryside.

The sun set, painting the sea and sky in colours few artists could capture.

During dinner, she polished off a bottle of wine. Afterwards, back at the pension, we sat on a balcony, and she started another.

"You're comfortable talking to journalists," she noted. "Most people are awkward and careful around me—in case they say something they shouldn't."

"So, this hasn't been off the record?" I said with mock concern.

She laughed. "There's no such thing." After a sip of wine, she continued: "So have you had training?"

"In handling journalists?" I asked. "Would have been a good idea, but no. Just experience."

She asked and I told her about my job in Penang, allegedly babysitting a journalist. We thought her report would be about ghosts and bad luck at the barracks. It turned out to be a twisty murder investigation.

"A woman reporter?" Hilary clarified.

"Yes."

"With access to the military—inside a barracks?"

"She had connections."

"Ah." Hilary took another drink, and I suspected she was becoming tipsy. "It's not easy being a woman in this industry."

She went on a brief rant before a sudden drop into contemplative silence.

After a while, I started to rise, planning to head for bed.

"Too early," she said. "And don't think I haven't noticed that you avoided telling me anything about your time in Singapore. Which was suspicious because you're happy to talk about Penang and Malaya."

I waited a beat. "You've been asking all the questions."

"Because it's my job." She giggled, confirming my suspicion that the alcohol was having a considerable effect.

"Providing you tell me about your past," I said.

She took a breath. "Boring."

"Let me be the judge of that."

"I'll need another drink." She ordered a brandy. I had to wait until it arrived and she'd knocked it back. Then she said, "It think it's about time I confessed to my nickname."

I waited.

"It's Wiggles."

"Nice," I said although there was little surprise.

She laughed and then started to recount her tale. She'd been born in the Philippines with an English father and Filipina mother. Her maternal grandmother was Spanish. That explained the British name, yet hint of Spanish heritage.

They'd lived in Manila where her father owned a hotel, two restaurants and a string of shops—clothing outfitters and grocers.

The evacuation of foreign nationals began in 1941 after the attack on Pearl Harbor. Her father had handed over the management of his businesses with the understanding that he'd return, and the family had boarded the *SS Corregidor* bound for Australia. Hilary had been fourteen.

She remembered the smell of oil and rust on the old steamer. It had been ill-suited for comfort and had been crammed with diplomats, military personnel and civilians all fleeing the encroaching Japanese forces. Despite her father's wealth, they had cramped quarters where they huddled for long days and nights. The heat and fear of enemy attacks weighed heavily on them and her mother had cried incessantly.

During the night, the steamer sailed *dark* to avoid detection. Hilary said she would slip out clutching her notebook when her parents were asleep. She'd listened to other passengers' whispers about the war and the uncertain future. She'd documented everything: the unfamiliar sounds, her fears, the distant drone of aircraft or other ships and the snippets she captured from other passengers.

I realized that she'd probably gained her passion for journalism on that voyage. And honed her skills, invisibly tailing people.

They'd landed in Sydney and been transferred to Holsworthy Internment Camp. Hilary had attended Sydney Girls High School—which was where the name Wiggles caught on. After school, she studied journalism at The University of Sydney. From there she'd returned to the Philippines and confirmed the family businesses were no longer run by the men her father had employed. After the occupation, ownership had transferred. She wasn't bitter about it, but I knew she'd avoided telling me the reason she'd been reluctant to talk about her past.

I said, "Can you talk about what happened to your parents?"

"My mother died of lung disease... my first year of university. And my father..." she choked up.

"It's all right," I said. "There's no need to tell me."

She took a ragged breath. "He enlisted a month after we landed in Australia. Did basic training and then got sent to somewhere in the Dutch East Indies. We got a few letters, but they didn't tell us much and we didn't know what happened. March 1, 1942..." she said and paused. "He was on the *HMAS Perth* which was sunk as they attempted escape from Java. If he survived—and some did—he'd have been a Japanese prisoner of war." She stopped and looked at me with liquid eyes.

"You don't know what happened to him?"

"No. I went through the War Office. Did what I could as a civilian and later as a journalist. They had a record of him going on board the ship but nothing after. He wasn't a recorded prisoner of war. Officially he died at sea."

"Is that enough?"

"For closure? Maybe not."

"What was his name?" The kernel of a idea formed in my mind.

"Charles."

"I'm sorry that you don't know what happened."

I thought—or at least hoped—that she'd forgotten about our deal. Her story for mine. She ordered another drink, and I think I should have stopped her. But then she fixed me with her sharp gaze and insisted I tell her about Singapore.

Relenting, I told her about my last two years: initially working for the government, supporting the army and finally becoming a private eye. A job involving Raffles Hotel had been a good impetus for private work. But she didn't care about that. What she really wanted to hear about was my love life. Perhaps because Hilary had had so much to drink at this stage. So, I relented. I told her about Su Ling and that I thought I could just walk away from Singapore. She didn't care about me. She'd used me. And yet I'd found a note from her in my luggage.

"Go back for her."

"I can't. It's complicated." And so, I went on to explain about her role and the Chinese secret society and her boss Andrew Yipp.

"Sounds like the mysterious Blind Man here in the Philippines," she said. "If I learned one thing from the war, it was this: don't cling to the past." She shook her head. "Something like that. Can't quite remember the insightful adage now that I try and tell you. But there's one thing that's clear."

I waited.

"You need to move on, Ash Carter. Stop pining for someone you can't have."

I nodded. She was right, of course.

We stared at the stars for a while, neither of us speaking. It turned midnight. She finished her drink, then pushed up out of her chair.

"Right," she said swaying slightly. "I think it's time you took me to bed."

Chapter 22

I was up early, before the sunrise, and went for a jog. Despite my aches and pains, I pushed through them.

Fishermen were already hard at work in Roxas harbour. I turned east along the coast and was soon away from civilization. Birdsong and monkey chatter were my only companions.

Run five miles out and back, a straight route to the south, away from the main roads. That was my plan but soon found that the tracks cut away from the coast because of rivers and inlets.

The sun came up, and I navigated by it each time I doubled back or got diverted. I passed through acres of banana and abaca plants, got lost and found myself at a high chain-metal fence. On the other side, I could see open land that looked like it had been cleared. There was also machinery and vehicles. After the beauty of the plantations and coast, this was an ugly scar.

That's progress for you.

I followed it and saw signs warning that trespassers would be shot. *The last frontier*, I reminded myself.

The fence went on and on. I'd been heading for a bay but was hopelessly lost. Keeping the fence on my left, I knew I could find my way back. Eventually, I figured I'd run three miles along the fence, and turned around. As I neared the town, I saw workers in the plantations. They stared at me, bemused, as I passed.

Hilary was waiting in the lobby when I returned, having taken twice as long as I'd intended. She looked concerned, but it was nothing to do with my sweaty, dishevelment.

"Ash," she said once I was close. "Last night... did we?"

"Did we...? You asked me to take you to bed," I said. "You'd had a lot to drink."

Her eyes flew wide. "I don't remember!"

I raised a hand, unable to put her through the torture. "No, we didn't do anything," I clarified. Last night, as I'd initially tried to leave, she'd clung to me in an awkward embrace. I didn't bother telling her about that, nor about the kiss she'd attempted.

"We went to your room, and you passed out," I said.

"And?"

I shook my head. "And that's all. I tucked you up in bed and left."

"You undressed me?"

"No. You undressed yourself... afterwards," I added, although it was a lie. It had been before she'd passed out. Luckily, she didn't spot the inconsistency. How could she have passed out and then undressed? How could I have left and yet known?

She nodded and smiled. "I shouldn't drink so much. And..."

"It's better that we keep this on a professional level," I said.

Just before the allotted hour, we knocked on Señor Rodriguez's oak front door. The butler chap answered and bowed his head.

"I am so sorry, but Señor Rodriguez has been called away on urgent business."

Hilary asked, "Will he be back later?"

"I don't think so. I am so sorry for wasting your time."

"You might be able to help us—in a small way," I said hopefully.

He looked dubious. "Yes?"

"A journalist called Martin Gillie interviewed Señor Rodriguez fairly recently." It was an assumption that got a positive response.

"Yes?" he said uncertainly.

"About a month ago," Hilary suggested.

The butler pouted. "No. It was closer to two months ago."

"About the attacks," I said. "The rebels."

He nodded.

Hilary said, "They weren't reported."

"No."

"Why not?" Hilary pressed.

The butler looked at me, considering. "It's not my place to comment."

"The attacks were on Señor Rodriguez's land?"

"Yes."

"Some workers got killed."

Again, the consideration. The butler swallowed, getting more concerned.

He said, "I think this line of questioning should be directed at Señor Rodriguez … or the police."

"They're just facts," I said feigning innocence. "Anyone could tell us that five… villagers were killed."

I saw it in his eyes. *Not villagers.*

"Workers?" I asked.

He nodded then shook his head. "Perhaps you could telephone and make an appointment. I don't believe I can be of any more assistance. Good day."

The door closed.

I walked back to the taxi, deep in thought.

Once we were on our way to the port, I said what was on my mind: "I think Señor Rodriguez is deliberately avoiding us."

"Or was told to avoid us," she said. "Ever since our conversation with the police captain in Puerto Princesa, I've had an uncomfortable feeling. The deaths occurred, so why weren't they reported? And why aren't people willing to talk about it?"

A few miles outside the port, the skies opened. The taxi had no roof and we used squares of tarpaulin to cover our heads.

"It'll stop soon," Hilary said.

It kept raining. At the port we found a place where we could dry and change, then waited for our boat to prepare for the journey back. We sat outside a café and watched steam rise as the sun blazed down.

"Tell me about the Blind Man," I said.

"Not much I can tell you. He's allegedly the head of the biggest Chinese gang here. However, I don't know anyone who's ever seen him. I understand that anyone who's tried to identify him has either been warned off or is no longer around to tell the tale. Why'd you ask?"

I told her about Wolfe's failed job: the kidnapping of baby Isa Galizina.

Hilary said, "Why?"

"Why, what?"

"Why would a gang kidnap a nobody? From the sound of it, the parents or extended family couldn't have paid that ransom."

"Mistaken identity," I said. "Or mistaken wealth. Her parents had been fairly well-off at one time."

"Let's hope they don't target me, then," she said with an ironic laugh.

We boarded the boat and tried to continue our conversation.

"Politics," I shouted above the engine noise. "We talked about the deaths near Roxas being kept quiet because of politics. The police and politics..."

"The Head of Police is also a politician."

"And he's regularly mentioned by Gillie."

"He would be."

"And he features in the committee reports."

She nodded. "You know what? I've interviewed him in the past. I bet I could get us in front of him."

★

It was very late when I got back to the bar in Manila. The last of the bar crowd appeared trouble-free, and Wolfe wasn't tipsy. More progress on that front, at least.

He followed me through to my room. As I unpacked my things and hung-up wet clothes, he told me that Mrs Gillie had returned, desperate for news. He'd told her that I was following leads and that these things took time.

I told him about the strange reaction from the police in Puerto Princesa and the feeling that the landowner had been avoiding us.

He pointed out that I was with a reporter, which sometimes opened doors but could also close them. Regarding the police, he reminded me that they weren't easy to deal with and he wasn't surprised at the lack of support from the captain.

He said, "If this is about the land reform... and Rodriguez has been buying up smallholdings, then it might be sensitive. I don't know"—he shrugged—"maybe there was trouble and he paid the police to keep schtum."

"Local farmers rather than rebels? Wouldn't that mean trouble for Rodriguez—damage to his land and property—rather than deaths of civilians and police?"

"You don't know for certain... It's just Gillie's notes. That's not evidence."

We sat pondering it for a few minutes before he spoke again. "Was everything reported in Malaya? You know it wasn't in Palestine. Freedom of the press only goes so far. I'm sure your new friend Hilary would tell you that."

He was looking at me with a sly smile.

"What?"

"She's keen on you. Did you...?"

"No."

He shook his head as though considering me a lost cause.

Then he said he'd tell me the rest of his story. What happened after the kidnappers failed to take the ransom.

Chapter 23

"If Margarita didn't pay the ransom, they said they'd kill the baby," Wolfe said. "They killed little Isa and it was my fault."

"You tried to pay. You followed instructions."

"They must have known I was waiting for them."

I shook my head. "It's more likely because of the police presence."

Wolfe shook his head. "I shouldn't have checked under the car. Everything calmed down after the Huks got away. No one was killed. No police force stormed the street. Just a couple of cops checked on the jewellery theft. I waited another two hours before retrieving the money. The kidnappers must have seen me. I must have scared them off."

I my experience, when ransom drops went wrong, the kidnappers tried again. But six-month-old baby Isa Galizina wasn't given a second chance. They'd killed her and dumped the body.

I could understand why Wolfe blamed himself, but they were the killers not him.

Things got worse, he said, because the police arrested the mother. Her estranged husband identified the body and helped point the finger at his Margarita. He agreed that the kidnapping and ransom was most unlikely and that she'd killed their baby because of their marital troubles.

Wolfe didn't believe it and spent a chunk of the ransom money on paying off a police inspector so that the case was dropped.

He'd needed that money as an instalment for his bar. Not only had the case ended horribly, but he'd become financially challenged.

In the morning, Wolfe pointed to my face. "How're you feeling?"

I'd been exercising at the YMCA gym and I guessed the exertion showed. The swelling around my eye had eased and become a purple arc.

"The eye's fine," I said, "but my ribs still hurt."

"When you're ready for revenge…"

"Cezar."

"Yeah, Cheatin' Cezar."

I shook my head. "Thanks, Bill, but I'd rather use your skills in the investigation."

"Not going to happen." He shook his head firmly. "I'm out of the business."

Hilary was trying to set up a meeting with civil police head, Emilio Santos.

The clock is always ticking on a missing person case. But sometimes, all you can do is wait and recognize the clues when they present themselves.

I decided to go back over my earlier actions. The *Manila Times'* building was my first visit. Gillie hadn't returned to work because his wife was still looking for him. However, he might have been in touch with someone at his office.

It was a long shot and turned out to be futile. His boss, Mr Edwards, was still anxious about deadlines and his assistant, Jasmine, made fleeting eye contact with me, but gave the signal that she wasn't to be involved.

From the newspaper's office, I strolled around the port and visited the shipping companies again, just in case. I showed Gillie's photo and asked them to check manifests but there were no more sightings.

I would normally visit the missing person's home, but Wolfe told me that Mrs Gillie had again asked that I delay that for as long as possible. The children still thought Daddy was away on business.

If nothing came of the meeting with the head of the civil police, then I'd be forced to look elsewhere. Mrs Gillie was in denial and, sooner or later, we needed to ask uncomfortable questions. The children would need to know. I doubted they could shed light on his disappearance, but clues can come from the most unexpected sources.

Quick had mentioned that Wolfe rejected his friends after the baby kidnapping case. He said they'd all originally stayed at the Bayview Hotel. He thought a couple of them were still long-term residents.

A solid guy met me in the hotel lobby. He had a hard-as-nails look like a man who hadn't left the military behind. Or at least, not long ago.

"You're one of Bill Wolfe's friends," I said as he greeted me with a strong grip. Maybe mid-thirties, I gauged. He wasn't as tall as me but he looked strong—beefy arms and broader shoulders than mine.

"More than a friend, mate. John Manners's the name. Bill fuckin' Wolfe's best mate." An Aussie.

"No, you're not!" an American voice shouted. A slim, good-looking man about ten years older. Manners was in short sleeve shirt and shorts whereas this other man had a smart suit. I figured him for a salesman-type in his mid forties.

"Spider Sullivan at your service," the second man said. Now I heard Irish heritage beneath the American accent.

We huddled in the bar, and I told them about my mission. Wolfe was the shadow of the man I'd known and I wanted to help.

"Don't push him, mate," Manners said. "We all tried and look what happened to us."

I confirmed that Manners was a few years older than me. A former Australian commando sergeant, he now worked security, mostly for foreign businesses."

"Z Special Unit," Sullivan said nodding towards the Aussie.

The other guy didn't comment. I'd heard about Z Special Unit in the second world war. A good reputation although I couldn't recall detail.

Sullivan, undeterred, added: "John's a hero. Part of Operation Jaywick, he was."

Manners's teeth were clenched.

Sullivan either didn't notice or didn't care about Manners's reticence. He kept talking. "As for me, I was a marine... also Pacific Theatre. Found this place and couldn't go home."

"Jumped ship," Manners said, an edge of aggression in his tone. "He doesn't tell people that.

"All in the past," Sullivan said. "Now I run a little import and export business... a bit of dealing"—he winked—"if you know what I mean?"

Black market, I figured.

I learned the group of friends had waxed and waned. Some had left, but there were a couple of others still around. One was the trumpet playing manager at the jazz club next to the Manila Hotel.

We chewed the fat, but my main purpose was to get them involved. Wolfe had been in a dark place for a long time. Now drinking less, his financial situation was improving, the bar business had picked up a little—probably because he was less aggressive.

I said, I'd involve them as soon as we were ready for the next phase. I planned to slowly draw him back into the investigation business.

"You know what happened to the baby," Manners checked.

I said, I hoped to get to the bottom of it.

"You'll need to be careful," Sullivan said. "Bringing all that up again."

Manners said he'd started to look into it and found a gang whose name translated as Black Flags.

"But just a dead end," he said.

Sullivan said that they'd both tried to meet up with Wolfe since, but he still didn't want to know.

"Figured, we just have to wait until he's ready," Sullivan said. You digging into it again..."

"Could set things further back," Manners grunted.

But waiting wasn't in my nature.

The slow progress I was making with Gillie's case was frustrating. He'd been missing for over a week and I knew time was against me. The longer it took, the less likely it was that I'd find him alive. But I still had to wait for an interview with the police chief.

I left the two old friends and caught a taxi to Quiapo in the north of the city. It was a working-class district with affordable housing, slightly better than the lowest earners could afford. Quick had given me the address in a tenement building for Margarita Galizina. However, when I knocked on doors, I learned that the Galizinas no longer lived there. After three enquiries I got a new address in Sampaloc near the river. This district was a mix of housing and small businesses. Being close to schools and the university, I sensed a bohemian vibe not evident in other areas of the city.

The home was on a single level, detached with a small yard. The door was answered by a plump, middle-aged Filipina who proudly invited me inside. The yellow-flowered dress she wore seemed to bring the sunshine into her home.

This was Margarita's mother, Evangeline.

Her English was peppered with Spanish, but we could understand one another. I was given a seat and water, and she started talking.

After the awful incident, Margarita had been too distressed. She couldn't work and had moved in here with her parents. Evangeline was keen for me to understand that they couldn't afford to pay the ransom. It was the same story Wolfe had told me. They used to own a business but had retired. Her husband now worked when he could to help their dwindling finances. They had moved twice to save money.

Margarita had married Pablo Galizina at the age of eighteen. The young man had prospects it seemed. He worked at a factory in the Pandacan district and got promoted. Margarita had a number of small jobs at first and later added the cleaning work for Major Wolfe and a big job for a wealthy couple—Señor and Señora Martinez. By the time Margarita became pregnant with the baby, Pablo was working long hours.

Evangeline shook her head. "*Muchas* hours but no more money." Again the headshake. "He no working more hours. *Usted sabe,* Señor Carter? He drinking and gambling."

It got worse. Pablo became an alcoholic and lost his job. When Isa was born, he lasted three weeks and then left home. Evangeline said that she believed he now lived in a poor tenement building in the Tondo district. She didn't care what happened to him. Margarita didn't care either. He was a bad husband and a bad father.

Señor and Señora Martinez kept Margarita on during her pregnancy and had her back after. Major Wolfe had her back as well. Margarita was a hard worker. And things went well for five months.

Then it all went wrong—or as Evangeline expressed it: *everything ruined.* First, Señor Martinez accused Margarita of stealing a silver candlestick. Without any proof, she was fired.

"She no steal anything, Señor. Never!" Evangeline insisted, and I felt her belief.

Then a few weeks later, Pablo turned up drunk. He insisted Margarita owed him money. They fought and he took some of her things.

Two days after that, there was a problem with the sewage. At least, that's what I think the mother told me. Then another week later, baby Isa was taken.

There was a photograph of a baby and Evangeline picked it up. After looking longingly at it, she handed it over. Isa had been a beautiful girl with dark curly hair, large, liquid brown eyes and pale skin.

I handed it back. "A beautiful baby."

She took a ragged breath and nodded.

"*Parusa ng Diyos ito,*" she said, and after clarification, I worked out that this meant it was God's punishment.

"Why would God punish her?"

"No her. He punish me." Evangeline shook her head and then crossed herself. "I no go to church. A month I miss it. Just!"

The grandmother blamed herself for the kidnapping, that was clear. She looked after Isa during the day. Margarita worked extra hard after losing the Martinez job. She got two small roles clearing rubbish from shops but still had Wolfe's cleaning work.

"Tell me what happened on the day Isa was taken," I asked gently.

It took a while to get the complete story, but she'd stayed the night at Margarita's home in Quiapo. Margarita had left before daybreak to start a new job at the port. It looked like a big opportunity, and she had to work for free for a week to prove herself. The money would have meant she could reduce the workload to two jobs. That one and Wolfe's bar.

Evangeline was in tears by the time she told me she'd got up in the morning and wondered why baby Isa wasn't crying for milk. The cot had been in Margarita's bedroom and was empty.

After panicking, Evangeline decided that Margarita must have taken the baby to work.

"But she hadn't," I said because the lady was crying too hard to speak.

Evangeline nodded.

Eventually, I learned that Margarita had found the ransom note in the cot. Evangeline thought she must have buried it in her desperation. It seemed she'd overturned the bedding and covered the note.

"Written in Tagalog."

"Yes."

"Did you recognize the handwriting?" I asked.

"No. Margarita, she… she think Major Wolfe will get Isa back."

I learned that they had asked neighbours, and no one had seen or heard anything. They couldn't go to the police. Margarita Galizina spoke to Bill Wolfe and believed in him. He would find her baby. But the ransom drop had gone wrong, and he'd failed.

Baby Isa was murdered.

Wolfe blamed himself. Evangeline blamed herself.

The mother was also wracked with guilt. I sensed she blamed no one but herself.

It was a heartbreaking tale. When I'd entered Evangeline's home, I'd sensed sunshine. When I left, it was as though the world had gone dark.

Chapter 24

Quick answered the ringing telephone and I gathered that it was someone asking for me.

I took the phone from him. "Hello?"

"Mr Carter?"

"Yes."

"George Edwards here—from *the Times.*"

"Yes." I said again, intrigued.

"When you came to see me. You asked about Gillie but you didn't tell me everything."

Did Edwards expect an update on the investigation? I was about to clarify that he wasn't my client when he spoke again.

"You've teamed up with a reporter."

"One of yours."

"You're trying to be funny, Mr Carter."

"I am?"

After a beat he said, "You're not?"

"Not trying to be funny? No." This conversation wasn't going well. "I'm working with Hilary Wigglesworth," I said. "We're looking into Gillie's investigations."

"You blithering idiot!"

I held the phone away from my ear, shocked by his loud outburst.

He continued: "Miss Wigglesworth is a pain in the backside. She's a scoop-stealer. Gillie complained many times… many times… that she was trailing him, trying to steal his leads."

"I didn't know," I managed to say as he paused for breath.

"You didn't know. You didn't know. Good God, man! Working with a competitor. It's… It was obvious she was up to no good. What have you given her? Tell me that, at least!"

"Nothing," I lied, thinking that he'd have an apoplectic fit if he knew I'd shared Gillie's notes with her. My head was spinning with implications, but I managed to keep any concern out of my voice. "We travelled to Palawan and tried to interview people who might have recently seen Gillie." I paused then added: "We got nothing," hoping that would placate Gillie's employer.

He grumbled for a few seconds. I think I heard liquid being poured and imagined him toping up a mug of whisky.

"Right!" he snapped eventually. "I want you to assure me that if you find out anything, you'll bring it to me first. First! If it's print-worthy, we'll print it. And if it's a result of Gillie's work, I'll give him credit. Better still,"—I imagined him licking his lips—"if there's a scandal or conspiracy that resulted in his murder… well, I should think that'll be front page news. Imagine that, Mr Carter. The publicity will do your private detective business no end of good."

I tasted bile as I handed the receiver back to Quick.

Edwards had called because of Hilary. He was more concerned about getting the scoop—or not losing the scoop to a competitor—than about Martin Gillie's safety. He practically relished the possibility that Gillie had been murdered as a result of his investigations.

I was angry on two counts. Edwards was a cold-hearted bastard. And, possibly worse because Edwards meant nothing, I was angry because Hilary had tricked me.

Chapter 25

I found Hilary Wigglesworth at the lounge bar in the Manila Hotel. She was perched on a stool, looking out of place among the well-heeled clientele in their pressed suits and evening dresses. Not because she wasn't well-dressed—she was—but because she was working, scribbling in a notebook while nursing what looked like a gin and tonic.

I could hear jazz coming up the stairs from the club next door. It reminded me to find Wolfe's friend, the trumpet playing manager. But not tonight. Tonight was about confronting Hilary.

I walked up and stood beside her. She glanced up, that bright smile appearing automatically, then faltering as she saw my expression.

"I take it you've spoken to Edwards?"

"You might have mentioned that you're employed by *the Chronicle.*" I sat down without waiting for an invitation. "Or that you and Gillie are rivals."

She closed her notebook carefully. "Would you have worked with me if I had?"

"That's not the point." I asked for water with ice from the immediately disappointed bartender. "You played me."

"I didn't *play* you," she said sharply. "You can't blame me for running down a story!"

"I'm blaming you for the deception, Hilary. You tricked me into thinking you cared about Gillie whereas you're more interested in the story than finding out what's happened to him."

"The two are undoubtedly the same. And it's not true."

I shook my head. "It's about motivation."

"All right, so I am a journalist through and through, but I also care. More than his colleagues at *the Times*, I bet. Why aren't they helping you look for Gillie? Answer me that."

The water arrived and I took a long swallow. Then I noticed the barkeep had poured me a shot of whisky too.

"You lied," I said.

"No, I just... omitted certain facts."

"Like the fact you've been trailing Gillie for months, trying to steal his stories?" I knew my argument was going around in circles, but I wasn't being totally rational. Neither was she, it seemed.

Her eyes flashed. "Is that what Edwards told you? Of course it is!" She took a sip of her drink. "Did he also tell you that Gillie and I were actually working on the same story? That we'd started sharing information?"

"No, he didn't. But then, why would he know that?"

"Exactly." She turned to face me fully. "Look, yes, Gillie and I were rivals. We worked for competing papers, chased the same leads. But about three months ago, we realized we were both onto something bigger than a simple scoop."

"The incidents in Palawan?"

She shook her head. "We hadn't figured it out yet. But we knew something was wrong. The big anti-corruption message of the new government, hints of unreported rebel attacks, the infighting between police and Constabulary. Suspicious activity—it all pointed to something systematic. Something neither of us could crack alone."

I thought about the documents we'd examined, the strange reactions on the island. "So, you started working together?"

"Secretly." She glanced around the bar. "We had to. *the Times* and *the Chronicle* are bitter rivals. If Edwards knew Gillie was sharing information with me..." She shrugged. "Well, you've met him."

"Why should I believe you?"

She reached into her bag and pulled out a folded piece of paper. "Because of this."

It was a note in Gillie's handwriting. I recognized it from the file Jasmine had given me. Short, but clear: *H – Meeting confirmed for Tuesday. Same place. Bringing proof. – M*

"That was the day after he disappeared," she said quietly. "He never showed up. That's when I guessed something was up."

I studied the note. It could be forged, but something about it felt genuine. "Who was he meeting?"

"I don't know."

"What was the proof?"

"I don't know. He was excited though. Said he'd found the missing piece." She leaned closer. "That's why I came to you. Not to steal a story, but to find out what happened to him. To finish what we started."

I sat back, considering. I took a sip of the whisky that was fire on my inexperienced tongue. But it sharpened my mind. "Edwards said Gillie complained about you following him."

"Of course he did. He had to maintain the appearance of rivalry. Just like I told my editor I was closing in on one of Gillie's stories." She smiled slightly. "It's how the game is played."

"I don't like games." I took another sip of the whisky. I knew the argument was still going round and round.

"Neither do I, Ash. Not anymore." Her smile faded. "Not since Gillie disappeared. This is bigger than newspaper rivalry now. You saw how those police officers reacted in Puerto Princesa. Something's very wrong, and Gillie found out what it was."

121

I took another sip of whisky, thinking about Lieutenant Zante's fear and Captain Mendoza's threats. About the suspiciously new and inappropriate police vehicles. About the mysterious landowner Rodriguez and his connection to it all.

The jazz music sounded good. The whisky tasted good.

She was watching me. "You don't drink."

I pushed the glass away. "You're right. Drink isn't the solution. It never is."

She raised her chin. "Do you trust me?"

"I want to, Hilary."

"I'll earn it. I'll show you…" I heard sincerity. I wanted to hear sincerity. I was pretty good at reading people. But she'd fooled me. Was her deception justified? No. If she'd come clean at the start, I'd have believed her, despite the competition between newspapers and Edwards.

"Total honesty going forwards," I said looking into her eyes.

She put her hand on her heart. "Girl guide's honour." Then she smiled. "Although I'll confess now that I was never a girl guide."

"All right, we work together," I said after a sigh. "But from now on, everything on the table. No more omissions."

She nodded slowly. "Agreed. Though I should warn you—there are some things I can't tell you. Not won't, can't. Sources I have to protect."

"Fair enough."

"Like Gillie," she said. "I have a few and I use false names in my reports. Something I should have told you, but forgot to mention. Topo won't be the source's real name."

"I figured," I said.

She gathered her things and stood. "I managed to get the meeting with the Chief of Police."

"Santos."

"Tomorrow at ten. Meet me outside City Hall. And Ash… Thank you for giving me a chance to explain."

I watched her walk away, her heels clicking on the polished floor. I still wasn't sure I trusted her completely, but I believed she was genuinely worried about Gillie. And right now, that would have to be enough.

Chapter 26

The Chief of Police had an office in the Manila Police Department HQ on United Nations Avenue. Most of the government buildings were in the old city, strung along Taft Avenue, which was the main throughfare. City Hall was the first, and most imposing, followed by the Legislative Building. After the United Nations Park was the Police HQ and a cluster of other offices including the National Bureau of Investigations.

But, at ten minutes before the appointment, I met Hilary outside the neoclassical City Hall building. Our meeting would be here.

If the architect had intended it to be uplifting or welcoming, he'd failed. The symmetrical front was adorned with columns and large arches. Detail and statues were gray whereas the concrete building was primarily tan-coloured. If the arches had contained large windows, the place might have looked brighter, but it didn't. Windows were small and square, in formal rows.

We were shown to a meeting room and at the appointed time, a young man entered. He wore a gray suit, one size too big, and a friendly smile.

"Chrisanto Cortez," he said as I decided his eyes looked anxious. "Mayor Lopez's junior assistant. There has been a delay. My apologies. Chief Santos has been called to a meeting with the mayor. Perhaps in the meantime, I can get you something?"

The room had a teak table with green leather padded chairs. Twelve of them. Add cutlery and wine glasses, and it could have been a dining room. Around the walls hung giant portraits. I guessed they were past government dignitaries, probably set here to look down on us and intimidate.

Hilary sat in the middle, facing the door. I stood.

Tea and cakes arrived.

While we waited, Hilary explained that traditionally the head of the police also had an office at City Hall because of reporting lines.

The Chief of Police was officially the Chief of *Manila* Police despite having national responsibility. He reported to the Mayor of Manila, Antonio Lopez, who didn't have national responsibility. It was complicated.

We waited an hour.

There was a strip of the square windows in the room, but they were closed, and the air was heating up.

Hilary seemed unperturbed by the delay. My mind went back to our failed meeting with the estate owner in Palawan. Would that happen here? How long would we wait before the young man came back and apologized that the chief had been called away?

No time at all, it seemed. But it wasn't young Cortez who next entered, it was Chief Emilio Santos. A hat tucked under his left arm, he wore a crisp, tailored police uniform with a gold badge.

I guessed him to be mid 50s and standing at about five ten. He had commanding presence, his salt and pepper hair and thick black moustache gave him a distinguished, yet intimidating look.

After closing the door behind him, his dark eyes flicked from Hilary and locked onto me.

"And you are?"

As I introduced myself, I felt his eyes boring into mine.

"Sit down," he commanded, and I obliged, taking the seat next to Hilary. Santos sat opposite, placing his hat on the table in front of him.

"We have a good relationship," Santos began. I noted that there had been no apology for his tardiness nor an introduction of himself. He'd met Hilary before so perhaps he thought it wasn't necessary. He continued, pointing at Hilary: "I will give you fifteen minutes because of the relationship we have with *the Herald*."

Hilary nodded. For the first time since I'd met her, I sensed that Hilary felt inferior, as though overwhelmed by this man.

"Before we start, sir," I said, "I'd like to explain that we are concerned about a missing colleague."

Again, his eyes attacked. "Why is this my concern?"

Hilary spoke quickly. "Señor Santos, I am trying to build an understanding of the investigation and the background to the—"

"Stop gabbling!" Santos snapped.

"Sir," I said, "we just a have a few questions that might help us."

Hilary breathed and this time spoke more calmly. "We wondered why the Huk would attack police outposts in Palawan and Quezon Province." We didn't know there had been attacks in Quezon Province, but we had Gillie's second map and he'd marked deaths and injuries in Palawan. Her assertion seemed reasonable.

Santos's face showed no recognition as he looked at her unblinking. "I know of no such attacks."

She said, "Hypothetically if…"

"Why would there be attacks in Quezon Province? The rebels are north, and you should be talking to the Police Constable not me."

"Of course," she said. "The funding of the civil police force has been challenging, with the focus on the military to address trouble. Perhaps you have a comment regarding reports of rebel attacks in Pala—?"

His eyes narrowed as he interrupted. "This is nonsense. The civil police are responsible for the maintenance of law and order in the provinces—the protection of land, businesses and the agricultural folk. It would be very easy to argue for more military funding because of rebel attacks, however the civil police have and always will be the bedrock of law enforcement, public order and the protection of civilians. The quote for your newspaper, Miss Wigglesworth, is this: While the military plays an important role in defending our nation, the real battle for the safety and security of our people happens every day on the streets and in the countryside. To truly protect the people of the Philippines, we need more funding for modern equipment, better training and additional officers on the ground."

It was quite a speech.

Chief Santos stood, tucked his hat under his left arm and gave us a curt nod. "I think we're finished here."

"Thank you for your time," Hilary said.

"Thank you," Chief Santos said less genuinely. Then he pointed at me. "And next time... if there is to be a next time, Miss Wigglesworth, I suggest you don't bring along a known troublemaker... someone arrested for disorderly conduct and violent disturbance. Yes, I know who you are ex-Captain Carter."

Before I could respond, the chief marched out of the room.

Hilary looked at me agog. "Would you like to explain?"

And so, I did, filling her in on the protest and how I got drawn in.

"You defended someone from being beaten?"

"And got arrested for my trouble."

She shook her head. "Maybe we should reconsider the land theft angle... although..."

"It doesn't fit with unreported deaths and injuries."

"But fits with funding issues. A stronger civil police to control the public rather than protect."

We thought for a moment before Cortez, the mayor's assistant came to show us out.

On the steps, I said what I'd been thinking. "When you suggested there had been attacks in Quezon Province, the chief didn't like it."

"He reacted."

"Got defensive."

Hilary blew out air and nodded. "That's what we do next. We go to Quezon."

Chapter 27

Wolfe's old Army Jeep coughed a few times as I coaxed it through Manila's crowded streets. Hilary sat beside me, one hand on the door, the other on the dash—a similar locked pose that she'd taken during our taxi ride on Palawan island.

Hilary estimated between five and six hours to reach Tayabas in Quezon Province. Based on the waves of anxiety coming off her, I doubted she'd make it that far.

As we left the bustling capital behind, the landscape gradually transformed. The often-crammed buildings of Manila's outskirts gave way to sparce towns, then to vast stretches of farmland. Rice paddies stretched as far as the eye could see, a patchwork of vibrant greens under the relentless Philippine sun.

I'd thought she'd relax once we got out of the city, but she was still tense and silent. Our initial conversation was about Chief Santos and his issues with funding. We went over what he'd said and his aggressive yet defensive attitude. However, the conversation soon dried up as I recognized it was one sided. Now all I got was sharp intakes of breath every time we jolted over a pothole or swerved to avoid a stray chicken. As we hit the rougher country roads, I noticed Hilary's braced knuckles turning white.

"Okay," I said. "You haven't said a word for a while except give me directions. I know you're a bad passenger, but I'm a reasonable driver."

She breathed loud and fast. "Sorry."

"Is it just—?"

"Look out!" She yelled and pointed at a water buffalo that was being led out of a muddy field.

I'd seen it in plenty of time and stopped.

I looked across at her. "Do you want to take the wheel?"

Her eyes flashed wide. "Can I? Would that be all right. Oh, Ash, that would be so much easier... I ... I can't thank you enough. It wasn't that you're a bad driver. I'm so sorry at being a bad passenger."

I got out and she scooted over into the seat I'd vacated. My shirt was sweat-soaked, and I felt guilty about my damp seat.

She grinned at me. "Let me know if I... if you need to drive again."

She quickly relaxed and drove faster than I would have. *Ironic*, I thought. Settling back in the seat, I was determined to enjoy the scenery rather than worry about the road.

As she drove, she had a story for every place, and I could hear the poetic journalist in her words. She painted pictures of a Philippines I hadn't seen in my brief time here, full of life and history and traditions.

We went south, following a massive freshwater lake that glittered to on our left, vast and calm. We stopped for a break and ate roasted fish on sticks. Out in the water, small boats with bamboo outriggers bobbed gently and fishermen cast nets. The glassy water stretched to meet the hazy outline of distant islands and hills.

There were bigger hills ahead.

"Makiling Mountain," Hilary said as we arrowed toward it. Eventually, we turned away when the bay swept left.

I know a lot of people prefer the American Jeep over a Land Rover, but in my opinion, it was style over substance. Land Rovers were more solid, and this Jeep of Wolfe's had seen better days. I suspected the US Army had sold it due to wear and tear. On rougher roads, the Jeep bounced and rattled, and more than once I was sure we'd lose a wheel.

Hilary, on the other hand, seemed perfectly at ease, bracing herself against the steering wheel like it was second nature.

"I'll say this for you," I said with a wry smile, "you drive like you're running from the law."

Hilary smirked but kept her eyes on the road. "I'm just giving this old Jeep a workout. Besides, the longer we take, the more daylight we lose."

The Jeep rattled over a patch of rough road, jolting us. Hilary expertly steered around a deep pothole, then slowed as we passed a small cluster of nipa huts. Children waved. Smoke from cooking fires curled lazily into the air, and the scent of grilled fish mixed with the earthy aroma of damp soil and rice paddies.

Another village and children ran and waved.

"Quaint," I muttered, my gaze flicking to the villagers. "But I'll bet this road's been the same since the Spanish left."

Hilary laughed. "This is nothing compared to driving the roads in Mindanao during monsoon season. Besides, where else can you get views like this?"

We passed through many more small towns, each with its own character. As we rounded a bend, the larger town of Santa Cruz came into view. It was bustling with activity, the streets lined with sari-sari stores. Vendors called out their wares, and a calesa—a horse-drawn carriage—clattered by.

The delicious smell of food made my stomach rumble and when she stopped to let a group of nuns cross the street, I suggested we find somewhere to eat.

"Just a little further."

Two miles later, we stopped at a town called Pagsanjan which had stunning waterfalls. We stretched our legs and ate at a café. Afterwards she led me to one of the many roadside stands selling fruit and drinks.

"Want to try green mangoes with bagoong?" she asked.

Based on the delicious mangosteen she'd previously introduced me to, I accepted. We took a cup each. She knocked hers back. I took a sip and discretely spat it out.

Fortunately, the vendor wasn't insulted. He laughed louder than Hilary.

"Bagoong is fermented shrimp paste," she explained. "It's an acquired taste."

My tongue felt like I'd licked a slug. I'd swill my mouth out with water as soon as possible.

"It was the alcohol," I said weakly.

"Hey, don't give me that, mister! I saw you drink that whisky in the Manila Hotel."

Guilty. "Fine then. Let's say it's no shrimp with alcohol, for me."

She laughed again. "Maybe next time, tough guy."

As we entered Quezon province, the air changed, filled with a sweet, floral scent. It brought back memories.

"Ylang-ylang," Hilary explained. "They grow it here for perfume. And look there," she pointed to the endless rows of tall, palm-like trees. "Coconut plantations. The lifeblood of this region."

I nodded but I wasn't listening. The scent had made me flash back to my first date with Su Ling. We'd been off the coast of Singapore. I'd been loaned a Japanese *sengoku-bune*—similar to a junk, but larger and more graceful—which came with both a crew and caterers. Su Ling had looked more beautiful than ever and smelled divine.

I shook the thoughts from my head. Wolfe was right. I needed to move on. I needed to get over her.

I cleared my throat. "How much further?"

"Not much."

Eventually, I saw signs for Tayabas, and twenty minutes later we rumbled into town. After the six-hour journey, the old Jeep was coated in a thick layer of dust.

We passed by an impressive church and Hilary told me it was the Basilica of St. Michael the Archangel. One of the oldest churches in the country. Tayabas had once been the capital of Quezon Province and despite being small, had grand buildings that spoke of a proud Spanish colonial history.

Eleven towns in the province had sub-police offices. Tayabas had a main police station, because of its historical significance and proximity to Lucena, the new capital.

The police station reminded me of the ones in Malaya. It was outside of the town and had a two-storey block on one end with a pitched roof. The offices and senior staff would be in there. The rest was a low-level, long stretch with a public reception area, squad rooms and holding cells. Like the police station on Palawan island, it had an undercover area with benches and tables, giving it the air of a café. This time there were no police officers outside, but there were two new-looking Volkswagens.

We went inside and asked whether we could meet the officer in charge. We gave our names, the desk clerk went away and returned. The officer in charge was not available.

"Who *is* available?" Hilary asked.

"No one," was the reply.

I showed the clerk Gillie's photograph.

Hilary said, "Have you seen this man? Martin Gillie. He's a reporter for the *Manila Times*."

Barely a glance. "No."

"Could you look more closely," I asked.

He took a long, world-weary breath, looked harder at the photo and repeated: "No."

I could see activity in the building. There must be someone we could speak to.

"We'll wait." I announced.

We sat in the reception area. The clerk looked at us, uncomfortable. After ten minutes, he went away and returned soon after.

"Lucena," he said. "The sub-station captain is in Lucena."

We stood.

"Do you need directions, to the main police station?"

We did.

We clearly also needed new identities since we got no luck at the province's police HQ. They couldn't tell us that there were no senior officers available. They tried, but I had seen an officer through the windows as we approached.

Eventually, a lieutenant was sent out to deal with us. He had a grim face, full of bitter police experience, I judged. As he talked, he rested one hand on his side arm. Not subtle.

He told us in no uncertain terms that we weren't wanted. If we persisted in our nuisance, we'd be arrested and thrown into jail.

Hilary wanted to argue, but I pulled her away. There was no point—unless we wanted to see the inside of that prison cell.

Chapter 28

The pension we found in Tuguegarao was cleaner than the one we'd stayed in on Palawan, though the ceiling fan worked just as poorly. We sat on rattan chairs on the small balcony, the night air thick with humidity. Hilary had loosened her collar and rolled up her sleeves, her notebook open on the small table between us.

She'd been fuming when we left the Lucena, talking about heavy-handed police. However, she'd calmed down since.

"Drink?" she asked, pulling a bottle of local rum from her bag. It was already a third empty and I suspected she'd been drinking before I arrived.

Maybe the heat and the day's frustration had worn me down. Maybe there was also something in her expression.

"Plain rum, no shrimp," she said. "I promise."

"A small one," I said.

She grinned and poured one generous measure and one small tot into glasses she'd borrowed from the pension's kitchen. "So," she said, taking a long sip. "Let's go over what we know."

"We've visited two of Gillie's locations. One with unreported rebel attacks that no one will talk about. One where they've clearly been told that they mustn't talk to us."

"Chief Santos," she said.

I nodded. "Chief Santos has warned them. Guessed we'd be coming here."

"I'm used to people being cautious. People in public office can be worried about a reporter."

"Especially one looking into unreported deaths and Huk activity."

She took a mouthful of rum and savoured it. "But this is more than that."

"It is," I agreed.

"Why?"

"That's the big question."

We sat in silence for a moment, each with our own thoughts. "Those Volkswagens," I said eventually.

"Those police Volkswagens," she repeated, pouring herself more rum. "They seem to be everywhere now."

"Not built for country roads. Or Palawan island."

"Exactly! Surely replacement cars aren't a priority. And yet there are the complaints about funding. It makes no sense."

We bounced around some more random thoughts until she stood suddenly.

"Map! I need a map!" She disappeared and returned with a large map of the Philippines, which she spread on the table between us. "Look, if we..."

She began drawing circles and lines, connecting our observations. The rum had made her cheeks flush, but her hand was steady as she wrote.

"Here's Palawan," she said, circling the island and marking Roxas with an X. "Then here's Puerto Princesa... the police station. Here's Quezon Province. The funding dispute between police and military..." She drew a circle around the towns we had visited. Then she went up north and drew another big circle her eyes bright with alcohol and excitement. "Here's Cagayan Valley. Three locations. Extremities... of sorts."

"Yes?" I said after she paused.

"She scribbled circles around Panay island to the south, then Negros below it, then Samas island to the east. What if...?"

I waited expectantly.

"What if, Gillie had only got as far as three. What if there are more…. The extremities!"

I said nothing.

She sat back, pondered then shook her head. "If only we knew."

"We have to stick what we do know," I said. "But there's a problem with your theory… Where we are tonight, isn't really an extremity. I traced my finger down the map round the coast from Lucena and down into the province of Negra—much further away, almost as far as Samar island. "It could have been much further."

She nodded, but she was still thinking. She put an X in the middle of Manila and another, just outside—Quezon City. Nowhere near the province of the same name.

I said, "You think Gillie meant Quezon City?"

"What? No." She shook her head. "I just thought, civil police versus the Police Constabulary. Their HQ is in Quezon City… outside Manila because of the overlap of responsibilities… I need to know where all the regional civil police stations are…. All the Police Constabulary stations."

"But why these specific locations?" I questioned the obvious. "Why rebel attacks in those places… assuming it wasn't just in Palawan? Why there specifically?"

"Exactly!" She threw up her hands, nearly knocking over her glass. "It doesn't make sense. What if there were no rebel attacks? What if they are all fake?"

She poured more rum, spilling some on the paper. I noticed her glass seemed to refill itself while mine was still on my first measure.

"You should slow down," I said.

She waved a hand dismissively. "I think better like this. Everything's clearer." She studied her diagram. "Or it should be. Why can't I see it?"

"Because we're missing something. Something Gillie found. Something Gillie was going to tell you… before he disappeared."

She looked at me, her eyes suddenly intense despite the alcohol. "You know what I think? I think the land reform issues is a distraction. They're obvious—too obvious."

"A red herring?"

"Maybe. Not newsworthy enough." She stood again, pacing the small balcony. "We're looking at the wrong pattern. The extremities. The funding budget. The attacks..."

"As far as we know there was only the attack on Palawan."

"Yes but..."

I watched her move, noting how the moonlight caught her hair. She'd taken it down from its usual neat style, and it fell loose on her shoulders.

"Alberto Flores," I said. "His name is on Gillie's list, and he has land in Quezon Province."

"Yes," she kept pacing.

"We were directed to another landowner in Palawan—Rodreguez. The police lieutenant... Two landowners..." I was thinking aloud. "De la Torres owns farms. Is this about landowners? Are the five men connected?"

She said something about big landowners being important, and Santos's assurance that the police protected the land and businesses.

"Could it be land reforms," she said, returning to something she'd previously dismissed. "It makes no sense."

"It will," I said, thinking a sober mind was needed.

She repeated her thoughts a few times then stopped pacing. "You're staring at me."

"You're wearing a hole in the floor."

She laughed, dropping back into her chair. "You know what else doesn't make sense? *You*, Ash Carter!"

"Me?"

"The tough ex-military policeman who notices details most people miss." She leaned forward, her face close to mine. "Who are you really, Captain Carter?"

"You know who I am."

138

"I know some facts." She was closer now. "But not the man. The man inside."

I could smell her perfume, mixed with rum and the night air. I was aware of my quickening pulse, shook unbidden thoughts away.

She was inebriated again. "Hilary..."

"Wiggles," she corrected softly. "When we're... alone, you should definitely call me Wiggles."

Her hand found mine on the table.

I looked down at it, then back at her face. The case, the mysteries, the patterns—they all seemed to fade into the background.

I stood and shook my head. "It's time for bed—alone. You're drunk and we agreed to keep this professional. We have a man to find and a mystery to solve. Tomorrow we find Alberto Flores and ask him questions."

"Spoil sport," she said. "But you can still call me Wiggles."

Chapter 29

The day dawned beautifully. I exercised and showered, then met Hilary for breakfast.

"I hope I didn't embarrass myself last night. I think I embarrassed myself. Blame the drink."

"It's fine," I said.

"So I did embarrass myself. Oh dear. Did I ask you to call me Wiggles?"

"You did."

"And you don't find me attractive?" Her tone was flat and I couldn't tell if she was genuinely hurt or just teasing me.

"You're attractive, Hilary," I said. "But we keep this professional. We've a job to do."

"As we'd agreed." She flashed a coquettish grin. "Although... you may call me Wiggles whenever you like."

After breakfast, we settled up and set off. Hilary had obtained directions to Alberto Flores's estate. It was west, along the coast.

The main building stood on a hill and probably had a view of the distant sea over a dark green canopy. The property was pink with many white-washed columns. Roof tiles were also pink and a white statue—possibly the Madonna—perched near the apex. I recognized the Spanish influence, although my initial thought was of a cathedral rather than a stately home.

Beyond it, half hidden by the trees, I spotted attap huts—presumably for the workers.

The drive swept around extensive formal gardens with fountains and tropical plants providing vivid colours. Hilary parked right in front of the main building's door. The old Jeep looked as out of place as a vagrant at a royal function.

There was no door pull. I knocked and waited.

"I need a pet name for you," she said. "I can't call you tough guy or boxer—by the way, your face is practically back to normal."

"Thanks, but no pet names."

She knocked on the door.

"Oh…"

"I'm not calling you Wiggles."

I knocked.

"You're no fun," she said.

I knocked again. No one was coming.

We got back in the Jeep and Hilary drove thirty yards before stopping and sounding the horn.

I hadn't spotted the old gardener on his knees by a perfectly groomed shrubbery. He stood up and doffed his cap.

Hilary jumped out. I followed.

"We're looking for Señor Flores," she said in English.

The old man, who had skin the colour and texture of a walnut, replied in Spanish.

The two of them chatted for a few minutes and he finally bobbed his head and touched his cap again.

We went back to the Jeep.

"And?" I prompted.

She shook her head, her mouth turned down. "Flores has a number of properties in various provinces. This is his main one but he's not here and… Juan… he's the head gardener… says he doesn't think Flores is coming back anytime soon."

I could read something in her eyes. A tease perhaps? They'd spoken too long for that simple message.

"Wasted trip, then?"

She started driving.

"He said something else. He told me that Señor Flores seemed downhearted and disappointed."

I cocked an eyebrow at her, although she was looking fixedly ahead. "We've got a long journey; I suppose you'll tell me eventually."

Now she shot me a mischievous glance. "Tell you what?"

"Hilary! Just tell me, what's got you so excited, you're pretending it's bad news!"

"Juan didn't recognize Martin Gillie's name or picture, but then he's just a gardener. But... It all changed in September last year."

"Flores's attitude?"

"Yes. Want to know what Juan told me happened in September last year?"

I had an idea, but decided to let her enjoy the moment. "Pray tell," I said.

"Four men on the estate got shot and one was killed."

My breath caught. "Huks?"

"That's the assumption. The police dealt with it and there was no further trouble."

"Interesting. Another location where there appears to have been an unreported rebel attack."

"Just like we assumed from Chief Santos's comments."

I said, "The deaths occurred, so why weren't they reported? And why aren't people and the police willing to talk about it?"

"That's the big question," she said. "Let me know when you have an answer."

She drove us out of the estate and in the opposite direction of Lucena. We weren't on the main road and going back through Tayabas would have meant a detour. But Hilary seemed unsure of the route. I was just thinking that we should have retraced our steps to the main drag, when I spotted a fence.

"Stop!"

She slammed on the brakes as though in an emergency and I collided with dashboard.

"What?" she asked alarmed.

I got out and examined the fence. It looked identical to the one I'd seen on the island. It stretched east and west, disappearing into trees.

I returned to the Jeep and suggested we drive along the fence, explaining I'd a similar one near Roxas on the island. It had seemed out of place at the time. Cleared land with no clear purpose and threats of death. The land in Quezon province hadn't been cleared, but I spotted the same warning sign. Trespassers would be shot.

"Is it relevant?" she asked.

"Just odd. Call it a feeling. Two locations with the same fencing."

We continued, following the fence for about six miles before it veered too far from the track, and we lost sight of it.

"Landowners and fenced-off land," I said. "If that's our connection, maybe we should think about land reforms again."

Eventually, we found the main road although we were going around the mountains in the region: south and west, clockwise. The opposite side to how we'd reached Tayabas yesterday. When we picked up signs for Calamba, Hilary knew where we were and drove with more confidence. Because of the speed, I preferred it when she drove with less certainty.

Less than halfway back, the skies opened, and we went through a sheet of rain. Hilary stopped, and I looked in the stowage for the canopy. There wasn't one.

That explained the Jeep's rust, poor suspension and solid seat cushions.

I was already soaked. "We could wait it out," I suggested.

"Let's press on," she said. "We're already wet, we can't get any wetter, can we?"

We could.

By the time the deluge stopped, my feet were in an inch of water and Hilary's hair and clothes were plastered to her skin. I must have looked the same—like we'd been swimming fully dressed. Much worse than when we'd been caught in the rain on the island.

I made a mental note to talk to Wolfe about getting a canopy for his Jeep.

We bailed out the water and pressed on with steam rising from us as the sun blazed down.

I asked, "Have you ever considered looking into the ownership thing? Have a lawyer check whether you're entitled to your old family businesses?"

"My mother did after the war. There were no papers, no proof." She shook her head. "And no political appetite, either. Think how it would look: Europeans fled when the country was in crisis and they return to make claims against the hard-working Filipinos. It doesn't make for good copy, let alone legal precedent."

She drove on and my thoughts wandered for a long time. We were running along with the massive inland lake, Laguna de Bay on our right, about twenty miles from Manila, when I had a thought. I saved it for a moment as Hilary complained about the Jeep's handling.

"I think it's getting worse."

"Stop again?"

"No, it's not that bad; just pulling to the left."

She drove on.

"Politics," I said, raising the thought I'd had.

"Politics?"

"We talked about the deaths on the island and near Tayabas being kept quiet because of politics. Could the five people named, be connected to politics as well as being landowners?"

"Wealthy people often are," she said. "Though I know of nothing specific. I've been thinking about the committee papers and the head of the civil police. Santos is also effectively a politician."

"The five people named by Gillie… Can you find out where they own land… how much they've recently acquired under the new law, and whether they are involved in politics?"

"I'll do that."

"What about Major General Valdez?"

"Are you asking whether the head of the Constabulary is political? I don't know."

"I think you were asking the right questions last night."

She shot me a glance.

"About the police and Constabulary."

"Ah, right!" She nodded. "Then we have a plan of action. Research the five names and interview the head of the Constabulary."

By the time we reached the outskirts of Manila, there was something seriously wrong with the Jeep's steering or offside front wheel. I could hear grinding, metal on metal. We'd make it back, I thought, but a mechanic was needed, urgently.

Hilary crossed the Pasig River on the Ayala Bridge by the island. The old city was ahead, but she turned away, round the Isla de Provisor and kept going on the south side of the river.

San Migel district was on the north bank. I could see Malacañang Park, ahead, but we veered right along a street with nice apartment blocks. They had views of the park with the river beyond.

"This is where I live," she said, pulling to a halt.

I nodded, impressed.

"I'll arrange for that meeting with the head of the Constabulary. And do some research into those other landowners. I'll let you know as soon as I have an appointment." She climbed out and I took the driver's seat. "And you?" she asked. "What will you be doing?"

"First off, taking the Jeep to a garage."

"And then?"

"I still want to find Isa Galizina's father—"

"The baby that was murdered?"

"Gathering all the information I can."

That would be tomorrow. I didn't bother sharing, but tonight was another scheduled Fight Night at the Olympic Boxing Club. And I was going to be there.

Chapter 30

After dropping the Jeep, I caught a taxi to the boxing club. Happy Jose was in his usual spot, a cramped office that smelled of liniment and stale cigars. I hadn't been at the club many times, but I'd not seen him smile. I figured he never did. His weathered face was a map of Manila's boxing history, each line earned from decades of training fighters.

"I want Cezar," I said without preamble.

Happy looked up from his ledger, dark eyes studying me. The fluorescent light flickered overhead, casting shadows across his face. "Too soon," he grunted. "Give it another month."

"You saw what he did last time."

Happy's expression didn't change, but something flickered in his bloodshot eyes. Of course he'd seen the illegal moves—the trips, the elbows. He hadn't gotten his position at the Olympic Boxing Club by missing things like that.

"That's why I want him again," I pressed. "Before the bruises fade too much."

He scratched his chin, the sound of stubble against calloused fingers filling the silence. "Odds would be long against you."

"I don't care about odds."

He grunted and I figured it was an acceptance. He scribbled something in his ledger. "I'll move things around. Last bout tonight. Don't make me regret this."

147

I nodded and left his office, my heart already beating faster. Outside, the sun was low. It would soon paint the Manila sky in shades of orange and purple.

I headed for Wolfe's bar, planning on rest for a few hours before my fight.

Word had spread quickly. By the time I arrived back at the gym, the place was packed tighter than I'd ever seen it. The air thick with cigarette smoke and anticipation. Money was changing hands. Concerning my fight, most of the money was against me. The smart money was on Cezar—after all, he'd beaten me soundly just a week ago.

I hadn't expected his unusual footwork last time. I'd fought kickboxers on the streets of Singapore—admittedly with little success—and reckoned he'd had similar training. He couldn't kick in our ring, but Cezar's clever footwork set up his trips. I'd played his illegal moves over and over in my head. Assuming he could still pull them off without being penalized, I would be better prepared this time.

The remaining bouts passed in a blur of sweat and cheers. I warmed up in the corner, shadow boxing, letting my mind settle into that calm place where nothing existed except the next move, the next punch.

Cezar appeared late, swaggering through the crowd like he owned the place. His supporters cheered, but I noticed others turning away, their faces hard. It seemed like I wasn't the only one who'd grown tired of his dirty tactics.

The ring announcer called our names. Cezar climbed through the ropes, bouncing on his toes, a predatory grin plastered across his face. I followed, keeping my expression neutral, focusing on my breathing.

We met in the centre. His eyes were cold as ever, but there was something else there now—a hint of uncertainty. He'd expected me to stay down longer, to nurse my wounds and my pride. My quick return to the ring against him had thrown him off balance.

The bell rang.

This time, I was ready for his opening rush. He came in hard, looking for an early knockout, but I kept him at a distance with my jabs. Left, left, right. Basic boxing, nothing fancy. Every time he tried to close, I made him pay with straight punches.

His first attempt at trick footwork came near the end of the round. I saw it coming—the slight shift of his weight, the way his eyes flicked down. When he moved to tangle his feet with mine, I was already sliding back, letting him stumble past. The crowd roared.

Round two started with Cezar looking frustrated. His attacks became wilder, more predictable. He threw a desperate hook that I saw coming from last week. I slipped under it and planted three quick shots to his ribs—right where he'd elbowed me in our last fight.

He backed off, respect finally showing in his eyes. But respect made him dangerous. He came in again, this time with a combination that drove me to the ropes. I covered up, absorbing the blows, waiting for my moment.

It came when he overextended on a right cross. I ducked under and came up with an uppercut that snapped his head back. Before he could recover, I stepped in close—too close for his tricks—and unleashed a flurry of digs to his body. He tried to clinch, but I wouldn't let him. Left hook, right to the body, left uppercut.

The last punch caught him flush on the chin. His eyes went glassy, his legs turned to rubber, and he went down hard.

The crowd erupted.

The referee started counting. Cezar tried to get up at six, but his legs wouldn't cooperate. At eight, he managed to get to his knees. At nine, he finally found his feet, but he was swaying like a drunk crawling between the clubs on Dewey Boulevard.

The referee looked him in the eyes and asked if he could continue. Cezar nodded, but his legs told a different story. The fight was stopped.

The roar was deafening. Money changed hands—a lot of money, judging by the grins and curses I could hear. More than a few people seemed happy to see Cezar taken down a peg.

I left the gym an hour later, after the congratulations and backslapping had died down. The night air was cool on my face, the streets quieter now. I felt good. Not just because of the win, but because I'd done it cleanly, no tricks needed.

I took the shortest route through the park.

That's when I heard them.

A rustle of bushes and a group of men stepped out in front of me. Cezar and four cronies. They flanked him, spreading out in a loose semicircle. They'd traded boxing gloves for brass knuckles and lengths of wood.

"Think you're clever?" Cezar spat, his face dark with rage. "Think you're better than me?"

I dropped my gym bag, keeping my hands loose at my sides. The street was empty except for us, the nearest streetlight casting long shadows across the pavement.

"Actually," I said, "I think this proves I was right about you all along."

He snarled and stepped forward. His friends moved with him, widening the arc.

I smiled, but there was no humour in it. Some fights you win in the ring. Others, you win by surviving what comes after.

The night was about to get interesting.

Chapter 31

I kept my ground and two of the gang had uncertainty in their eyes. They'd expected me to run.

It was still an option, but if you don't get away, running can fuel the bloodlust of the chasing mob. That's what experience told me.

I'd fought groups before. Sometimes I won, sometimes I lost. It depended on their skill and teamwork and attitude.

I could tell from Cezar's face that there would be no backing down. But maybe…

"Just you and me," I said calmly.

Cezar grinned.

I said, "You want to prove you can beat me? Have a go… and kicking is allowed."

He chuckled. "You'll allow it, will you?"

"Just you and me," I said again. "Prove who's the better man."

He jerked his chin up. An acknowledgement. The others saw it and took a step back. Not far, but enough to say this was one on one.

"No rules," he said.

I nodded and suddenly there was a blade in his hand.

"Cezar…" I started, sounding disappointed. I was still calm, I had an ace up my sleeve. Or more specifically, a Beretta in an ankle holster.

Then the cold reality hit me. I'd not put it on this evening. In Singapore it had been second nature. Every day, I'd clip on the ankle holster and carry my gun. I'd learned it in Israel. In fact, Wolfe had provided it. But here… I hadn't done it. I was unarmed and vulnerable.

My heart rate kicked up a notch further. Maybe I'd have to run after all.

I could see Cezar tense his fingers. Any second now…

He lunged and I grabbed my bag off the floor, swung it and deflected the blade. I'd hoped to counterpunch, but he kept his distance.

"Enough!" A booming voice cut through the tension. I recognized it: Boxing coach, Happy Jose.

Cezar hesitated like a dog reacting to its master's whistle.

The coach closed the gap. I heard other footsteps and realized there were more men coming quickly in his wake.

Happy Jose spoke sharply in Spanish and then in English: "What happens in the ring, stays in the ring!"

It was a good principle, and I'd heard it the world over. Boxing was a civilized sport. It didn't spill over into street-fighting and if it did, club members were usually expelled.

Cezar spat something back. I didn't understand the words, but I got the sentiment. He was less than impressed.

To me, he said, "Looks like you've been saved, English pig. This time." He pointed his knife at my head and grinned viciously before swivelling and marching away.

Chapter 32

The following day, Hilary stared at her notes until the words blurred.

She'd researched the five names on Gillie's list and confirmed that wealthy individuals with those surnames all owned land. None of them appeared with any reference to politics or politicians.

She'd arranged an interview with Valdez, the head of the Constabulary, but it was scheduled for tomorrow morning at ten. When she called the Crazy Bear, with a message about the meeting, she already knew Ash wouldn't be there. He'd gone off to work on the old kidnapping case. Looking for the baby's father. He said the distraction would help.

Hilary had recognized how different they were. Ash was methodical and logical. He wouldn't be rushed and could find solutions to one problem while focused on another. She, on the other hand, was laser focused. At work they said she was a worrier... like a dog with a bone. She had it and wouldn't let go.

She also recognized that a break would help them remain professional. Too easy to fall into a relationship with him.

Focus, Hilary! Worry this problem out.

She went back to her notes, the words no longer blurred. Landowners, the police, politics... Topo. Martin's source was called Topo.

That's it! She slapped the table with excitement. Topo is Spanish for mole. It's not a name, of course it's not, but it's a clue. The source is a mole. An informer. If she could tap into him, she'd have the same insight Martin had gained. It might make this whole thing fit together. Maybe it would even lead to Martin. Someone surely knew where he was hiding.

"Topo, the mole," she whispered. "The mole. Politics. Someone in government?"

Her hands shook slightly as she reached for the phone. She got put through to City Hall and asked for Manuel, her own inside man.

Not available.

She tried Sergio at *the Chronicle*—he allegedly knew everyone in Manila with shady political dealings.

"What trouble are you in now?" Sergio asked by way of greeting.

"I need to know about a mole. Someone inside the government who sells information."

A long pause. "You know I don't talk about such things."

"It's important, Sergio. Life and death important."

He sighed. "No promises… tell me more about what you need."

Hilary gave him some details and explained they had a name: Topo.

"Give me at least half an hour. Where are you?" She gave him her number, put the phone down and waited impatiently.

More than an hour later, the phone rang. "There's a club. The El Nido on Tuberias Street. Ask for Carmen."

"Does she know about Topo?"

"I can't tell you. All I know is that I have a contact for you."

"That's it?"

"That's all I could get…. Without…" His voice softened. "Listen Hilary… Be careful. Some doors shouldn't be opened."

She telephone the Crazy Bear again and left another message with Quick, letting Ash know what she was doing tonight: a meeting—7 PM at El Nido

Then she returned to her research, looking into land acquisitions by the five men. She was disappointed. They'd all acquired but also sold land. However, there was nothing on a scale implying aggressive expansionism at the expense of little farmers. Not linked to land reform, then. What was it?

Did Topo have the answers? Would she get a clue tonight?

The sun was setting as she made her way through Manila's old quarter. The El Nido was exactly the kind of place she usually avoided—a concrete building with blacked-out windows and a sign that flickered half-heartedly in the growing dark.

A heavyset man blocked the entrance. She mentioned Carmen's name and he grunted, stepping aside.

Inside, the air was thick with cigarette smoke and something sweeter, less legal. A band played American jazz, badly. There were only about 12 patrons but it was still early.

She made her way to the bar, feeling eyes follow her.

"Carmen?" she asked the bartender.

He pointed to a booth in the corner. A woman sat alone, middle-aged but still beautiful in a hard way. She smiled as Hilary approached, showing gold teeth.

"Sit," she said in English. "Sergio said you might come."

Hilary slid into the booth. "I need some information about—"

"Quiet!" Carmen lit a cigarette. "First, you tell me why I should help you. What do you offer?"

Hilary pulled out an envelope. "Money."

Carmen laughed. "Money I have. Information..." She blew smoke toward the ceiling. "That's more valuable."

"I'm looking for someone who sells government secrets," Hilary said, guessing. "They call him Topo."

Carmen's eyes narrowed. "Many people sell secrets. Why this one?"

"Because he knows something about the police... or rebel raids. Maybe fake. Maybe real and not reported."

The change was subtle but immediate. Carmen's smile remained fixed, but her eyes went cold.

"You should leave," she said quietly.

"Has Martin Gillie been asking—"

"Leave!"

"Please. I have—"

"Now!" She said more urgently glanced over Hilary's shoulder. "While you still can."

Hilary turned slightly. Two men had come in. Wearing suits, they were smarter dressed than other patrons. And moved with the casual menace of professional soldiers.

"Last chance," Carmen said, but she was already sliding out of the booth, disappearing into the crowd.

Hilary stood, trying to look calm. The men were between her and the main exit, and closing in fast. She remembered seeing a sign to the restrooms. Would there be a back door?

The band started a new song, the trumpet sounding flat. She moved toward the restrooms, forcing herself not to run. The suited men followed, not bothering to be subtle now.

A dark corridor then a back door. She could—

"Looking for something?" One of the men had reached her. His breath smelled of anise and stale cigarettes. "Maybe we can help."

"I was just leaving."

"But we have so much to discuss." He placed his hand on the wall beside her head, put his body between her and the rear exit. "About moles and the police."

The other man boxed her in. He showed her something in his hand—a switchblade. All pretence of casualness was gone.

"I think there's been a mistake," she said, her voice steadier than she felt.

"No mistake." The first man leaned closer. "You've been asking questions. Wrong questions. Now we need to know who else you've been talking to."

Chapter 33

While Hilary was arranging a meeting and researching land ownership, I went to the boxing club. I took my gun this time but there was no sign of Cezar or his mates. Some of the lads shook my hand. I'd gone there specifically to thank Happy Jose. In return, he gave me a respectful nod, which I figured was the equivalent of a smile for him.

Afterwards, the air smelled fresh, and I walked. With a clear head, I wandered the streets, thinking about what I knew... trying to put the puzzle pieces together. Where was Gillie? What did he know that made him run away?

I was hoping for inspiration.

None came.

When I returned to the Crazy Bear, Quick passed on a message from Hilary. She'd arranged the meeting with Colonel Valdez for tomorrow morning. I was to pick her up at nine.

I would help out in the bar tonight, but had the day to kill. Mentally parking the Gillie problem, I decided to spend the time more constructively on the other issue: helping Wolfe by unpicking the kidnapping case. So, I went to Tondo district looking for Pablo Galizina.

According to grandmother Evangeline, Margarita's estranged husband lived in the rough area. He was a drunk who'd first lost his job and then abandoned his family.

Tondo was walking distance, north of Wolfe's bar. I passed the railway terminal that fed the North Port district and followed the tracks to a street called Buchaneg.

Evangeline had known the street because Margarita's father had found Pablo shortly after he'd left Margarita and Isa.

The old lady hadn't admitted it, but I suspected there had been more fists than words exchanged between the two men.

I located the tenement building, which was one of the worst in the area. Most properties were used by low-income working families. These weren't slums. They were poor but respectable. However, some appeared to be last resorts, and Pablo Galizina's place was one of the worst. The brickwork needed repairing, the windows were too grimy to see out of and frames appeared rotten.

There was also a pile of stinking rubbish outside that attracted mangy-looking cats.

I knocked and asked, but Galizina wasn't there. In case Evangeline had been mistaken, I tried other buildings along the street. No luck anywhere.

Before things deteriorated, Galizina had been employed in the warehouse at a sugar refinery in North Port. I knew he'd been dismissed, but I found another employee who had worked with Pablo Galizina. The colleague called Galizina a lucky bastard.

"He landed a good job," I was told.

The guy didn't know where Galizina worked now, but he knew he'd moved to Malate district.

He *had* gone upmarket.

I strolled. No hurry. My mind wandered. I started by considering the district. Just knowing the area, wasn't much help. Thousands of people lived there. Needle in a haystack. I needed more to go on. Just like the Gillie case. Maybe he was holed up in one of the houses too.

Or perhaps he was dead.

If someone was after Gillie, then the longer it took me, the more time they had. Isa Galizina had been kidnapped

159

and murdered. I knew that as time progressed, in a missing person cases, the likelihood of a successful outcome shrank exponentially.

I shook my head. I couldn't think like that. This was different. There were no indications that Gillie had been taken. Nothing suggested he was dead.

He was out there somewhere.

But where?

I walked the streets of Malate and picked up no clues about Pablo Galizina. With aching feet, I rested in the Manila Hotel.

A silver-haired man dressed in a white coat and tails walked by. Someone greeted him as Frankie and I figured this was Frankie Dee, the jazz club manager. One of Wolfe's old pals.

I followed him into the club, which was being set up for the evening's entertainment.

A quick introduction and we were sitting at a table with a couple of cool drinks.

Dee was another ex-US Army guy, I discovered, although he had never seen combat. Easy-going and from Chicago, he'd been in the army band his whole service and, like the others, had met Wolfe in the Bayview Hotel.

I warmed quickly to Frankie Dee. A big personality, he was unlike the other two I'd met. They were tough ex-army men whereas Dee exuded suave sophistication, like he'd missed his calling to classy productions on the Silver Screen.

"Tried to improve his trombone," Dee said with a shake of the head.

"His what?" Then I understood. Something I'd never known about my old colleague. "Wolfe used to play the trombone?"

"Not very well, I'm afraid. I think he learned at school. When he told me, I had hopes he'd join the band, but... it wasn't to be."

I also learned that Dee, along with the other friends, had helped decorate Wolfe's pub. In fact, Dee had provided the bear. He'd found it gathering dust in a Manila Hotel storage room.

"He hated it at first," Dee laughed. "Grew to love the poor creature and of course it gave the bar its name." He laughed again. "Boy, we had fun choosing the name!"

We could have talked for hours, but Dee had to prepare for the evening, and I hurried away.

Evening was closing in fast. I strolled back, switching my thoughts to Hilary, wondering whether she'd learned anything about the landowners.

Back at Wolfe's bar, Quick passed me her second message. Following a lead in the old quarter? It sounded dangerous and Quick told me the El Nido Club had a rough reputation. Not the place for a woman on her own.

I didn't like the sound of it.

Hailing a cab, I raced to Tuberias Street and charged into El Nido Club. It was busy but not crowded. I guessed the bad jazz didn't encourage business. Anyone with taste would be at Frankie Dee's place.

I scanned the small crowd. Then I saw them.

Two men at the rear were standing close to Hilary. One threatening, one towering over her as he leaned in. It didn't look good.

I drew my gun, closed in fast, stuck the gun behind the ear of a man with a knife.

"Drop it!"

The knife dropped. The man who was leaning in swivelled and went to draw a gun.

I punched him with my free hand.

"Don't!"

He stopped. "This isn't your business," he said, his eyes full of questions. He hadn't expected me.

"The lady *is* my business." My voice was cold. "Now move away. Slowly."

The man hesitated, then stepped back. His companion, the one with a gun under his ear, looked a question at me.

I eased the pressure from his skull. "You step away too."

He moved.

I positioned myself with the rear exit behind me. The two men in front, the club beyond. No one else was coming. The bad music continued.

Hilary darted behind me.

The first man looked at us hard. "What do you know?"

"I'm asking the questions. Who are you?"

The man shook his head. "No answers."

"You're military," I said.

Neither man responded.

"You certainly aren't communists. You aren't gangsters. Police then?"

The second man dropped a hand beneath his jacket. I thought he was going for a gun.

I swung mine toward him. "Don't!" I warned.

Damn! The first man used the distraction and drew his weapon.

"Stalemate," he said.

"Who are you?" I asked again.

He smiled wryly. "More than my life is worth."

He wasn't going to reveal anything useful, and neither were we. He was right. Stalemate.

I said, "We're leaving. Don't follow or I'll shoot."

The man with the gun just continued to glare with hard eyes.

Hilary and I backed up toward the door.

The second man drew his gun. Both pointed at me. I aimed back.

Behind me, I heard her fumble with a latch and a handle. Then fresher air blew in.

She went through and I followed.

The door thudded shut, us on the outside, the gunmen inside the club.

I counted to twenty. No one followed us out.

We walked quickly through the darkening streets, not speaking until they were several blocks away.

"That was foolish," I said finally.

"I know."

"You should have waited."

"I know that too." She stopped walking. "I thought I had a lead on the Topo the mole. I thought it might lead to Martin Gillie."

He was quiet for a moment. "And now they know we're looking for him."

She shook her head. "No, they came in looking for me. They already knew."

"They wanted information. They wouldn't have shot you."

"How do you know?"

"Because they weren't thugs. They were probably military or ex-military and were following orders. Information, that's all they were after."

She breathed out, long and hard. "That's good."

I touched her arm. "No more risky solo missions."

She nodded, knowing I was right.

I hailed a cab and took her home. The lights of San Migel, across the river, sparkled in the darkness.

When we arrived, she said, "Thanks for coming to my rescue."

"Promise me. No more risks like that."

She kissed me on the cheek, then stepped out of the cab. Looked back at me. I wondered if she'd invite me inside, despite our agreement to wait.

"Do you need someone to stay with you?" I asked. "You had a scare, this evening."

She looked conflicted, eyebrows knitted. "No, I'll be all right."

"You're sure? You've had hell of a fright."

"I'm sure," she said. "I can be strong. And, I need you to show willpower as well."

"I can. I'll just come up and make sure you're all right."

She smiled wryly and shook her head. "Nuh uh, mister."

I grinned. She was fine. "Good. You know where I am if you need me. I'm sure Wolfe will be happy with my help at the bar."

"Go," she said. "I'll be fine. See you tomorrow."

Chapter 34

Wolfe's Jeep was still in for repairs, so we took a taxi to Quezon City, just outside Manila.

Twelve days missing. However slowly, I sensed we were moving forward. The incident at the club on Tuberias Street told me that someone was rattled. We'd have to take care, but a meeting with the head of the Constabulary, felt good... Almost as good as the high from defeating the thug called Cezar.

On the way to Quezon City, Hilary reminded me of the structure of the various divisions. The Chief of the Constabulary reported to the Chief of Staff for the armed forces. Despite the title, the Police Constabulary was in fact a paramilitary branch of the Armed Forces of the Philippines.

The national police reported up to the Chief of Police but worked closely with the Constabulary's Provincial Command. In theory, the provincial police had to involve the paramilitary if there was trouble from the rebels in their region.

I said, "As far as the Chief of Police is concerned, the Constabulary *is* the Army. There's an uncomfortable overlap of responsibilities."

The Constabulary Headquarters was at Camp Crane and was military through and through. The perimeter, marked by high, barbed-wire fences also had concrete walls. Armed soldiers guarded the main gate.

We weren't allowed to drive in, and when we climbed out of the taxi, I immediately heard the familiar sound of drills and marching soldiers.

The guards methodically checked our identification and confirmed our appointment with Major General Valdez.

We left the taxi at the gate and climbed into one of their Jeeps. It looked and smelled like it had come off the production line that morning. I felt relief that Wolfe's old boneshaker hadn't been available.

A new Jeep. Which made me think of the police's new VWs. Jeeps would have made better police vehicles in remote and hilly areas.

A driver took us into the camp, which opened up into a large, structured compound with barracks, parade grounds and training areas.

Officers in crisp uniforms moved purposefully between buildings, while recruits performed manoeuvres, some practicing combat techniques. A rapid burst of gunfire made Hilary wince. But it was just training on a shooting range.

At a typically ugly, square army office block, we stopped and were taken inside.

No portraits adorned these white walls. The chairs had metal frames and hard wooden seats. Classic, no-frills military efficiency. A million miles away from what we'd been treated to at City Hall.

"The tension is palpable," Hilary whispered to me.

I smiled. "Feels like home to me."

The Major General didn't keep us waiting. He strode in briskly with an aide and shook our hands.

Valdez was about my height with a lean but muscular build. His angular face was marked by deep-set dark eyes, framed by thick eyebrow, and a square jaw. His hair remained jet-black despite his age—I guessed he was about the same as Chief Santos in his mid-fifties. Like Santos, Valdez had a piercing gaze. The chief had appeared intimidating, whereas I sensed Valdez radiated both intelligence and authority. But maybe that was my military bias or because of Santos's animosity towards me.

The aide introduced Valdez, although not himself. He told us that the Major General was happy to provide information that might help our investigation. He also stressed that no material from the meeting could be published without prior approval.

We agreed and introduced ourselves. The Major General showed interest in my background.

"Did you fight against the communists in Malaya?" he asked.

"No, sir." I paused, seeing his disappointment. Then I added: "But I came across them multiple times and exchanged a few hot bullets with them."

He liked that, and seizing the opportunity to get him to warm to us, I then recounted a brief story from my time near Ipoh in the north-west of the country.

He nodded, impressed.

I had no doubt that the Major General was a busy man, but he didn't put time pressure on us and Hilary quickly relaxed and asked questions.

Valdez claimed to know of no rebel trouble in Quezon Province or Palawan. Most of the attacks occurred in north Central Luzon, he assured us.

When she asked about working with the provincial police departments, he told us that the police provided a crucial role in reporting incidents and calling for assistance.

He was open about the support the Constabulary was receiving from the new government. Funding wasn't an issue and even if it were, his duty was to perform with the resources available.

I sensed from his answers that he was genuine and a pragmatist. However, with the government on his side, he was in a more comfortable position than the Chief of Police.

Hilary asked whether he had heard of the rebels receiving support.

"Of course they are," Valdez said. "They're getting support from the Chinese. They'd be delighted if the Philippines became communist. However, I can assure you it will never happen."

I said, "How do you feel about the US military presence, sir?"

"I'm no politician, Captain." He smiled and I thought he'd end the subject there, but he didn't. "It's important for the US to maintain its presence and support the US—Philippine alliance. The Philippines is the first Southeast Asian democracy and seen as critical to the effort of containing communism. Their objective is to stabilize the Philippines, and we receive their support."

Despite his claim, Valdez *was* undoubtedly a politician.

"So, they are nothing but a positive influence," Hilary said.

"No comment," Valdez said and then laughed.

Hilary asked some more questions but received only bland answers.

I waited until it seemed like we'd run out of steam, wanting to catch Valdez off guard.

"Martin Gillie…" I said, watching for a reaction.

He knew the name.

"Did Martin Gillie come and see you, sir?"

"Yes," Valdez said without hesitation—so much for trying to catch him out. "About five weeks ago. He mentioned the same unsubstantiated rumour about Huk attacks. I gave him the same answers."

"Did he raise anything we haven't covered?"

Valdez didn't respond immediately. After a pause he said, "The reporter had a theory. He wondered what motive the regional civil police would have in orchestrating a rebel attack. I told him it was nonsense, of course. The police wouldn't do anything like that to support their case for increased funding."

Chapter 35

"The major general was a straight talker. Unlike Chief Santos," Hilary said once we were back in the taxi.

"And effectively pointed the finger at the police, telling us it was easy for him to obtain funds because of the military support."

"Which is what Santos said as well."

I nodded. "The tension between the two functions—or at least the heads of them—has been confirmed."

She said, "What did you think of Valdez's comment? Without prompting, when you mentioned the unreported attacks, he said the police wouldn't do anything like that to support their case for increased funding." She waited for my nod, then added: "Was he implying the opposite?"

"I think so. He chose his words carefully throughout and I got the impression he was making that insinuation."

We crossed the Manila city boundary and continued on the Quezon Boulevard but then got redirected because a lorry had spilled its load. We diverted through milling traffic around Old Bilibid Prison. There had been extra police at the incident, and I noticed another squad outside the prison.

Had Gillie been investigating police funding? Was this about Chief Santos and his ambitions?

Hilary must have been thinking along the same lines, because she said, "Rebel trouble directly targeted at the police... in regions with less Constabulary presence..."

"Like Palawan and Quezon Province," I added unnecessarily.

"This could be about funding and responsibilities... Perhaps Gillie also found evidence of rebel support."

I let her explore the idea for a few minutes. She was connecting dots and coming up with a potential puppet master. Could someone be aiding the rebels? Encourage rebel attacks in areas that weren't expected. The Constabulary weren't informed or involved. The provincial police handled it—or attempted to. Despite official protocol, it wasn't being communicated to the Constabulary. The military had bigger issues than random skirmishes in remote locations.

As we pulled up outside Wolfe's bar, Hilary drew a conclusion: "If Gillie had evidence against—"

I held up a hand and stopped her saying the name again until we were out of the cab. When she resumed, I noted how bright her eyes were. She was also breathless with the revelation. "If Chief Santos is behind this, then no wonder Gillie went into hiding. This is huge, Ash!"

I took her into the bar, where she knocked back a double brandy.

"There's only one problem with the theory," I said.

She frowned at me.

"Why *not* report it?" I explained. "This whole thing makes absolute sense if the trouble in the regions is reported. More trouble equals more funding. But the opposite has happened. Gillie's investigation seems to have been about a coverup. The police captain on Palawan denied it and we both felt that Rodriguez, the estate owner had avoided us. The police in Quezon Province wouldn't see us and we only have the gardener's word for it that there was trouble last year." I paused and shook my head. "If Chief Santos wanted to use the attacks to support his funding ambitions, then, surely... surely, he'd be shouting about it."

Hilary slumped at the table. "Then it makes no sense," she said.

Before we could discuss it further, Quick approached with two hot drinks and a concerned expression etched on his face.

I asked, "What's the matter?"

"I'm sorry... I forgot... Two nights ago, you were out boxing and then you didn't hang around much when you came back."

I hadn't. I'd walked off the adrenaline from the confrontation with Cezar, using the time to think about the case, wonder where Gillie was and hope our meeting with the head of the Constabulary shed some light on the problem.

I'd returned the Wolfe's bar, had a brief chat with him and then gone to bed, happy that he wasn't drunk. Quick hadn't had chance to speak to me.

"Slipped my mind. I was so busy. Should have remembered when Miss Wigglesworth left her messages yesterday... but I didn't." He pulled a folded piece of paper from his pocket and handed it to me. My name was on the front. There was writing inside.

Maybe I did need a proper office and secretary. I hoped not. Despite my frustration, I said it was all right.

"Who left the note?"

Quick shrugged. "Someone came in, ordered nothing, left this." He mimicked the action of placing the note on the bar. "Sorry. I was so busy, and—"

"It wasn't Martin Gillie, then?" Quick had used the journalist's photograph. Surely, he'd recognize him if he came into the bar.

"No." He blinked, thinking. "The man had a hood, and now that I think about it, it was hiding his face. I don't think he wanted to be recognized, whoever it was."

"What did he sound like? Local, English, Spanish?"

Quick shook his head. "I don't think he said anything except for get my attention so I'd see the note. I didn't even pick it up straight away." He shook his head again. "I'm so sorry, Ash."

"It's fine. It's fine."

I unfolded the paper carefully. The writing was illegible. Then Hilary explained.

"Shorthand. Here let me…"

She started to interpret then shouted, "Oh my God! It's signed *MG*."

"So… what does it say?"

"He's in hiding. They are after him—although he doesn't say who 'they' are. We shouldn't trust authorities, because they're involved. He's linked rebel activity to land sales… wait… here it is: he says he doesn't know who's behind it. We need to get the proof and expose them." She was breathless, her spirits raised. "Ash, he mentions the places we've been… Roxas and Tayabas, but also Bayombong."

"Bayombong?"

"That's in the Cagayan Valley."

Ah, the other map. I wondered whether Gillie hadn't been there, hence the lack of detail on the northern province's map. Or maybe the file from Jasmine, the editor's assistant, hadn't included everything.

We talked about the note. Hilary questioned whether it could be fake… a trap. It wasn't, I was sure. Anyone could sign *MG* but he'd used shorthand. That convinced me it was genuine, but also that he expected Hilary's involvement. If I needed further evidence that she wasn't conning me, this was it. However, I resisted announcing my conclusion, since I imagined she'd be offended that I still needed proof.

"We have the connection," I said. "The list of landowners. Not land acquisition. They're people selling land."

"What should we do now?" she asked.

"How far is Bayombong?"

"Way up north. It'll take more than a day to reach it."

"We go to—"

I stopped. Mrs Gillie had stepped into the bar.

Chapter 36

Rena Gillie was as elegant as ever in a pale blue dress. Her eyes found us immediately.

"Captain Carter." She smiled warmly, hurrying over. "I hoped I might catch you."

I offered her a seat, noticing how her gaze lingered on me before she held out a hand to Hilary. "Rena Gillie."

"Hilary Wigglesworth." They briefly touched hands.

Mrs Gillie looked at me again. "You seem happy."

I nodded. "We're sure Martin's still alive."

She gasped and put a hand to her heart. "You are?"

I told her about the note.

"Oh my goodness. Oh my! He's all right. Where though, where do you think he is?"

Quick replenished our drinks and brought Mrs Gillie a cup of coffee.

"We don't know," Hilary said. "But—"

"But?" She shook her head, a look of confusion clouding her features. "Surely this is all about finding my husband. I've paid for your services, Captain."

I nodded understanding. "We've been following his trail. We'd been to Quezon and Palawan provinces. Gillie had been investigating possible rebel attacks that hadn't been reported."

"And in Cagayan Province," Hilary added. "Martin thinks there's land purchase linked to the attacks although we don't understand what it's got to do with police funding—"

"Police funding?" Rena Gillie's eyes flew wide. "The police are involved?"

"Somehow," I said. "That's the way it looks."

"We've a pile of government meeting minutes about arms and police funding." Hilary said. "There's tension between the police and the Constabulary."

"I don't understand," Mrs Gillie said.

"Nor do we," I explained. "But we're following the trail to expose the truth."

"Expose the truth…" she said, as though tasting the words. "Captain, I want my husband back."

I nodded. "The way to get him back is to expose what he was investigating."

She frowned deeply. "There has to be a better way."

"I can't think of one," I said.

"But he's hiding because he's in danger?"

"Yes."

"But then if you are investigating…"

"That puts us in danger too." Last night's incident ran through my mind. "We know."

She sipped her coffee, thinking. We waited until she said, "I have a better plan."

"You do?" Hilary prompted.

"Martin has family in Australia… Sydney." She nodded as she spoke. "I will book us tickets. We'll catch a steamer to Sydney and stay with his family. A night boat… I'll book it in my maiden name… I'll organize it for two days… Do you think he'll still be all right in two days?"

I had no idea and didn't want to respond, but Hilary said, "Yes."

I said, "Rena, you have to appreciate that we still don't know where he is. You can book the tickets but he still hasn't revealed himself."

"That's what I want you to focus on, Captain. You must!" She sipped her coffee and searched my eyes with hers. "You simply must."

"Rena," I said, "In that case, I think we're at the point when I need to go through the house… We've had no other clues."

"You've had the note!"

"But we don't know who delivered it."

"Someone out there knows."

"True," I said.

She shook her head decisively. "No, I seriously don't believe there are any clues at home. Otherwise… Well, I think I would know."

"Sometimes—"

"I would know, Captain," she said firmly. "Find the person who brought the note. Have you located this Topo person? Perhaps it's him."

"Not yet."

"You need to find him."

"We'll try but if we don't have any joy…" Hilary said brokering peace between us.

Mrs Gillie shook her head again and said, "I don't want to upset the children, Miss Wigglesworth. You can appreciate that."

"I can. Will you agree to give us two days? Book the tickets for three days' time. If at the end of two we haven't located him, we search the house."

Mrs Gillie sighed. "I suppose so." She wrote a telephone number on a piece of paper and handed it to Hilary. "You call me as soon as you have news."

I got the symbolic message. Hilary was in favour. I was not. My client wasn't happy on two fronts. I hadn't been giving her updates and I was chasing Gillie's investigation rather than him.

We watched her leave and resumed our conversation about the case. Yes, we had the note, which implied he was still alive, but he wanted us to expose the truth, and I didn't like Rena Gillie's plan of escape.

"She needed a deadline," Hilary said.

"Spoken like a true journalist."

She shrugged. "If we don't expose the truth within three days, we can continue the investigation after he's fled."

"Assuming we find him. We have no idea where to look."

"Someone brought the note," she said.

"So, someone is harbouring him. And probably a man."

Wolfe stomped into the bar. "That was fuckin' expensive." He'd been out to collect his Jeep from the garage. "Damaged tie rod and ball joint failure, apparently. Said it must have been driven very hard."

"How much did it cost?" I asked.

"Almost twenty dollars—Very hard driving, they said... treated my Jeep worse than an enemy fuckin' soldier! Carter, you—"

"I was the driver," Hilary said. "Sorry."

I dealt out the cash which Wolfe accepted without comment.

He was still grumpy an hour later and Hilary suggested we get out.

"Where are we going?" I asked.

"You'll see." A smile played at the corner of her mouth. "We need to eat, don't we? And we need peace and quiet to think about the case."

She hailed a horse-drawn calesas when she spotted one and we continued, by carriage. The air filled with clicking hooves as we crossed the river and went into the old walled city.

She took me to a small restaurant tucked away in a colonial building. The owner greeted her by name and led us to a corner table.

"This used to be one of my parent's businesses. I come here to think sometimes."

"And you don't mind that it should really be yours?"

She shook her head. "It shouldn't be mine. The past is the past, Ash. I can't dwell on it. That road only leads to ruin."

We spent an hour there, talking through the case again. Then the owner brought out plates of local specialties.

By the end of the meal, I said, "The only clear action is Cagayan Valley."

"A taxi will be expensive and, again, too far for a day trip."

"Wolfe will lend us the Jeep," I said feigning confidence. "Quick said he's expecting it to be busy tonight, so he'll be grateful for my help... and someone else's."

The other person was Spider Sullivan.

I'd hoped Manners could make it as well, but he was working evenings on a security job.

The Juke Box belted out rock and roll and the beer was flowing fast.

The bar had started with a few locals and then a bunch of sailors came in. It was the usual slow build up and then a large crowd of rowdy American GIs on liberty bustled in. They'd already been drinking, but Wolfe had them under control.

Last time they'd met, Wolfe had told Sullivan to bugger off. A year later, Wolfe ignored him at first, but it was because of the trade.

Wolfe eventually came over and thumped Sullivan's shoulder. "About time you showed up, Spider," Wolfe said.

Sullivan raised an eyebrow at me. Wolfe wasn't drunk. Not even tipsy.

Sullivan showed his palms. "You didn't want me around. You didn't want any of us around."

Wolfe shook his head. "Weak excuse, Spider Sullivan. Weak excuse. Now, jump behind the bar and give Quick a hand. You have some making up to do."

Wolfe was still in good spirits later, so I mentioned borrowing the Jeep again. He shrugged and shortly after, tossed me the keys.

That was before a fight broke out when a group of rowdy sailors bustled in. Damage was done, including a broken window, but Wolfe, Sullivan and I managed to get between the two groups, help the sailor boys on their way and calm it down.

"Reminded me of Palestine," Wolfe said afterwards.

"Because of the wreckage?" Sullivan asked, wringing spilt beer from his shirt.

"Going into bars and dealing with troublemakers." Wolfe nodded at me. "I'd forgotten that feeling—much better sober than when I've had a skinful."

More progress, I thought.

I needed to resolve the Martin Gillie case, then focus more on understanding what had happened to baby Galizina. He was getting better, but addressing the old issue was the only sure way of getting Wolfe back to the man he'd been.

Chapter 37

The route was almost straight north, through the towns of San Migel and San Jose. Hilary and I crossed from Central Luzon into the Cagayan Valley. For a while, the going got tough. We'd been following a river most of the way, but the route to the Valley now involved over two miles of climbs and switchbacks through the hills. After that, we picked up the Sante Fe River and Hilary finally decided she could relax and let me drive.

The road stretched out before us, a ribbon of asphalt cutting through the Philippine countryside like a lifeline. To the left were mountains, to the right, hills and forests. It all looked rough and wild, except in the flat river plain where the land was prime agricultural.

We passed through Nueva Ecija where I saw farmers in wide-brimmed salakots bent double in the fields, their movements a choreographed dance passed down through generations. The air was thick with the earthy smell of newly tilled soil and a sweet scent.

"Rice, before it's harvested," she said. "It's called palay. Nueva Ecija is known as the Rice Bowl of the Philippines."

After a ten-hour journey and about 20 miles short of our destination, in the town of Bambang, overlooking the confluence of two great rivers, we found a pension. It was basic but the rooms were clean.

In the morning, refreshed from our break, we drove into Bayombong.

We'd talked about our approach. We thought there'd be a low chance that the police would help, and we were right. Again we sensed they'd been forewarned about our investigation.

According to Gillie's map, there had been incidents of some sort in Cagayan Valley although, of the eight question marks, only one was marked near Bayombong.

Was there a rebel attack here recently? Late last year? At any time?

Asking locals, drew nothing but dismissive grunts and headshakes.

We left the town and the main road and went east. I used Gillie's map, and we tried to find the location of the nearby question mark, although based on the scale, it could have been anywhere within a five-mile radius.

At villages, Hilary spoke to the locals. In the town many people had spoken Spanish. Rural inhabitants only spoke Tagalog.

No one could help.

Then we came to paddy fields that were barren. We were used to seeing an expanse of green—little shoots in neat rows.

"Drought?" I suggested.

She shook her head. "No. Other fields aren't like this. Same valley, same water source. It doesn't seem natural."

We got out at a village, crossed the cracked earth to a small cluster of nipa huts. An old woman sat in the shade, weaving something from palm leaves. When she saw us approaching, her hands stilled.

Hilary spoke to her in Tagalog. The woman's eyes darted between us, then to the road behind. She shook her head and returned to her weaving.

"What did you ask her?"

"I asked what had happened to the land."

"Ask about a rebel attack."

Hilary tried again, but the woman merely shook her head more vigorously.

A young man appeared from one of the huts. He spoke rapidly to the old woman, then turned to us with forced politeness.

Hilary listened and explained: "The man says his grandmother is confused and we should leave."

To the villager she said, "We just want to know what happened here."

She translated his reply: "Nothing happened here. You are mistaken."

His smile was tight.

Hilary pulled out a notebook. "But the land—"

"Nothing happened!" The young man's voice rose sharply. His grandmother reached out and grabbed his arm, speaking softly. He took a deep breath and spoke again.

Hilary said, "He's begging us to leave."

We walked away, the grandmother's anxious eyes following us.

"They're terrified," Hilary said once we were out of earshot.

"Of what?"

She shrugged. "Rebels?"

"But if there was no attack...?"

"Something happened here," she said.

We got back in the car and drove further. At the next village we decided to change our approach. Gillie had told us the alleged rebel activity was linked to land acquisition.

Were the rebels taking the land? Was that what the people were afraid of?

At the next village, we asked about land ownership.

We got nothing.

In fact, we got nothing from the next two villages, but at the third we were pointed away from the main track.

"About a mile, that way," Hilary explained as we bumped over rough terrain. I grimaced at each heavy jolt, praying that Wolfe's Jeep wouldn't suffer more damage.

We reached a small rise overlooking the valley. Below us, a car kicked up dust on the dirt road. Even from this distance, I could make out the official markings—another police Volkswagen. Then I spotted a fence.

"Like at the other places," I said.

"Yes," she agreed. "But what connects a failed rice paddy in Cagayan to the jungle coast of Palawan and the coconut plantations of Quezon Province? If they are being acquired, then why?"

I studied the valley. Something had caught my eye earlier, although I'd thought nothing of them. Fresh survey markers, barely visible in the tall grass.

"What are those for?"

Hilary followed my gaze. She walked to the nearest marker, brushing away the grass. Her intake of breath was sharp.

"These are property boundaries," she said, already moving to the next marker. "The land's been divided up."

"But who would buy failed farmland?"

"Let's check the land registry," she said. "There should be records in Santiago.

"How far?"

"Twenty miles. A little more because we need to get back to the main road."

"Quicker straight on?" I asked, picturing where we were.

She looked at me, doubt on her face, probably thinking about the Jeep's suspension or axles or…

"All right," she said, "maybe we'll see more of this land acquisition and learn something before Santiago."

It took us twenty minutes of treacherous driving before we came to a fence. The same no trespassing signs were there. We learned nothing new until we drove another two miles. Then we saw activity on the far side.

Heavy equipment had driven along, leaving deep tracks in the earth.

We got out and found a higher vantage point. I used binoculars and said, "They're laying infrastructure." This wasn't agricultural development—this was major engineering work.

A flash of sunlight on metal caught my eye. "Vehicle coming."

We pressed lower into the grass. A pickup truck appeared on the dirt road, moving slowly. Two men in uniform stepped out.

"Security," Hilary whispered.

I agreed. They were alert, scanning the fence with military precision. Then they started walking toward where we lay.

"Time to go," I said quietly.

We began crawling backward through the grass.

A bird burst from the grass nearby, startled by our movement. One of the men's heads snapped toward the sound.

"Run," I hissed.

We broke cover, staying low. Behind us, I heard sharp commands and the sound of pursuit.

The Jeep was thirty yards away. Hilary was faster than I expected, keeping pace beside me. More shouting.

We jumped in, Hilary at the wheel, me now with my Beretta in my hand.

Another shout, a warning, followed by the crack of a pistol.

She hit the accelerator, and we thundered off the track, bouncing like a boat on choppy seas. Another shot and ping of metal on metal as it hit the rear.

I pointed my gun and fired, a wild shot because of the jolts but it let them know we were also armed.

The shooting stopped.

But we kept going until I eventually put my hand out to calm Hilary down.

She slowed. "No one's ever shot at me before," she said breathless. "I don't know whether I'm scared or exhilarated!"

"Both," I said. "Those men meant business. They aimed to kill... those weren't warning shots. No wonder people around here are scared."

Chapter 38

Hilary was wrong. Santiago didn't have a registry office. In the town hall, she was told that the provincial office was located in Tuguegarao, sixty miles north.

If we went up there, we'd spend another day away from Manila… which was where we judged Gillie must be hiding and was also the deadline that Rena Gillie had agreed to. Time was short, so we tried a desperate measure.

I dealt out the cash and we paid an official in Santiago to find out for us.

We showed him the location and asked who owned the land. Within the hour, he was back with the information.

"The registered owner is Enexacion Agriceutial Inc." He gave us a date last September. A few months after the purported rebel activity in Palawan. "What's interesting," the man went on, seemingly relishing his role, or maybe the payday, "They made a number of acquisitions in the Valley."

He showed us three places on a map along the Monaceon mountain range that ran up the east coast, much further north.

He touched his nose, indicating that he had more to say. Once I'd provided more cash, he said, "I'll tell you something, these are not agricultural sites."

★

We drove back south. The sun was low, casting long shadows across the valley. Another new police vehicle passed us, and I watched it in the mirror until it disappeared in our dust.

In Santiago, I'd asked who owned this mysterious company called Enexacion Agriceutial Ltd. The man in the town hall didn't know. He said the only way to find out was through company registration records in Manila.

So, we were going home.

We debated where we'd stop for the night, but agreed we needed to get back as soon as possible. We knew land had been acquired in multiple locations at around the same time last year. We knew they were probably owned by the same company, based on the fencing and warning signs. But we still didn't know who was behind the company.

And we didn't know how the rebels featured.

We bounced around the idea that the Huks were behind the land acquisition. Force the sale through fear. But why would they want it?

If the land had been agricultural, Hilary argued, she'd understand. The communist rebels had an issue with land ownership and workers' rights. They could conceivably develop commune farms… but the land acquisition in the hills didn't fit with that logic.

No, we agreed, this was something else. Maybe even linked to the issue of police funding or political conflict between the police and the Constabulary.

We still had a bunch of questions and prayed the answers lay in Manila's company registration records.

Hilary's grip tightened on the steering wheel as she navigated the twists and turns with skill, the hum of the engine filling the air with a low, steady thrum.

I hadn't mentioned it, but since we'd been shot at, my senses were on high alert.

I'd adjusted the passenger side mirror and kept my eyes on the road behind. And trouble, it seemed, was not far behind.

It had disappeared for a while and I'd relaxed slightly, but a sleek black Ford was back, the last rays of light glinting off it. Seeing it in Santiago when we left the town hall and again on the road south was too big a coincidence. The hairs on my neck prickled with a sense of unease.

"Hilary," I said quietly, my voice low and urgent. "That car behind us has been following for a while now. I want you to pull over."

Hilary glanced at me, her brow furrowed in concern, but she did as I asked, easing the car to a stop on the shoulder of the road. The Ford slowed to a halt about eighty yards behind us. The windows reflected sunlight, betraying nothing of the car's occupants.

I watched with a wary eye as the seconds ticked by, tension thickening the air between us like a suffocating blanket. Then, without a word, I nodded to Hilary, and she started the Jeep once more, the engine revving to life with a low growl.

The Ford followed suit, falling into line behind us as we resumed our journey southward. But I was not about to let them dictate the terms of this encounter.

"Stop," I said abruptly, my voice tight with urgency. "Stop right now. Here, in the road."

Hilary obeyed without hesitation, bringing the Jeep to a halt once more. I threw open the door and stepped out into the road, Beretta drawn, eyes fixed on the approaching vehicle.

As the Ford drew nearer, I could make out the figures of two people inside, presumably uncertain of how to deal with me standing in their path.

The Ford stopped twenty-five yards away, the engine grumbling impatiently. It waited like a predatory beast biding its time.

I raised my gun.

The driver clunked the Ford into gear. I heard the grinding noise. I readied, but instead of coming toward me, it began to reverse. Slowly at first and then faster.

I broke into a run. They'd have to stop and turn around. I'd confront them.

The Ford braked. Then it was lurching forward suddenly, its engine roaring as it accelerated toward me.

I dived aside just in time, the rush of air from the passing vehicle whipping at my clothes as it thundered past. I scrambled to my feet, adrenaline coursing through my veins as I watched the Ford disappear into the distance, leaving behind nothing but a cloud of dust and the lingering scent of danger.

I'd seen the men's faces and I'd seen them before.

The men who'd cornered Hilary at the club in Manila's old quarter.

Chapter 39

I kept my eyes peeled, looking for the black Ford. Maybe it had followed. Maybe I hadn't seen it in the dark, but I got the sense they didn't need to follow us.

They knew where we were going.

I wondered whether they'd tailed us yesterday, maybe all the way from Manila, checking where we were going.

We talked about the men. They undoubtedly had weapons and could have confronted us. Why didn't they? Like when we'd met them before. It had been the same two men who'd confronted us at the Tuberias Street jazz club. They had guns. They were professional.

Professional enough to only get caught on our way back.

Not killers. They'd wanted answers.

Were they who Gillie was hiding from or were they working for someone else?

We bounced it around but had no answers.

I dropped Hilary off in the early hours. She said she'd spend the morning investigating Enexacion. It would be boring and be no faster with two of us—especially since I had no experience of company registrations in the Philippines. I accepted on the grounds that she'd take no risks.

She promised and we agreed to meet in the National Library at 1 PM.

I returned to the Crazy Bear and was relieved that there was no sign of more trouble. I was also intrigued to find my camp bed had been replaced with a proper one.

Curtesy of Sullivan, Quick told me in the morning. The ex-Marine had also supported them in the bar last night and Wolfe hadn't been too drunk.

After helping Quick tidy, I still had three hours before my rendezvous with Hilary. And I knew exactly how I'd fill the time.

Three days ago, I'd gone looking for Pablo Galizina. I'd been to the rundown property in Tondo, and I'd found an old workmate at the Sugar Refinery at North Port. Mr Galizina allegedly now lived in upmarket Malate. If he was there, then in the years since losing his job at the sugar refinery, he'd sorted himself out. Big time.

Government employees and other professionals lived in the coastal area of Malate and the neighbouring district of Ermita. In fact, the Martinez family, where Margarita had worked for years, had a house in the area. I doubted Galizina was *that* successful and started my search at the other end of the district, where there weren't any parks or views of the sea. I'd previously covered half of it, now I started in a sector between a tributary and the southern rail track.

I got no hits until I progressed west.

"Galizina?" an old chap said as he and a friend smoked and watched life pass along their street. I could see money was required, so I pressed some notes into his hand. The old guy pointed his thumb at his friend. "He can tell you."

The second guy put out his hand, but once bitten... I held onto the notes until he told me.

He duly obliged. There was a café called Galizina's, just two blocks further on.

I parted with the extra cash and soon found the place. It was the local equivalent of a Malayan shophouse. The ground floor was a small café. Upstairs would be the living quarters.

189

"Pablo Galizina?" I said, greeting the man behind the counter.

He smiled before his brain kicked in. Then he frowned.

"Who are you?"

"Just someone looking for you."

"Why?" He glanced past me at the other people in his café. At least that's what I thought. I was wrong. He'd been considering his options, because he immediately darted in the other direction.

I could have chased after him, but figured there would be doors involved, maybe locked ones. And I know this type of shop. So, I sprinted out of the café and round the side, hoping to cut him off.

There was a narrow service alley behind the properties and that's where I found Galizina. He was no runner, and it took me less than minute to catch him.

A sharp push into a wall stopped him dead.

"Why'd you run?"

He gasped for breath. "You're the police."

"I'm not."

"Who are you then? What do you want?"

"I want to understand what happened to your daughter."

"Isa?" he said as though unsure of his own daughter's name.

"How many daughters have you got?" I asked.

His breathing calmed. He shook his head. "What? One... none. You know she died?"

"She was murdered by kidnappers a year ago," I clarified.

"Yes... yes." He shook his head again. "Terrible."

I asked if he knew why they had targeted his daughter. Galizina said he didn't know. I asked why he'd lost his job at the sugar refinery. He said the boss didn't like him.

I fired other questions hoping to learn something that made sense. Did he owe money? Did he know any gang members? Had he been in trouble? Was it someone getting revenge against him?

Nothing.

He told me it was Margarita's and her mother's fault that the baby had been taken. They should have been looking after her.

The urge to punch Galizina welled up inside me. Maybe it was a hangover from yesterday's adrenaline fuelled confrontation with the men in the black Ford. Or maybe I just plain disliked him. He was cold, with no empathy. No distress at the loss of his child.

But I didn't hit him. I took a breath and asked what he'd been doing on the day Isa was taken.

"I was drunk. I was in a bad way then. I think the shock of Isa's murder helped me sort myself out."

"I'm glad some good came of her death then," I said bitterly. "Did you help look for her?"

"Not with Margarita, no. The ransom note said to keep it quiet. No police. I asked around and then she employed a detective, and I thought he would find Isa."

I said, "You identified the body."

"Yes."

"What was it like?"

"What? Isa's body?"

He was twitchy. I didn't like the way he responded and knew something was amiss. So, I fired more questions at him, made him more and more uncomfortable. And finally, he broke down, unable to look me in the eye.

"It was awful. She'd been bloated in the water. There were cuts from a propellor or something. She was sliced up." He paused and gulped air. "Her necklace. She had nothing on, just her necklace. It had her name on. It was her."

Chapter 40

My head ached and my heart was heavy. Pablo Galizina's grief both disturbed and troubled me. Plus, my idea of a distraction this morning had been a mistake. There was enough to think about with the problem of Martin Gillie's investigation. The kidnap and murder of Isa Galizina wasn't straightforward. I'd been a fool to think otherwise.

Shortly before 1 PM, I climbed the stone steps of the Bureau of Public Libraries. That was the official name, changed a few years ago. Carved into the stone was the old, more popular name: *The National Library of the Philippines*. It was a giant, neoclassical building on the edge of United Nations Park.

After five minutes, searching, I'd wished Hilary had been more specific. Where was she?

I told a curator that I needed information on a company and he directed me to the Public Record Archives department.

There I spotted Hilary at a desk surrounded by stacks of papers. With her hair tied up, she looked ready for business—the determined investigative reporter.

"There you are!" I said, approaching.

A man looked up, disapproval on a weathered face.

"Sorry," I mouthed.

He turned his cold eyes back to the ledger he was reading.

"Well," she whispered as I sat down and slid a document toward me. "I've had some success... This is from the business registry: Enexacion Agriceutial Inc was incorporated seven months ago."

I studied the paper. The company details were sparse—just a Manila address and a generic business activity: agricultural investments.

"That's their registered office," she said, pointing to an address. "I went there this morning. It's just a lawyer's office. One of those that handles hundreds of companies."

"Enexacion's a shell company?"

She nodded with a little smile playing at her lips. "Not just one, but I've found six. It took some digging because there's a web of them. Company's owning companies."

"Is that allowed?"

"Of course, but someone must benefit somewhere down the line. I just had to untangle it."

"Who?" I asked.

"Carlos Delgado."

I shook my head. The name meant nothing. It wasn't a name on Gillie's list.

"He's a senator. Big and rich."

I said, "So he's the one buying land in remote spots."

"Nothing wrong with that," she said, looking disappointed. "That's what's been bothering me. Delgado is very active with the government and chairs committees. Maybe we're wrong. Maybe this is something else entirely."

"Too big a coincidence, Hilary. There must be a connection between the unreported rebel attacks. Just like Gillie said in his note."

"If they were real."

I caught the man with the weathered face and cold eyes glaring at me. The volume of our conversation had increased, and I mouthed "Sorry" again. Whispering to Hilary, I said, "Gillie sent us to Cagayan Valley."

"You know," she whispered back, "there is a something we're ignoring. I find it hard to accept, but it's possible... just possible Gillie is wrong. He's hiding, presumably afraid for his life and yet we both agree that the men in the black Ford weren't out to kill us."

I nodded. "Paranoia?"

"It's not unknown," she said, "amongst the journalist community. It's a stressful job, and people do get murdered."

"Sounds real enough to me." I could have added that Gillie's caution was sensible. Hilary had gone bundling into the jazz club and could have got into serious trouble. The outcome could have been very different if I'd not arrived in time.

No point in discussing it again though.

She said, "Where do the police and Constabulary fit in… the budget issues and tensions between divisions?"

We kept coming back to the big question. If there had been rebel attacks and the police were covering them up, it made no sense. The Chief of Police, responsible for both Manila and the regional divisions, would surely use the trouble to get more funding.

"Unless the budget problems aren't real," I said.

"The new police vehicles," she said.

"Even if they aren't exactly appropriate. It's—"

A shadow fell across our table. We both looked up to see a librarian giving us a stern look. Hilary quickly gathered her papers.

"We should go," she whispered. "There's nothing more for us here."

We went outside, hit by a blast of heat as we exited the cool building..

The urgency of Gillie's investigation suddenly appeared to pale. The calm of the library. The tranquil beauty of the United Nations Park. Or perhaps I was again distracted by what Pablo Galizina had revealed. I don't know why I'd hoped the father of baby Isa could help, but I needed to get Wolfe back to being the man he used to be. Which meant cracking the kidnapping case that had led to the baby's murder and Wolfe's depression.

"What do we do?" I said as we strolled. If I'd been thinking more clearly, I wouldn't have needed to ask.

"We talk to Senator Delgado," Hilary said.

The logical next move.

City Hall was just ahead, and we went inside hoping to arrange a meeting with the senator.

He wasn't available. Not only that, but his diary wasn't available. We couldn't make an appointment.

"I could go through official *Chronicle* channels," Hilary said.

"Or we could find out where he lives… pay him a visit there."

She looked at me askance, then inclined her head. "Wait for me outside. Give me ten minutes."

Intrigued, I retreated to the exterior heat and sat in the shade of a tree.

Hilary was less than ten minutes.

"I have a contact," she said grinning. "He felt terrible about sending me to the Tuberias Street jazz club. Ordinarily—"

"You got an address?"

She grinned and waved a piece of paper. "I got an address. Just outside the small town of Maycauayan. He's there now."

"Maycauayan? Where's that?"

"North. Central Luzon, on the other side of the city limit. He has a nice big house. My man described it as a palace."

It seemed straightforward, turn up to the senator's residence and ask him questions. But would he let us in? I guessed we'd find out. We had to. There were no other obvious leads.

As we walked, I thought more about the investigation. I wanted Martin Gillie to be wrong. Hiding because of paranoia. Hilary would be disappointed, but I wanted it over.

"What are you thinking about?" she asked.

"How we could flush Gillie out… if he's not in danger."

"He's not? What about the men in suits with guns!" she said, reminding me of the men from the club and black Ford.

Yes, there was that dimension. Plus, the security at the fence in Cagayan Valley. We'd been shot at. *Trespassers will be shot.* We hadn't even been on their land!

Jones Bridge was ahead. We'd cross the river, go to Wolfe's bar and borrow his Jeep again. He'd start charging me rental for it soon.

Ahead were police. They were on the bridge, and for a second, I flashed to concerns about Manila police. But the men in khaki weren't there for us. They were barricading the bridge and embankment. There was a body in the water.

Chapter 41

A police launch bobbed on the gray water while a crowd of onlookers gathered behind temporary barriers. A body lay on the concrete embankment under a canvas sheet.

We could have taken a detour over MacArthur Bridge and round, but everyone was watching and waiting, so we did too.

Police photographers snapped pictures. Hilary mingled with newsmen and heard whispers of murder. A body in the river wasn't a daily occurrence, but neither was it rare. It would be in the newspapers tomorrow. Or Hilary could use her contacts and find out before it made the presses.

But we had Senator Delgado on our minds.

Finally, a Black Mariah took the body away and we were allowed to cross the bridge.

When we got to the Crazy Bear, Wolfe and Quick were outside.

"Just talking about getting tables out here," Quick said.

It sounded like a good idea since business was picking up.

"You had a bit of trouble, last night" I said to Wolfe. "Sorry I wasn't here to help."

"We coped. You were busy," he said casting a glance at Hilary and getting the wrong idea.

"We're still busy," I said, then filled him in on the investigation.

At the end he sighed. "I'm not your partner, Ash."

"No," I said, "But I'm leading up to a request... Can we borrow the Jeep again?"

"Next time, I'll have to start charging," he said.

Forty minutes later, after filling the Jeep's tank with much more fuel than I needed, we drove through the poor town of Maycauayan.

Senator Delgado's place wasn't poor. Nor was it the 'palace' we'd been led to believe. But it was nice. There was a ranch house and horse farm on one side. It had a stream running through the grounds and there were great views of distant hills and forests.

The main house was modern, maybe styled on something American. It was white and with pillars like the neoclassical National Library, but where the latter was imposingly tall and blocky, the senator's house was on two floors with curves and arches. It also had a pond with a fountain and a swimming pool at the rear.

Ideal for entertaining, I thought.

On the way, we'd braced ourselves for rejection. Either Delgado wouldn't be there, or he'd refuse to see us. We bounced around ideas we could use to encourage an interview. The best seemed to be around the secrecy behind the companies. Why hide the ownership unless there was something suspicious. The new government had been elected on an anti-corruption ticket. Hilary would tell the senator she'd dig until she found out what he was up to.

Threats made me nervous, but what else did we have?

A goliath of a security man stopped us at the estate gate.

There was a tall fence around the property, not unlike the one around the land acquired by Enexacion.

"Trespassers will be shot," I whispered to Hilary.

"It's not funny," she said.

"I wasn't joking."

The gate security guy rang through to the house. We waited. He pressed the phone to his ear and looked at us through narrowed eyes.

I watched his mouth say "Si" at least four times before he replaced the receiver.

"Just how tall are you?" I said, being friendly when he came back.

"Six eight." Six inches taller than me. Three inches more reach. At least. Although, based on his weapon, I figured he would shoot rather than punch.

"Impressive." I smiled disarmingly. "So, can we come in?"

"Yes."

Hilary and I exchanged disbelieving looks.

"But not an interview," the big guy said. "Just a conversation. Off the record. You agree to that, and you can meet with the senator."

"We agree," I said.

The big man opened the gate. "Leave your Jeep here and walk."

We started walking and the big man followed. I didn't look, but imagined he had his hand on his holster. He didn't ask if we were armed, which was a good sign. I'd switched my Beretta from my ankle holster to my pocket while Goliath wasn't looking.

The driveway was a hundred yards, at least. Just before, on the right, was a garage. There were multiple cars parked up, most of them fancy. One of them wasn't.

A black Ford.

Hilary noticed.

"It's a common car," I said unconvincingly.

She winced.

A pretty, young woman opened the door before we reached it.

We stepped inside. The big guy didn't come in. I breathed with relief. But where were the two goons from the black Ford?

She introduced herself as the senator's assistant, then led us through a sumptuous reception area with wooden flooring and thick rugs. There were giant paintings, far better than the ones in City Hall, and every console table had a vase that looked like it should be in a museum.

A crystal chandelier, larger than any I'd seen, hung in the middle and a staircase swept up to the second floor.

We took two turns, right then left, before being shown into a study.

A silver-haired man with tanned skin and piercing blue eyes, stood and smiled. He was at least an inch shorter than me, wearing a white suit with a colourful cravat. Charisma came off him like sun beams. He reminded me of Wolfe's friend, Frankie Dee. Whereas Dee didn't have a hard edge, I sensed the senator's charm was pure veneer.

"Welcome," he said. "Captain Ash Carter and Miss Hilary Wigglesworth, the journalist. Welcome." He indicted two captain's chairs on the opposite side of his table. "Please take a seat."

We sat.

"So, we meet," he said. "So, we meet."

Hilary leaned forward. "Enexacion Agriceutial Inc."

"Yes," he said, his face giving nothing away.

"There is a web of shell companies that leads to you."

"Yes," he said again. "I'm not denying it, Miss Wigglesworth. What is your point?"

I said, "Could you explain why it was so hard to unravel the web and determine you are the beneficial owner?"

He cleared his throat. "Very well... and this is why I've agreed to meet with you... on the basis this is kept out of the press." He waited for Hilary's nod before continuing. "I am the owner of multiple sites throughout the Philippines. The reason for the caution is simple. Rebels. Communists. They don't like the rich. They don't like speculation at what they see as the expense of the people. Now, obviously, I'm a capitalist. I won't deny that. However, I do not want to paint a target on my back. So, I keep my activities under wraps. I had some trouble a couple of years ago... hence the security fence and guards… I live in Central Luzon and don't want to move, because I love it here… but there's a calculated risk. I calculate the risks and so far, touch wood"—he made a show of tapping his ornately carved desk—"I've been relatively unscathed."

Hilary said, "Your two men threatened me at a club on Tuberias Street."

"Yes," he said, surprising me with his frankness. "I asked them to find out what you were digging into. I have a natural wariness of the press."

"They threatened me with guns."

"That's regrettable, although I understand you, Captain, drew first."

Hilary said, "They could have just asked me."

"They tell me they tried."

"We were shot at outside one of your properties near Bayombong," Hilary said.

He shook his head. "I know nothing of that. But my guards must be vigilant. Perhaps you appeared to be a threat."

"We don't look like rebels," Hilary said.

"We were simply looking," I added. "We made no move to enter."

"Then I sincerely apologize," he said. "I'll find out who was responsible and fire them. They should only deter trespassers."

Hilary said, "Tell us about the rebel attacks."

He shook his head. "You'll have to forgive me. Which rebel attacks are you referring to?"

"Unreported ones," Hilary said pointedly.

The senator shook his head again.

She said, "It looks like the regional police are covering up attacks, Senator."

"Where?"

"At locations near where your company has bought land."

He scrutinized her for a moment with his piercing eyes. "That is ridiculous. Do you have evidence of attacks by rebels outside Central Luzon?"

Hilary blew out air, frustrated. "No, but we think another journalist—Martin Gillie of *the Times*—found out about them."

"What does the Chief of Police say? I assume you've approached him."

I said, "He denies it."

"And the head of the Constabulary? Have you spoken to him as well?"

"Also claims he knows nothing."

The senator hitched his shoulders in a tiny shrug. "Then I think you are barking up the proverbial wrong tree."

Hilary said, "Are you looking for Martin Gillie?"

"The reporter you just mentioned? I don't know the man," Senator Delgado said. "Why would I *look* for him?"

"Because he was investigating you and your company."

Delgado shook his head sadly. "Really? This is the first I'm hearing of it."

"And yet you knew *we* were investigating." Hilary pressed.

"I received a report from Palawan. I purchased land there. After your questions there, I asked my men to keep tabs on you. Again, I apologize if they overreacted."

That sounded reasonable.

"Did you buy the land after a rebel attack?" Hilary pressed.

The senator shook his head with a sad expression. "It sounds to me like you have got some good information about my activities. You've promised to keep it under wraps because of the potential threat to my life."

"I—" Hilary started to protest.

"Anything else... this bogus rebel activity... questions about the police... I think you are in danger of stirring something up. You're in danger of creating news rather than simply reporting it."

"I—" Hilary began again.

Delgado cut her off again. "Ethically, I'm sure that's not your intention. I'm praying and trusting that you do the right thing, Miss Wigglesworth. Do not build this up into something that it is not."

On the way back from Senator Delgado's, we were both lost in our thoughts. We'd hoped for a *Eureka!* moment, joining all the dots. It had been a long shot.

We hadn't expected a confession from the senator. I reflected that we'd been lucky he'd seen us. But his objective appeared plain. We'd uncovered his secret land acquisition activity, but he denied any of the rest.

I went back to wondering whether Martin Gillie had been mistaken. I didn't know him, but even Hilary had admitted he might be paranoid.

As we neared her building, I caught a whiff of Coca Cola. The wind was southeasterly, blowing the sweet caramel scent from a massive factory towards the river.

When Hilary spoke for the first time since we'd crossed the city limits, she confessed to a problem with her editor. He'd been tolerant when she'd told him about a conspiracy theory, involving unreported rebel attacks, but now we still had nothing concrete.

She had other stories and suggested they might have to receive more attention than Martin Gillie. We'd burned two of the days that Rena Gillie had given us to find him.

It couldn't be helped. Arbitrary deadlines were for journalists not detectives.

We were both exhausted from missing a night's sleep. I left her with a peck on the cheek and a promise that we'd have dinner tomorrow night.

Then I drove to Wolfe's bar and helped him for the evening.

He'd boarded up the broken window and we prepared in case more trouble arose tonight. But none came.

That had to wait until the morning.

Chapter 42

Hilary hadn't told Ash the full story. When they'd returned from Cagayan Valley there had been a letter waiting for her. She recognized who it was from—*the Chronicle*. Her boss.

She called him and received the same warning. Wrap this up tomorrow or find another job. He was angry. She'd missed deadlines in favour of Martin Gillie's case. As her boss became more frustrated, she'd argued more strongly that it would be big... the exposure of government corruption.

And all she had was Exenacion buying remote plots of land which could be tied to Senator Delgado. She could write about that, but ethics prevented her. The story wasn't huge, it was more personal. And she'd given her word to the senator.

There was no big story.

Martin Gillie was probably paranoid after all.

There might be a smaller story, she thought. One about the tension between the regional police and the Constabulary. Perhaps she could build out on the suggested deaths and injuries.

She spent the early hours working on an outline, trying to pull together quotes and threads that were gossamer-fine, but maybe...

In the morning, Hilary went to *the Chronicle's* office. Once she'd confessed that she hadn't got Martin Gillie's big conspiracy, her boss gave her fifteen minutes to convince him she had something that justified two weeks without a submission.

She delivered her planned speech. Most of it hinged on the unofficial statement by the police lieutenant Zante at Puerta Princessa, practically admitting to unreported rebel attacks last July. If she could...

Hilary's editor didn't give her the full fifteen minutes.

As she walked out of the office, she could feel everyone's eyes on her. Like they knew. On the steps outside, she let the tears flow freely. She'd been a fool. As a female journalist it was tough. It was a man's world. To prove herself, she'd known she'd have to do far more than her junior counterparts. She'd seen an opportunity with Gillie's conspiracy theory and thrown everything at it.

She should have let Ash investigate and stay on the periphery. In the meantime, she could have fulfilled her menial tasks, writing copy, meeting deadlines.

But no. Hilary Wigglesworth was better than that. She knew better. All or nothing.

And now she had nothing.

Fired from *the Chronicle,* none of the popular newspapers would take her. Not after this. She'd have to start at the bottom... either a dogsbody to a news office or a journalist for one of the minor rags. Whichever, she was starting again. Four good, solid years scrubbed out by her stupid, single-minded focus.

She wiped away the tears, stood up, and steeled herself.

News of her firing would take a few days to filter through. While she could still hold her head high and get a face-to-face with a senior editor. She'd go and talk to Martin Gillie's boss, Edwards.

She'd pitch herself as a junior, wanting to prove herself to him.

After sorting her smeared makeup, Hilary strode into the office of *the Manila Times*. Jasmine, Mr Edward's assistant met her.

"I know you," Jasmine said.

"Hilary Wigglesworth, the Chronicle."

"Martin Gillie—"

"Sometimes confided in me," Hilary said. "He's a nice man."

Jasmine struggled to speak but finally got the words out. "I'm... I'm really worried about him."

"No news is good news," Hilary said, immediately regretting the trite remark. Nerves, she told herself. "Sorry. I've been working with an ex-British military investigator."

"Ash Carter?"

"Yes. Do you know him?" Then Hilary got the connection. "You gave him Martin's notes."

Jasmine's eyes flew wide. "Don't tell anyone!"

"I won't. Don't worry."

Jasmine breathed. "Okay, thank you. Were they any help?"

"Some. We've pulled on a few threads and..." she couldn't bring herself to keep up the pretence. "I'm afraid we've not uncovered the conspiracy that Martin appears to have believed in. He may be hiding for no reason."

"Oh." Jasmine's eyes narrowed. "So why are you here?"

"I'm hoping... I need a job, Jasmine. The Chronicle have fired me."

"For investigating Martin's case?"

Hilary shrugged. "Mostly... if I'd come up with answers, it would be a different story... literally."

Jasmine nodded. "Mr Edward's diary is full. I'll let him know... try and get you a meeting tomorrow... with Martin Gillie missing, there's workload pressure. He might give you some freelance work."

"Don't mention that I've been—"

"I won't but... he'll find out, Hilary. He'll ask the Chronicle for a reference."

"Of course. Thanks." At least, a meeting with the big man, was better than none. Tomorrow would give her time to think about angles... maybe even discover more information.

A thought struck her.

"Mind if I use the telephone?" she asked.

Jasmine showed her one in the lobby and left her. Hilary picked up the receiver and asked for the number that Rena Gillie had given Ash.

"You have an update?" Mrs Gillie asked.

"Would you meet me at your house?"

"No. As I told—"

"Rena, please. I will go through everything we've learned. I'll explain why Martin might be unnecessarily worried. And I'm hoping that we can work out where he is."

It was a long shot, but Martin Gillie's home might hold a clue they needed.

"Just you? On your own?"

"Yes."

"Give me two hours," Rena Gillie said, and Hilary grinned. Despite everything, despite the likelihood that it would be another dead end, Hilary felt like she could take some positive action.

Two hours later, Hilary knocked on the Gillies front door.

"The children are with their grandparents," Rena said. "And I'm sorry it's not... we'll I've also spent little time here since Martin disappeared... Since Captain Carter warned me."

"It must be difficult for you."

Rena took a long breath and nodded.

"Come in. We'll have tea and you can update me."

Hilary reminded Rena that they had received a note that confirmed her husband was alive. He'd instructed them to investigate Cagayan Valley, and it matched the pattern they'd seen elsewhere—a company buying land in remote areas.

She said, "Your husband thought the police were covering up the rebel and it was linked to the land purchases, but we've not confirmed any rebel connection." She flashed back to the fence near Bayombong in Cagayan Valley. They'd been shot at. When they'd told the senator, he'd been shocked. What they hadn't done was confirm that it was one of his properties. Could this all be about the police?

"The police?" Rena asked as though reading her mind.

"They're involved somehow, I'm sure," Hilary said. "Budget issues, tension with the Constabulary."

"It's a concern. No wonder Martin is worried." She paused. "I know I said to find Martin rather than investigate but perhaps Captain Carter was right to find the truth."

"Or expose that Martin's fears are unfounded."

"Or that," Rena agreed. "If there is anything, then it all comes down to the information available from Martin's source. Topo isn't it? You should find that man."

"You might be right," Hilary said, then asked if she could search the house. Rena agreed without hesitation. Perhaps Hilary wasn't an experienced investigator like Captain Carter, but perhaps a woman's sensitive approach could get results.

Rena guided Hilary, steering her away from the children's room and personal things. As Hilary searched the modest property, it struck her that it didn't feel like a family home.

"We've had problems," Rena said in response to a question. "Doesn't every marriage? The children and I spend more and more time at my parents' house. I think this case Martin has become obsessed by... Well, let's say I'm hoping this time apart has helped."

Hilary, looked under furniture and tapped walls. There was an office with paperwork, but it was household rather than journalistic.

Until she found one piece of paper. Martin Gillie used old paper for lists of things to do. They were mundane items like paying bills and repairs, but that's not what caught Hilary's eye.

The reverse was part of a formal document. Something about public safety. It was old—over nineteen months. Then she noticed the government department logo at the bottom. Concentric circles had the department name inside: *Transporte, Orden Público y Operaciones.* Transport, Public Order and Operations.

Hilary stared at it, her hands shaking.

"What is it?" Rena Gillie asked.

Hilary's heart pounded. "We thought Topo meant 'mole' but it doesn't." She spluttered a laugh. "I can't believe it… look, it's not mole it's an acronym. TOPO."

Rena pointed to the officer who'd signed it. It said 'Mayor's Office' but it wasn't the mayor's signature.

"You think he's Martin's contact?"

Hilary grinned. "He may well be! I've got to tell Ash."

She hurried out of the house and started running.

Chapter 43

Martin Gillie was dead, but I didn't find out until late morning.

I went to the YMCA gym and then returned to find Father Reyes sitting at my usual table, his face ashen.

Wolfe was busy behind the bar. Quick put a jug of water and two glasses on the table and nodded at me.

"Good morning," I said to the priest warily.

"It is not," he said. "It is not a good morning." Reyes had a newspaper open on the table. He pointed at a column—an inside page, just a small header with about ten lines of print. No photograph. Too minor a story.

It was about the discovery of a body in the river—the one we'd seen. There were scant details except that the body was of an unidentified male shot in the back of the head. No witnesses. Washed down river and snagged on debris caught under Jones Bridge.

A sinking feeling built in my gut.

"Was it Martin Gillie?" I asked.

He looked wary. "Did you know?"

"I'm adding one plus one and hoping I'm mistaken."

He breathed heavily. "You're not. The report says 'unidentified' but I found out. It's Martin all right."

I tried to shake crowding thoughts from my head. We'd convinced ourselves that he'd been paranoid. He had bits of stories but had imagined a huge conspiracy connecting everything. The body that had snagged in Pasig River had been his.

Reyes was watching my thought process.

"I need to confess something," the priest said. "About Martin Gillie."

I poured him a glass of water. He stared at it for a long moment before speaking.

"I was hiding him," he said finally. "In the crypt under the cathedral."

The words hung in the air. Wolfe stopped wiping glasses and leaned against the bar, listening.

"He came to me two weeks ago," Reyes continued. "He'd tried to leave the country—buy a ticket for a steamer to Hong Kong, I think. But someone recognized him. He knew then that they were watching the ports."

Ironically, it had been an inquisitive member of staff at the Holand America Line, rather than someone looking for him. But the story tallied with what I'd learned.

"Did he say who 'they' were?"

"No. I got the sense it was what he called 'the authorities'."

I nodded. "I have to ask this, Father. Why, oh why didn't you tell me this before?"

"Because... because he was still alive then." Reyes's hands tightened around his glass. "He knew about your investigation. He watched from the tower, when you came to ask questions. He was... pleased at first. Then worried you weren't making progress. That's why he wrote you a note."

The shorthand note that sent us to Cagayan Valley and led to Enexacion the company who were buying land.

I said, "You delivered it."

"Yes. I was nervous that you wouldn't see it, but I couldn't risk being recognized. If the wrong people found out..."

"Did Gillie tell you what he'd discovered?"

"Not everything. He said it was safer if I didn't know the details. But he talked about a conspiracy—something possibly involving the highest levels of government. I think he'd uncovered irregularities in police reports about rebel

212

activity. Questions about whether the attacks were real."
He paused and shook his head. "He was afraid but also desperate to find the complete story."

"Did he know who was behind it?"

"No."

"He seems to have believed it was about land acquisition," I said. "Although we don't know why yet. If there are rebel attacks, they may drive down prices in specific areas. But we only confirmed a possible rebel attack in Palawan."

Reyes nodded slowly. "That fits with what he said. But Gillie... he couldn't stay hidden. He couldn't just rely on you. The journalist in him couldn't let it go. He set up a meeting with someone from City Hall."

"When?"

"Two nights ago." The priest's voice cracked slightly. "He said this person had proof—documents that would expose everything. He just needed to persuade them to share it."

"Was it Topo?"

Reyes nodded as though saying the name, even acknowledging it, was dangerous. "Although, that's not his real name."

"He was selling Gillie information?"

"No. I think you'd call him a whistleblower... but Martin said he needed convincing. Topo was worried too. He'll be even more worried now that Martin's been murdered."

"I have to ask," I said. "Are you sure it was him in the river? The body—"

"A source in the police."

"Martin Gillie didn't trust the police."

"No, he didn't, but this is one of my congregation. I trust him."

"Did Gillie mention Senator Delgado?"

"No."

I figured Gillie hadn't gotten as far as us. Either he hadn't known about Enexacion or hadn't untangled the shell companies to arrive at the senator's name.

"Did he give you any clues as to who Topo might be… anything at all?"

"No. He wouldn't tell me. Said it was safer that way… for everyone concerned." After a sip of water Reyes said, "It must have been someone he trusted."

I agreed.

Reyes looked up, his eyes haunted. "What will you do now?"

"Find the truth. Expose whoever's behind this." I hesitated.

Reyes shook his head. "Be careful. Martin said these people… they'd do anything to protect their interests."

And they'd taken his life. Gillie had been hiding for two weeks. Despite sending us to further his investigations, he'd been unable to resist. He'd surfaced, tried to get the missing facts we so desperately needed. And had been murdered.

"Have you informed his wife?" I asked, realizing someone should tell her.

"His wife?" The priest's head snapped up. "Mrs Gillie?"

"Rena." I could immediately tell by his face that something was seriously wrong. The attractive woman who had hired me to find her husband. She'd discouraged my investigation into his research. The sickening truth dawned on me. Why she'd been so pushy. Why she'd refused access to their family home. Nothing to do with children.

"Mrs Gillie?" Reyes said again. "No… Martin wasn't married."

Chapter 44

"Where have you been?" I challenged as Hilary strode into the bar. "I've been looking for you."

She grinned. "I've had my worst day. I've had my best day."

"Explain." I said frowning deeply.

"This morning, I got fired."

"What?"

"My editor said he'd had enough. 'No more latitude' was one of his expressions. Another... and this really rankles... was that 'girls can't be trusted with a proper man's job'."

"I'm so sorry, Hilary."

"But the good news is that I think I know who Topo is." She paused, teasing me. "Remember the mayor's assistant?"

"Young man... Cortez."

"Chrisanto Cortez. He handles the mayor's affairs and frequently signs documents on his behalf. Including notes from the department of Transport, Public Order and Operations. In Spanish the initials are TOPO."

My mouth dropped open. "An acronym!"

She winked and grinned. "I'd bet my pay packet on it... the one I no longer receive, that is."

"Well done!" I hugged her. "How did you work it out?"

"I hope you don't mind, but I searched Martin's house. He'd used piece of an official document for personal notes."

"You searched his house?"

"I called Rena—"

My elation turned to utter dread as I stopped Hilary mid-sentence. "She's fake. Rena's fake!"

"What?"

"Martin's dead and he's not married." I blurted it out and she couldn't have been more shocked if I'd pointed a gun at her.

I supported her, afraid she'd faint.

"Oh no… Oh no…"

Now it was my turn: "What is it?"

"She knows about Cortez… I worked it out with Rena. She knows, Ash. She knows!"

We ran for Wolfe's Jeep, my mind racing. I'd already spent time thinking there was something off about Rena Gillie. She wasn't a frightened wife. She was part of the conspiracy. They'd wanted to track down Gillie, believing my investigation would either flush him out or lead his hiding place.

But he'd been impatient and presumably blundered into another trap they'd laid.

They'd removed Gillie, and now they had the name of his informant. Then it struck me. Cortez had been their main target all along. They worried less about our investigation and more about the informer. He was a whistleblower, after all.

Within minutes, I was screeching to a halt outside City Hall.

We abandoned the Jeep and charged up the stairs to the mayor's assistant's office. It was empty. A secretary asked if she could help.

"Chrisanto Cortez…" Hilary said breathlessly. "Where is he?"

"Mr Cortez stepped out. He had an urgent call." The secretary frowned. "From someone about the land survey files."

My blood ran cold. "When?"

She checked her watch. "Less than ten minutes ago. He seemed quite excited. Said something about a breakthrough he'd been waiting for."

"Where's the meeting?"

She hesitated.

I pulled out my old credentials. "This is a matter of life and death."

"You're…" Her voice faltered, her eyes wide.

"I'm a private investigator."

She swallowed, looking paler by the second.

"What is it?" I pressed.

"You! He's gone to meet you and that reporter."

"Where?"

"The old warehouse district." She was breathless with worry now. "Near Pier 9. Mr Cortez wrote it down… Let's see… Where is it?" She shuffled through papers on her desk. "Here… It says: Meeting MG. 4PM. 23, 18th Street."

MG. Martin Gillie. It hadn't been public knowledge. Cortez didn't know Gillie had been murdered.

I checked my watch. Nine minutes.

"Call the police," I said.

A throw of the dice. Neither of us had confidence in the police, but if there was a patrolman nearby… Maybe just maybe…

"Tell them to send everyone they can to that address," Hilary yelled as we ran for the stairs.

We knew we would barely make it in time. The killer— probably the same one who'd murdered Gillie—would be waiting. And Cortez was walking right into his trap.

The Jeep's engine roared as I threw it through the old town's streets. Hilary braced herself against the dashboard, her face tight with tension.

"No way through," she yelled. The old town walls prevented me from going directly to the port. I should have let her drive. She would have known the best route.

"Where?" I asked, turning the Jeep around.

"Past the port. Out and down by the park, then back."

"Got it," I said, correcting my route. I was soon turning hard right alongside United Nations Park.

"If they kill Cortez..." she started.

"They won't," I said, but pressed the accelerator harder. Somewhere ahead, a frightened government clerk thought we'd exchange the final piece of the puzzle.

Instead, he was walking straight toward his death.

Chapter 45

The warehouse district was a maze of corrugated metal and concrete. The port stretched out before us. Pier 13 was ahead. There was no Pier 11, I don't know why. Pier 9 was the next. The sun was low and I was driving toward it. The late afternoon wind channelled down the streets from the port. We turned onto Chicago Street. The next turn would be 18th Street, toward Pier 9. Approaching the turn, high stacks of crates lined the end of the street, ready for loading. The way was blocked.

I pulled over, jumped out and started running. Behind me Hilary's door slammed. I didn't wait. At the corner, I saw building numbers painted in fading white on a rust-streaked walls.

"There!" Hilary shouted behind me. "Number 23's three-quarters of the way down."

Someone was on the street, walking toward it. Chrisanto Cortez, clutching a briefcase. He looked different outside his City Hall environment—smaller, more vulnerable. He glanced down the street, the opposite way, then darted from view.

"Cortez!" I yelled but doubt he heard.

I ran harder.

"Don't come in!" I shouted to Hilary somewhere behind me, as I reached number 23. I drew my gun and burst into the warehouse. Two men ahead, approaching one another like they were business associates.

"Cortez!" I shouted.

The mayor's assistant turned my way.

Everything seemed to slow down. I saw Cortez's expression shift from confusion to recognition as he saw me. He clutched his briefcase tighter. He began to turn back toward the other man.

I recognized him. The man with the weathered face and cold eyes I'd seen at the library.

An assassin.

Behind me, I heard the door. Hilary had followed.

"Run!" I shouted. "Cortez, run!"

But he didn't. Instead, he smiled—the relieved smile of someone who thinks help has arrived.

The killer's movement was almost too fast to see. A simple gesture, like straightening Cortez's tie.

Cortez's froze. The briefcase fell from his fingers.

The killer lunged for it and started running. I heard Hilary coming up fast behind me.

"Hilary, stay back," I yelled and fired at the killer's fleeing figure. My shot went wide, the sound echoing off metal walls.

I reached the mayor's assistant. Cortez looked down at his chest where a dark stain was spreading. He opened his mouth, but no sound came out. Then his knees buckled.

Nothing I could do for him. I ran on as he fell.

The assassin was fast and burst through the rear door before I could get off another shot. I went through cautiously in case he was awaiting on the other side.

He wasn't. He was well ahead of me when I came out of the building.

I chased hard. The gap between us closed.

He was fast, but I had rage driving me—rage at Gillie's murder, at Cortez dying in front of us, at all layers of corruption undoubtedly involved.

The assassin went right, then immediately left behind a building. A feint—he was trying to double back. I cut through an empty warehouse, bursting out the other side just as he passed.

He didn't break stride, changing direction, heading for a rusty fire escape. I was close enough now to hear his laboured breathing. *He's tiring*, I thought.

The fire escape groaned under our weight. He climbed fast, the metalwork ringing with each step. Four flights up, he swung himself onto a flat roof scattered with old machinery and ventilation tubes.

I followed, the ancient metal swaying as I pounded upward. The roof was a patchwork of different levels, some concrete, some corrugated metal. The killer moved across it confidently, running to an edge. Then he jumped a gap between buildings.

That first gap caught me by surprise—wider than it looked. I landed hard, rolling to absorb the impact. The killer glanced back, those same cold eyes and annoyed look. Then he was running again, heading for the higher roofs of the commercial district.

Sunlight bounced off metal surfaces. I blinked sweat from my eyes. The killer reached another gap, this one wider still. He backed up for a running jump.

"Stop!" I raised my gun. "It's over!"

He turned, and for the first time, I saw doubt on his face. Then he was running, launching himself across the void.

I fired. The shot caught him in the leg, just as his feet left the roof. For a moment he seemed to hang in the air, arms spread. Then reality took over.

He hit the opposite roof badly, landing on the edge. His hands scrabbled for purchase on the smooth concrete.

The briefcase fell.

"No!" I shouted. I needed him alive. Needed to know who he was working for, who had ordered the killings.

He found a grip, hanging by his fingers. Blood from the gunshot wound in his leg dripped. I looked for a way across—a lower roof I could use, a drainage pipe, anything.

The killer looked over at me, that same cold expression. But then he smiled and let go.

His body made a wet sound as he landed.

I found my way down through an internal stairwell. Found the briefcase and then the assassin. He was still breathing, but his eyes were glazing over.

"Who do you work for?" I demanded, kneeling beside him. "Who wanted the reporter and Cortez dead?"

His mouth opened, blood oozing through his teeth. He tried to speak, but only a wet cough came out.

"The police chief? The head of the Constabulary? Someone else? Tell me!"

He spluttered blood and spasmed. His eyes closed.

Then he was gone, taking his secrets with him.

I stood slowly, pocketing my gun. Nearby, police whistles sounded—they were finally responding to our warning. On 18th street, a crowd was gathering, drawn by the sound of gunshots maybe.

My hands were shaking with adrenaline and frustration. We'd lost our chance to prove who was behind it all. The killer had chosen death over betraying his employers.

I ran back to the rear of Building 23. Hilary was outside, huddled on the floor, her blouse and hands covered in Cortez's blood. Her face was streaked with tears.

"Dead?" I said, but already knew the truth.

She nodded and cried some more.

"We need to go," I said, helping her up. I swung my jacket over her shoulders, hiding the most obvious blood, and led her away. The Jeep could wait. Walk around onto 18th Street and we'd be walking right into the authorities.

I hailed a taxi.

First, I needed to get Hilary safe. Get her home and cleaned up. Then we'd find out what was in the briefcase. Documents. Hopefully the evidence. We'd follow the paper trail and see where it led.

Because somewhere in Manila, the people who'd hired this killer would soon realize their assassin had failed. Which meant they'd be coming for us themselves.

Chapter 46

The briefcase was empty.

I thought back to the killer's smile before he fell. He'd emptied it. Just in case I'd caught him or retrieved the briefcase. He'd fooled me.

Hilary came out of the bathroom. She looked fresh, her wet hair dripping onto a clean blouse. Colour had returned to her face.

I handed her a glass of brandy. She breathed in the fumes then knocked it back.

"Nothing," I said when she looked a question at me.

"The briefcase?"

I nodded.

"He said something to me," she said quietly. "Before Chrisanto Cortez died, he tried to speak."

I waited.

"He said something about Delgado having the proof. And someone else."

"Senator Delgado?" I said, my jaw tense. Had I fallen for his charms? I'd been wondering whether Enexacion and the land purchases were circumstantial, that it was the police…

"Someone else," she said. "It's more than the senator."

"So more than just land speculation?"

She handled the briefcase. "Do you think Cortez had evidence in here, or… hold on!"

She pulled a back flap away. I hadn't noticed a slot for documents.

Hilary fished out pieces of paper. The first was a page from a diary—the mayor's, dated July 1953. Two pieces of paper looked more formal—like pages from a contract. There was also a sketched floorplan that looked to me like the senator's main house. I recognised the layout from our brief visit.

I set the floorplan aside and we studied the contract. Hilary needed to translate the Spanish.

"Looks like an agreement to buy arms," she said. "But this is City Hall paper not the military's."

"Arms for the police?" I asked. "That's nothing suspicious. Civil police have guns."

"Maybe," she said, "But I did research on this a while ago. The police still use US Military surplus weapons: Colts mainly. Also Smith and Wesson revolvers. But the point is, they are supplied by the US Military. This is a private contract for rifles and machine guns. And it's small scale." She shook her head. "It's odd."

"No doubt that's why Cortez included it."

"The second page isn't from the same contract," she said reading it. "It's part of a report, I think. Oil and Minerals Survey. The author's name is here: S. Acosta."

"Mean anything?"

She held up a hand and I let her finish reading it.

"No," she said with wide eyes. "But, get this… there's mention of a number of exploratory sites including Bayombong and Tayabas."

"Where the senator's company bought land?"

She nodded.

I had glanced at the diary entries and spotted 'SA'. "This could meet the report's author, Acosta. There are a lot of meetings over a short period."

I ran my finger over the appointments. "And with the senator. Could be coincidence. The mayor has numerous meetings, including with the police chief."

Hilary said. "That comes as no surprise." She felt inside the document slot again and pulled out a postcard. No, not a postcard. It was an invitation.

"The senator's hosting a party in five days' time," she said. "The grounds will be full of guests."

We sat at the table and looked at what we had. It still wasn't the complete picture. I was sure the weathered-faced assassin had disposed of the loose papers.

This was possibly linked to an arms deal. There was a minerals survey by someone called Acosta. The Mayor had numerous meetings with Senator Delgado around the same time and the senator had bought land through his secret web of companies.

"Delgado has the proof," I said, paraphrasing Cortez's final words to Hilary.

"Maybe…" she said. "Maybe Cortez was going to use the event as cover. If he was attending, he might slip away, try and find it."

"If it's proof, it'll be secure. In a safe. There was a safe in his study."

That might have been their plan. Gillie might have even been part of it. I wondered if Cortez knew the code to the safe. Or maybe he just hoped he'd get lucky.

He'd need more than luck.

"We should try. It's too good an opportunity," she suggested.

We bounced around ideas. Could we get an invite? Could we break in? And even if we did, how would we find the evidence?

Hilary poured herself another drink. She was still in shock but handling it very well.

As I was thinking about the problem, she gathered the documents carefully and put them back in the case. "The thing I'm afraid of… what if we're caught…"

"You won't be there," I said firmly. "No arguments. I've had experience. It's what I do."

"But how."

"I don't know yet. I need to come up with a plan." I looked at the papers one last time and imaged them stained with blood. "Two good men have died trying to expose this. I owe it to them to finish what they started."

Outside her window, Manila's lights were coming on, the city settling into evening. Somewhere out there, in a heavily guarded estate, a senator was sitting on evidence worth killing for.

In five days, we'd know exactly what that evidence was. At least, that's what we thought.

Chapter 47

I worried that Hilary was in shock, so I stayed the night on the sofa. In the morning, after checking she was all right, I went to 20th Street behind the warehouses and found the rear of Building 23. There must have been a hundred places the assassin could have dumped the contents of the briefcase. We were certain there had been more documents, but I found nothing.

Retrieving the Jeep from where we'd abandoned it, I drove back to Hilary's, my mind already working on how to convince Wolfe to join me. Together, we'd break into the senator's house.

I couldn't let Hilary do this, and I couldn't do it alone. Wolfe was the perfect partner when it came to an endgame. Early on, not so good. But the physical side of things—when the bullets started flying—I wouldn't choose anyone else to be by my side.

Hilary accepted my logic and said she'd focus on her writing. This would include working on the exposé—the report that Gillie would have written if he'd still been alive.

Contented that she'd wait for me to obtain the evidence, I set off again, thinking of arguments that would encourage Wolfe's help.

Justice was my motivation. But I suspected Wolfe would be persuaded because I needed him. He'd never admit it, but he had an ego that could be stoked. He was undoubtedly better than me at some things, and that's what I'd focus on.

The smell of smoke hit me before I turned the corner. Quick was standing outside the bar, his face and clothes blackened with soot. All windows were shattered, glass crunching under my feet as I ran the last few yards.

"What happened?"

"Fire," Quick said, his voice hoarse. "Around three this morning. Luckily, I was kipping here last night. Caught it early enough."

Early enough? I thought, surveying the damage.

The front door hung askew on its hinges. Inside, the bar was a mess of scorched wood, broken bottles, and water damage. The ceiling was black with smoke, and, near the back, many of the floorboards were burnt through. The proud stuffed bear that had given the bar its name was a sodden, singed mess.

But the bar wasn't completely destroyed. The basic structure had held. The beautiful bar top still looked solid.

"We fought the flames ourselves," Quick said, following my gaze. "And then neighbours joined in. It was pretty much out by the time the fire department got here. The boss was the real hero. He fought it like a demon. Made sure others didn't take risks but kept going back in."

Something in Quick's tone. My stomach twisted. "Quick... Where is he? Where's Wolfe?"

"Hospital. Smoke inhalation. Some burns. They said he'll be okay, but..." Quick gestured to the bar. "Someone did this... deliberately. They poured gasoline around the building. Started multiple points of fire. Professional job. If I hadn't been here..."

"Was Wolfe drunk again?" I asked, wondering what his state had been.

"Not too bad last night, despite you not being here."

I nodded, grateful.

I ran my hand along the bar top, got to the end and touched the burned frame. My eyes raked the ugly scene again and again.

This was my fault. I'd brought this danger to Wolfe's door by staying here, by involving him in the investigation.

I walked through to the back and looked at my room. It was burnt out. One of the fires had started here and destroyed everything. I'd stayed at Hilary's last night. If I'd been here... I shook away the thoughts of what might have happened.

"The alcohol?" I asked Quick, remembering the stored cases in the back.

"Some exploded. That's what woke us, I think. Could have been much worse if the fire had reached the main storage." Quick managed a weak smile. "Wolfe says at least it was the cheap stuff that went up."

I looked at the devastation again. The bar could be repaired—the structure was sound, the damage mostly superficial. But the message was clear. This was a warning, a demonstration of what they could do.

"Which hospital?"

"San Juan de Dios. But Ash..." Quick hesitated. "Don't let him react. You know what he's like. We don't know which group did this. And..."

"I agree," I said, holding back on what I knew. "No hasty reactions."

I clenched my fist. They'd tried to burn us out, maybe hoping to kill me, maybe hoping to destroy Cortez's documents. Instead, they'd nearly killed my friend.

The taxi ride to the hospital seemed endless. Manila's streets were busy with morning traffic, everyone going about their normal lives while my world had shifted on its axis. I might have taken Wolfe's Jeep, but my head was still full of dismay and anger. Crashing on the way to the hospital wouldn't have done either of us a favour.

I found Wolfe in a small ward, oxygen mask covering his face. His eyes were red and swollen, but they opened when I approached.

"Don't start," he said, voice raspy as he pulled the mask aside. "Don't give me a lecture."

"A lecture?"

"Some pissed off group of GIs…"

I shook my head. "No, Bill, it's my fault."

"This isn't your fault!"

But it was. I'd stayed at his bar, made it a target. I'd effectively involved him in my investigation, putting him in the line of fire.

He continued: "You've been trying to change my ways. I'm my own damned worst enemy. I should have expected it. Fighting arrogant pricks, chucking them out. Someone was bound to come back at some point."

"Bill…"

"Shut up and listen." He coughed, replaced the mask for a moment.

"No," I said, now that I could get a word in. I told him what I thought had happened. Not disgruntled GIs after him, but a senator or his henchmen after me and what I had.

He sucked in the oxygen, then removed the mask again. "Bloody hell. Bloody fuckin' hell!"

"The bar can be fixed. Quick's already organizing a cleanup," I said.

"We're going after the bastards who did this, right?"

I nodded.

"Good. Because this isn't just about your case anymore. They brought this to my door. Endangered my people." His eyes were hard despite the redness. "So, whatever you're planning, I'm in."

"You need to recover."

"Three days. Doctor says I'll be good as new in three days." He grinned, then winced. "Just enough time for the smoke to clear and for you to tell me how we're going to make these bastards pay."

I sat beside his bed, guilt warring with gratitude for his friendship. "It's dangerous, Bill. These people… they've already murdered two that I know of. They won't hesitate to kill anyone who gets in their way."

He looked at me critically, then reached for water, his hand shaking slightly. "It's more reason not to let them win. You think I built that bar, made a home there, just to let some corrupt politician burn it down?"

A nurse appeared, frowning at Wolfe's removed oxygen mask. She shooed me away, saying he needed rest.

"Three days," Wolfe called after me, then coughed with the effort. "Come up with a good plan, Captain."

I threw him a mock salute. Normally, I didn't like him calling me captain—it made me recognize his superiority. However today was fine. It felt like he was showing his fighting spirit.

Outside the hospital, I stood in the morning sun, letting its warmth fight against the cold knot in my stomach. They'd tried to intimidate us, to frighten us away from the investigation. Maybe they'd expected to kill us.

Instead, they'd given us one more reason to bring them down.

I thought about Cortez's words, about the evidence hidden in the senator's house. We'd need help to get in there.

Three days to come up with a plan. And this time, we wouldn't just be chasing proof of.... land fraud or weapons shipments… whatever it was.

Now it was personal.

Chapter 48

"How is he?"

Frankie Dee snapped me out of my reverie. He was loitering outside the hospital unsure whether he should go inside. Unsure how Wolfe would react to a visit.

"He'll live," I said.

"But it's not good? You've seen him?"

"Looks like he'd damaged his lungs. He's on oxygen. The docs say at least three days in bed."

We stood in silence for a while. Our shadows were long, stretching beyond the wall, into the river. Wolfe's bar was front and right. To the left I could see the old town and the broken cathedral. Very different venues but both damaged refuges.

Dee sighed. "Maybe it's a sign. Will Wolfe take it as a sign?"

I turned to look at the affable musician. "Something religious, Frankie?"

"No, I mean… well,"—he spread his hands—"He started as a private detective, then things didn't work out, so his focus became the bar. But he's been in decline. Rejected friendship. Drinking too much." He spread his hands again and shook his head. "Time to move on. A lot of ex-pats come and go. For Wolfe, what's left?"

"From what I've seen," I said, "the friendship's very much still there. It may be a little one-sided at the moment, but under that gruff exterior, the old Bill Wolfe is underneath."

Dee nodded but looked at me critically. "You think you'll bring him round? Solve his old case?"

"Not solve it," I said. "I can't bring the baby back to life. But if we can find who did it...?"

Dee turned away, looking down the river again. "And if you can't?"

He was right to be concerned. No one else had mentioned the risk, but I knew Dee was thinking it. What if I dug up the case and we got nowhere? Would that reinforce Wolfe's depression? Maybe it would, but I sensed it was the only option. I'd probably get shot down by a psychologist, but I had been brought up to address issues head on. I'd hated my father for most of my life. The school of hard knocks, he called it. After a bad crash, he made me get straight back on my bicycle. I'd cried and got no sympathy. My knee was bleeding, my palms and a forearm were grazed. Once on, I wobbled. My hands were shaking. My left leg hurt when I put pressure on the pedal. But after a couple of seconds I was cycling again. I did it and learned a powerful lesson. It wasn't the bike's fault. Accidents happen and life is about recognizing the risks and learning how to avoid or deal with them.

"I have to try," I said. "The bar... He's all fired up..."

Dee chuckled at the irony of my unintended pun.

"Poor choice of words," I said. "The fire could have depressed him further, but he's showing spirit. He wants revenge."

"Revenge?" Dee's face fell as he shook his head. "Surely he can't go after a bunch of GIs? How's he going to pinpoint—"

"Not GIs," I said. "They burned Wolfe's bar because of me. I took a case, looking for a missing reporter and it's uncovered a conspiracy. He was murdered and they've killed his informant."

"Who... who the hell are they?"

So, I explained about the senator and his company acquiring land—not just from small farms, but also wealthy landowners. It wasn't about land reform and

233

bigger farms. We didn't understand it all but there were potential issues between the Constabulary and police as well as suspicious contracts—City Hall buying small arms. Worst of all, and something the murdered reporter was investigating, were unreported deaths and rebel activity that may have been linked to the land acquisition.

Dee took a long breath. "I can't claim to understand everything you said. But it's good to hear there may be a specific target responsible for burning the Crazy Bear."

"Senator Delgado," I said. "Or at least, he has the evidence that'll blow the conspiracy wide open."

"I'd like to help." Again, he raised his palms. "But I'm no soldier. I'm sure Spider and John will want in… with whatever you have planned. You do have a plan…?"

I stared down the river as an idea started to form.

"Ash?"

"We need to get into the senator's place and find the documents. He's having a party in four night's time. There are bound to be musicians—"

"You're thinking of infiltrating the party?" he interrupted. "Four nights… so Bill will be up to it, if the doctors are correct."

"That's what I'm hoping. I'll do him good. A bit of excitement… a bit of revenge."

"Greater chance of success than the dead baby case?"

I sighed. He was probably right. I had gained information about the case but was no closer to finding the perpetrators than Wolfe or, later, Manners had been.

Dee grinned at me. "I know everyone in the music business in Manila. Shouldn't take long to find out who Delgado has commissioned and then apply a little leverage." He patted me on the shoulder. "However, whatever you do, don't let Wolfe play his trombone. You do that and any subterfuge will be blown sky high."

We agreed we'd meet later at his club. I'd bring Sullivan and Manners along and we'd discuss plans.

Dee nodded towards the hospital. "Will he see me? It's been—"

"Go and say hello. He'll be grumpy but it'll do him good to see a friend."

"He was always grumpy." Dee grinned.

"And tell him about the plan to infiltrate the party. He'll be involved."

Dee patted my shoulder again and headed for the hospital entrance. He'd go and check on Wolfe and then get to business.

As I walked back to Wolfe's bar. I went from enthusiasm to doubt. I'd had no plan before, and with Frankie Dee's help we'd get into the house. I knew the location of safe. It wasn't in my nature to send someone else in there, so I'd need a disguise. The senator would surely recognize me if I waltzed in there pretending to be one of the musicians. And then there was the other problem. Getting into the party was just the beginning. I'd wondered how Cortez had planned to get into the safe. Maybe he had details. Maybe it had been included in the notes lost from the briefcase. No way could I crack a safe. I'd ask Sullivan and Manners. Maybe they knew a safe cracker.

I walked and thought. There was armed security. We'd need to prepare for taking the senator at gunpoint. Force him to open the safe. There could be a gunfight. There probably would be a gunfight. How many people would be at the party? Civilians in the way. I didn't like that risk.

We had the beginnings of a plan. But this mission was far from straightforward.

Chapter 49

When I returned to the Crazy Bear, there were already men working. The morning sun caught the glass they were sweeping from the street, making it sparkle like cruel diamonds. Quick was directing operations with impressive authority.

"The whole bloody bar's history," Sullivan called from behind a scorched panel. "Seems an age ago... Wolfe standing there with his big plans; none of us believing this dump could become anything."

"You were wrong then," Manners grunted, pulling away damaged wood. "Wrong now too, if you're thinking this can't be fixed."

I watched them work efficiency. A good team. These men had built the bar once before, I realized. Now they were here to rebuild it.

There were faces I didn't recognize, others I did. Locals who worked nearby or drank at the bar. Men who thought of Wolfe as a good man despite having their friendship rejected.

Quick introduced me to Miguel who called himself Wolfe's financial advisor. Although he hadn't been in touch for a couple of years. Wolfe had rented the detective agency office from him in the Santa Cruz district. Later, he'd found the bar opportunity and persuaded Wolfe to invest.

"I didn't expect him to just work here," Miguel said.

"Wallow here," someone else added.

"You could help, rather than chat," Quick said after watching me. He held out a broom.

"In a minute," I said. "First I need to talk to Sullivan and Manners."

I called them over and together we walked to a quiet spot along the street. Quick was two paces behind.

"Don't exclude me," he said. "How'd the boss?"

I nodded and they gathered round. I gave them a brief update then said, "Before I tell you the plan, I need to explain."

"We think it was angry GIs from the other night," Manners said. "We need to root them out."

"I should have been there," Sullivan added.

Manners shook his head. "Or maybe someone else the boss crossed. But not your fault, Spider. No one's fault."

"It was," I said. The guilt churning inside. "This is because of me."

They stared, faces full of questions and doubts.

"Your fault?" Sullivan clarified.

"Better explain yourself, mate," Manners said.

I did. I told them about Martin Gillie, about the land grabs and possible link to rebel attacks, about Cortez's murder and the documents that suggested something even darker at the senator's estate.

"Maybe he's the one getting the arms. Maybe it's a private militia!" Manners's eyes narrowed. "That's what I think. No other reason to arm up like that. Too few guns for the police or military, that's for sure."

"Could be for self-defence," Sullivan suggested. "A man like the senator, in this country..."

"No." Manners shook his head. "Not with those quantities. Not with that level of organization."

They were connecting dots that might not have existed, but I didn't argue. They were as riled up as me now, and I let them vent.

"We go after the focker now," Sullivan said, hand straying to where a weapon might once have been. "Tonight."

"We need proof first," I said. "Something solid enough that the police have to act. According to Cortez, the senator has the evidence and it's likely to be in his study."

"Which is heavily guarded?" Quick asked.

"The property is. And I expect professionals," I said, remembering the killer at the docks. "One of them was the man who murdered Cortez—the whistleblower. He's dead but there's at least three more." I described the giant and the two from the black Ford.

Manners's face hardened. "Planning a break-in then?"

"No," I said and explained the idea of disguising ourselves as musicians for the senator's party.

Sullivan shook his head. Manners voiced his concern.

"We can't wait four nights."

"Wolfe will be out of hospital in three days," I explained. "So, we'll have him and an ideal opportunity." Even as I said it, I remembered the doubts I'd had."

"Tell us the plan," Sullivan said.

"I outlined as much as I had."

Manners wasn't impressed by the lack of detail and I couldn't blame him. But we had three or four days to perfect this.

"You know we aren't likely to get in and out easily," Sullivan said.

"May as well go in shooting from the start," Manners grumbled. "Get the bastard. Stick a gun up his arse and force the truth out of him."

"And the evidence," Sullivan said. "We should go tonight."

"Agreed," Manners said. "Been too long since I had a proper operation."

I let them talk. These were good friends. Their energy was palpable. I liked that they were committed and or involved. Totally. But I also feared their approach was too gung ho. We needed cool heads for this operation. I was about to bring them back to the plan when Quick piped up.

"We should ask Patel," he said. "He's smart."

I looked at him. "Who?"

Sullivan said, "Raj Patel." There was something in the ex-marine's tone—derision maybe.

But Manners jumped in: "Agreed. Ex-military intelligence. Smart guy. He'll know what to do."

Chapter 50

Frankie Dee's jazz club was packed, the air thick with cigarette smoke, sweat, and the sticky scent of rum. A trio was on stage, the piano man hammering out a slow blues number, but the real noise came from the crowd—sailors on shore leave, hotel residents nursing drinks, and tired men trying to forget the heat.

I pushed through the bodies, past a couple of American GIs playing dice at a table near the bar, and slipped through the side door into the backroom.

The air changed the moment the door shut behind me.

Frankie Dee was leaning over the table and looked like he'd just been talking. Manners sat with his arms crossed. Sullivan sat opposite, flipping a coin between his fingers with the air of a gambler. Leaning against the back wall was Miguel, the financial advisor. He raised a cigarette to his lips, casual like he had all the time in the world.

I hadn't expected him. I'd met Raj Patel earlier and he'd gone off to the senator's ranch with Quick. We would all reconvene in the back room of the jazz club.

We were now back and waiting for them.

"Ash," Frankie Dee said, "we were just debating again. I can get you in as musicians. Two of you at least."

"I still vote we hit them tonight," Sullivan said. "We should have been preparing this afternoon."

Dee said, "We agreed to hear what Raj has to say."

Miguel pushed away from the wall. "They torched the bar. They damn near killed—"

Manners grinned, the kind of grin that doesn't reach the eyes. "The kid's got fire. But fire gets you burned, mate."

"Is that a joke about the bar. If so, it's not funny."

"It wasn't intended. Doesn't change the truth. We go in blind, we probably die. Simple as that."

"You don't have the numbers," Dee cut in. "Or the intel."

Miguel shook his head, like that wasn't enough of a reason.

I looked at him, wondering why he was in the team. "Are you ex-army?"

"No, but I can handle myself. Give me a gun. Point me in the direction of the bad guys…"

Sullivan checked his watch. "They're late. Look, if Raj can't come up with intel, and we're not going tonight, I was wondering…" He paused, making sure he had our rapt attention. "I could go in there…"

"Go in there?" Manners challenged.

"Wait… hear me out. I go early tomorrow and see what they need. Everyone needs something. And they're having a party. I could say I'll supply it."

"Black market?" Dee asked.

"Probably. Don't actually have to get it, but I have the gift of the gab. I'll charm a girl… bound to be a girl who needs something for the party. Then, maybe, I get some inside information. For a price, I could get her to talk. Would be good to have someone on the inside."

Sullivan may have been about to explain more, but at that moment, Raj Patel and Quick entered the room.

Patel was originally from Bombay and claimed to have been a simple analyst, but there was something about him that suggested he'd been much more. I suspected his natural modestly prevented him from telling us otherwise. He was older than the rest of us by at least ten years. But he was still slim, with angular features, and tall—about my height. His skin tone was paler than the average Indian and dark eyes held an unusual piercing intelligence.

He nodded a silent greeting to us all.

Manners cleared his throat. "Let's have it, Raj."

Quick tossed a hand-drawn map onto the table. "Your money's worth," he said, grinning.

"The dimensions aren't perfect," Patel said apologetically. His voice was quiet but firm, the Queen's English rolling off his tongue with precise diction—a remnant of an Oxford education.

"He had me pace the whole thing out," Quick said.

Patel pointed. "Main house, here. Garage along the front to the left. Looks to me like there are rooms above."

"Probably the guards' barracks," Quick added.

Patel raised a gentle hand letting the young man know that he would be doing the talking. Quick nodded and took half a pace back.

"The fence around the main house is eight feet and there are ditches, here and here," again he pointed them out. "The adjoining horse ranch has a lower fence that would be easily scalable, but the only access from the ranch to the main house is through this gate." He indicated a gate in the fence behind the stable section. There was an office or lockup of some kind beside the stables that they hadn't been able to see into.

"That's where they'll keep food and medicines," Sullivan said. "I've seen something similar before."

"The staff live onsite," Patel continued, "in the ranch house. They'll be out of the way at night. Just the guards to worry about."

"And the dogs."

"Dogs?" Manners said, frowning. "I hate dogs."

I said, "We don't need to worry about the dogs. They won't be out during a party."

Patel met my gaze and shook his head. In the corner of my eye, I caught Quick hopping about, desperate to speak.

"We're not waiting until the party, are we?" I said.

Patel shook his head. "We asked in the town. People know about the party and they talk to the staff. There will be over a hundred guests at the party, but that's not the reason. We can't wait for the party because Senator Delgado is doubling his security for the event. We have to go sooner."

"Tonight," Sullivan said, suddenly alive with anticipation.

"Not tonight," Patel explained. "We need more intelligence. We have the layout, but I want the exact number of guards and their shifts."

We agreed I would go tonight. Then Manners and Sullivan started talking about the approaches while Patel wouldn't get drawn into the debate. His eyes suggested he had a strategy but wasn't ready to discuss it. Like he'd said, he wanted more information.

"We'll need equipment," Manners said.

"I can source it," Sullivan promised. "Just need to know what's needed."

"We're going in hard," Manners said raising an eyebrow. "Mate, we'll need…"

Sullivan shrugged. "They don't call me Spider for nothing."

"Why *do* they call you Spider?" Quick asked.

Sullivan waggled his fingers. "Many hands, my friend."

Manners shook his head. "Spiders don't have hands, mate."

"Whatever."

"I'll provide the outfits," Patel said, cutting through the abrupt tension. "Black clothes for everyone… unless you have…?"

Except for Manners and Sullivan, we accepted the offer, although I saw doubts. What would the Indian come up with?

"Transport," Patel then said showing his palms. "I have a truck we could use, but it has the company name. Perhaps…"

"We won't use your truck, Raj," I said. "We've got Wolfe's Jeep."

"We need another," Patel said. "Even if everyone squeezes into the Jeep. Backup. Contingency. We need at least two vehicles."

"I'll source other wheels," Miguel said. He was still leaning against the far wall, and I'd almost forgotten he was there.

We talked about specific requirements, but I could see Manners's and Sullivan's minds were elsewhere now.

Finally, Manners said, "Raj, what's the most likely approach?"

"This route," Patel said after a moment's consideration. He tapped the northeast corner of the map, "this provides cover all the way to the main building. The trees are dense here. Then circle round to the service gate entrance."

Sullivan turned to Manners. "How long to crawl through that... half a mile of jungle?"

"Doesn't matter how long."

"Not to you, maybe but the rest of us..." Sullivan traced a line with his finger along the eastern perimeter of the property. "I prefer this route then cut the fence. Approach from the rear."

Manners sighed because he'd already argued against it.

"Probably suicide," Patel said. "It's open ground about two hundred yards."

Sullivan pushed away from the table. "And your way takes too damn long. We'll be spotted before we even reach the gate."

I watched them from a few feet away, letting the argument play out. When assembling a team like this, you had to know when to intervene and when to let men work out their differences. Patel was methodical to a fault— years of intelligence work had made him cautious, deliberate. Sullivan operated on instinct and opportunity, seizing openings without question. Both approaches had their merits.

Manners was different again. I figured he was fearless and would happily charge in, but he also knew the importance of a plan and intelligence. Probably learned by bitter experience.

Sullivan interrupted, leaning over the map. "You've been reading too many British field manuals, mate. In the real world, shit happens. Guards smoke, take leaks, change routines."

Patel's face remained impassive, but I noticed his jaw tighten slightly.

"Men who rush in without proper planning tend not to rush out again."

Sullivan snorted. "Worked well enough in Guadalcanal."

"We're not in Guadalcanal," I said, finally joining the conversation. "And this isn't a war."

Both men looked up at me, momentarily silent.

Manners said, "Sure as hell feels like a war."

I shook my head. "There are too many civilians. Our objective is the extraction of the evidence from the senator's safe. I'll go tonight, gather the intelligence Raj needs, then we agree our plan."

Everyone was silent although I thought Sullivan was brooding rather than focused.

"We move tomorrow night. Get some rest, get what we need"—I looked hard at Sullivan, who nodded—"and we reconvene here tomorrow at midday."

Chapter 51

"You ever been to Borneo, Ash?" Manners asked me. We'd driven to the senator's once the meeting ended. I was going to get the guard routine. Manners insisted on joining me. He wanted to see the lay of the land for himself.

Others had also wanted to be part of the overnight reconnaissance, but Patel persuaded them that everyone else should get rest. I would take Quick in the morning so that he could be the scout. While he checked for any changes and counted people, Patel and I would finalize the plan.

I'd suggested a 4 AM attack. Patel wanted to know guard movements for at least two hours before that.

The moon was nearly full and the sky clear. Perfect for surveillance, not so good for a sneak attack. The weather could change abruptly, and I prayed that tomorrow would be less clear and bright.

I found a secluded spot, hidden from the road half a mile off. Then we hiked to the senator's place. I found a good tree and climbed. Manners headed out and round to check the approach from the far side.

I made myself as comfortable as I could. It was quarter past one and I had about three hours of surveillance ahead.

From my elevated position, I used binoculars and took notes of people-movements and timings. Time dragged, but it was worth it. Two guards permanently circled the grounds in opposite directions. Not perfect synchronisation, but reasonably predictable. They changed every ninety minutes. Two new men came out of the garage block. I saw the gatepost guard change twice and judged they rotated every two hours.

No guards came and went from either the main building or the ranch. Downstairs lights were on in the ranch but then in darkness before two. The main house had lights on upstairs and down throughout my watch. I saw movement inside, downstairs. Possibly two separate people. Possibly guards.

At four thirty with a stiff neck and aching right side, I returned to the Jeep. Manners was waiting.

"All good?" he asked.

I nodded and pulled away. "Providing they don't change the routine tomorrow. How's your route?"

"It's achievable, but challenging," he grumbled.

"Even for you?"

"Even for me. Daylight recon, would identify the best route. In the darkness, it was hard to judge. Can't risk using a light." He breathed out loudly. "Looks like Spider might have been right."

We returned to the Bayview Hotel. I couldn't sleep at the ruined Crazy Bear but there were no available rooms.

Manners offered me his bed. I declined and he rigged up something on the floor for me using cushions.

Before retiring, he poured himself a tumbler of whisky and asked me if I'd been to Borneo. The ceiling fan spun lazily overhead, barely stirring the humid night air.

I shook my head. "I never made it that far west. Spent most of my service in British Palestine."

Manners nodded slowly, his eyes focused somewhere beyond the hotel room window. "Jungle's different there. Thicker. More alive somehow." He took a measured sip of his drink. "Spent eight months there with my commando unit. Six of us dropped in to work with the locals against the Japanese occupation."

Sullivan had told me that Manners didn't talk about his war service much. Something about the coming operation must have stirred old memories.

"We called it Operation Semut," he continued, rolling the glass between his palms. "Ant, in the local language. Because that's what we were—tiny, almost invisible, but everywhere at once. We'd move at night, always. No flashlights, no cigarettes. Just the moon when we had it, and our hands when we didn't."

I stayed quiet, sensing he needed to talk, perhaps as his own way of preparing for what lay ahead.

"Had a guide, local Dayak tribesman. Man could walk through a dry riverbed without leaving footprints. Taught us to move like shadows." Manners's voice dropped lower, almost a whisper. "The Japanese had this garrison near Kuching. Intelligence target. High-value officers coming and going."

He finished his whisky in one swift motion. "Three weeks we watched them. Learned their rotations, their blind spots. When they ate, when they slept, which ones drank before their shifts."

"Like we'd ideally need at the senator's place," I observed.

Manners gave me a look that made me feel like a schoolboy who'd missed the point. "Difference is, we weren't planning to get out, Ash. Not right away. The oppo called for intel gathering, but also disruption. Long-term harassment."

In Malaya I'd come across men from Force 136. They'd been a clandestine unit during the war. Working with Chinese communists, teaching them guerrilla tactics and jungle warfare. It had changed them. And I wondered how much Manners's experience had change him. Did he have crazy thoughts? Did he wake up screaming at night? Maybe staying in his room hadn't been such a smart move.

Manners was still talking. "After we hit the garrison that first night, we didn't leave. We stayed for five days, hiding in the jungle not five hundred yards from their perimeter." A ghost of a smile touched his lips. "Every night, we'd take something else. Ammunition one night. Radio equipment the next. Small things. Nothing they'd immediately notice was gone. By the fifth night, they were shooting at shadows. Turning on their own sentries. Command was breaking down. When we finally pulled out, we left behind forty-three dead Japanese soldiers. Only three by our hand. The rest they did to themselves."

The implications hung in the air between us. "Psychological warfare," I said quietly.

Manners nodded. "The jungle taught me patience. Taught me that sometimes the greatest weapon isn't strength or even surprise—it's doubt. Plant enough doubt in a man's mind, and he'll defeat himself."

He leaned forward slightly, his voice dropping to barely above a whisper. "That senator, he'll be privileged and cocky. He'll think his walls and guards make him untouchable. Men like that, they panic when their certainty cracks. Makes them dangerous, yes. But also vulnerable."

I considered his words carefully. I'd told the team that it wasn't a war. "You disagree with my approach?"

Manners leaned back, his expression shifting to something more neutral, as if closing a door on those memories. "I think we should remember that we're not just going after documents, Ash. We're going after a man who believes he's untouchable. Those are always the ones who fall hardest."

He finished his second whisky and stood. "Get some rest. Tomorrow, we become the jungle."

As he walked to his bed, I couldn't help but wonder what other shadows Manners carried with him from those Borneo jungles. And whether those shadows would prove to be an asset or a liability when we stepped into the senator's world tomorrow night.

Chapter 52

Raj Patel was in his clothing and fabric shop on Rosario Street in the Binondo district. The street was bustling with Chinese, Indians and Arabs with a dense concentration of similar small businesses serving these communities.

Patel greeted me with a serious nod and showed me to the rear of the colourful store. Ladies in bright saris tracked me with something between intrigue and suspicion.

In a small back room, I talked through what I'd seen last night. Over the sketched map, I indicted the guard's routes and talked timings.

He asked about the dogs. I hadn't seen them actively used.

"Perhaps they are pets," he said.

"We can't assume they're not guard dogs."

"Agreed. We need to neutralize them beforehand."

We talked about the approach, options and scenarios. He didn't like that Manners hadn't found an easy route through the jungle.

"There's Spider's strategy," I suggested. "We go through the fence."

"It'll be a clear night again tonight," he said shaking his head. "Maybe one man could get across without being seen. The more men you use, the greater chance of being spotted. This plan requires stealth. Get inside and persuade the senator to provide the evidence."

Even as he said it, doubts crowded my mind. Stealth meant one man, a maximum of two, inside. But there were the interior guards. They'd need to be neutralized. And assuming we achieved that, we then had to get into the safe. Once they knew he was at risk, there would be an escape plan. We might get in undetected, but would we find the senator? Would he get away without revealing what was or had been in the safe?

We bounced around ideas, some crazy, some foolhardy, some downright impossible.

As we talked about requirements and strategies, it became clear to me that Patel had been more than the desk-bound intelligence officer he claimed. I let him lead the planning, his approach second to none. Every detail was considered, every contingency planned for.

I drove to the Crazy Bear and found Quick supervising the clean up again. He was full of nervous excitement as I showed him the map and talked him through the plan.

Then I drove him to the senator's place and left him with instructions. We needed final numbers and a way to deal with the dogs.

I'd brief the others, then return ahead of them, because Quick was going in first.

The rest of the team were already in the room at Frankie Dee's club when I arrived at midday. I could tell they were still waiting to hear the plan.

"Eastern approach?" Sullivan said expectantly. "Across the back garden?"

"No," Patel said. "Nor the jungle route." He looked at Manners who reluctantly nodded back.

I said, "We like the idea of stealth, but it won't work on its own, so we're going with both stealth and distraction."

Patel pointed to the map—the far side of the ranch house. "This area is hidden from the main gate and patrolling guards." He then drew a line from there to the edge of the paddock. "This route is exposed while the guards are here." He drew the route taken by the guards then marked when they could see the stretch of paddock. "It'll take forty seconds to sprint from the fence to the sheltered spot. There's just enough time during the patrols' blind spot. From there they wait until the guard is at the bottom of the garden. It's risky but they circle the ranch to the stables and wait there. When the time is right, they go through the side gate and get into the house."

Sullivan snorted. "You make that sound easy, but that'll be harder than crossing the paddock."

Patel nodded. "Yes, but that's where the distraction comes in. Quick will be the diversion. He'll go the same route and be prepared." He described what the young barman would be doing.

Sullivan said, "I'll need grenades."

"We'll need grenades," I confirmed. "Can you get them?"

"At this short notice?" Sullivan paused, thought then nodded. "I'll get them."

"What about the dogs?" Manners asked.

"They'll need to be neutralized," Patel said.

"I've already got quick working on it," I said.

I saw doubt in Manners's face but he didn't express it. "So who's going in?"

"You and I," I said. "There's security inside so it'll take at least two of us."

Patel said, "And more than two increases the risk of being seen. Spider and Miguel will go through the main gate. Maximum noise and confusion. All the timings have to be right. Quick will distract the exterior guards so that Ash and John can get inside. Spider and Miguel's job is to prevent any of the guards getting inside to help the senator. Frankie and I will be driver's and additional back up. We're not good for much." He bobbed his head in a kind of apology to Frankie Dee. "But we can drive, throw grenades and shoot when necessary. And we need to watch for the senator trying to make a run for it."

No one challenged this.

"So, the timings? When do we leave? When do we go in?" Miguel asked. Previously he'd been supremely confident. Now, as the mission became more real, I heard worry in his voice.

"Quick needs to be in place first. Fifteen minutes before, or earlier if the dogs still need to be neutralized. Then Ash and John need to get in place. I want them to go through the gate at about two fifteen." This was near the end of the gatehouse guard's two-hour shift. Patel argued that we should start when he was tired, looking forward to the end of his shift, and before the next guard was ready. I'd wanted to go later—around four o'clock—but accepted Patel's argument. He said, these were professional guards. Catching them half-asleep in the night, was unlikely.

Manners said, "Why about two fifteen? Why so vague?"

"Because of what you said yesterday," Patel said. "There can be variations. Quick needs to start the distraction at the right time. Get that wrong and we won't have the exterior guards running around, we'll just have a dead young man."

Manners nodded. "Fair enough."

Patel went over the plan, showing people's movements, the approximate timings, but more specifically, the triggers.

Dee had been quiet throughout the discussion. After the room quietened for the first time since Patel had started, he moved to the table and looked at me.

"I think I've a problem. The timing... When do we leave here?"

"I'll go first and brief Quick. The rest of you need to arrive by midnight. That'll mean leaving here at least an hour earlier."

Dee shook his head. "I don't think... I won't be able to get away by then because of the show tonight. I could cancel?"

"No," I said.

"Just a driver, Frankie. We'll be fine," Sullivan said.

"Last time, I was just a driver," Dee said sounding a little hurt. "I was needed last time. Raj and I may have different talents to the rest of you, but we contributed last time."

I looked at Patel. He gave a slight shrug, but I sensed there was something he was holding back. "You want to be involved, Frankie, but Spider's right. We've enough bodies for tonight's mission. That's no disrespect to you."

"I could cancel," he said again, less convincingly.

I shook my head firmly. "No. And if there's more to this. If we need you and your skills later, then you will be involved. No question."

Dee let out a long breath.

Patel changed the subject. "What transport have you got us, Miguel?"

The financial advisor grinned. "US Army truck. Old but works just fine. Acquired it from someone who owed me. Doesn't expect it back. Thought we might need a people mover, but it sounds like—"

"Can you modify it," Patel interrupted Miguel's rapid speech. "Steel bars on the front."

"Battering ram," Manners grunted.

"Sure, yes. I can get some bars welded on the front. Turn it into a fucking tank."

I caught Sullivan's eye and wondered if he was picking up the same nervousness that I was sensing from Miguel.

"Somewhere you can go—you and Miguel here? A bit of shooting practice? Get used to each other?" I asked.

"Two hours to get the equipment, then sure…" He gave an address in the shipyard. "A lot of noise and the sound is muffled."

"Anything else?" I asked. I looked at each of them and paused when making eye contact with Patel. He shook his head.

"I'll go ahead, and brief Quick."

"Collect your arms and the grenades for Quick at the shipyard," Sullivan said.

"Meet the rest of you here." I tapped the map. The rendezvous point. "Meet here at midnight."

Patel said, "The rest of us convene at the Crazy Bear at ten-thirty."

They nodded. We shook hands, full of bonhomie and eager anticipation. It could all go horribly wrong, but for now we weren't allowing ourselves to think about the negatives.

Everyone left to make final preparations.

I hoped Quick was all right, alone up north. I also hoped he didn't report significant change when we returned. The senator might realize that he needed more than four armed men to keep us out. Hell, it wouldn't have been enough to keep me and Wolfe out if it'd just been the two of us.

Chapter 53

I found Spider Sullivan and Miguel in a disused shipyard shed. Outside, the afternoon shadows were deep and clangs from the yard covered any unusual sounds.

I slipped inside, avoiding any curious eyes on the street.

"No, no, Christ's sake, hold it like you mean it," Sullivan was saying, his wiry frame bent over Miguel's trembling hands. "It's not a fockin' snake. Won't bite you unless you tell it to."

Miguel was holding a Smith & Wesson revolver like it might explode. His knuckles were white and sweat beaded on his forehead. When I first met him, Miguel had been cocky, a confident young man. I figured it went with his job and success. But I'd seen that confidence fade and now he looked scared. He had no military experience, not like Spider Sullivan. I figured this was getting real.

"How's it going?" I asked.

Sullivan straightened up immediately and scowled. He was a chameleon. I figured Sullivan could look like a businessman or a beggar depending on who he was selling to. This afternoon, dressed in dark clothes and a camouflaged baseball cap, he looked like what he was: dangerous. I noted canvas bag at his feet.

"Guns?"

"This one revolver and five Colts." He dipped into the bag and handed me a gun. A Colt 1911.

As I checked it, and the magazine, I asked how Miguel was handling the Smith & Wesson.

"It's not loaded. Just teaching him the basics."

Miguel winced.

"He's a long way from being a natural."

"Let me see," I said. "Aim and pretend to shoot at the target."

The young man raised the revolver, both hands wrapped around the grip like he was strangling it. Pointed at the bottles lined up less than fifteen paces away. His aim wavered as he pulled the trigger.

Click.

"How was that?" he asked anxiously.

"If there had been a bird in the rafters, you might have got it," Sullivan said.

I approached Miguel. "May I?" I asked, holding out my hand.

Miguel practically threw the gun at me, relief washing over his face.

The revolver was heavy, well-maintained. One of Sullivan's black market specials, no doubt. I stuck it in my waistband. Then handed Miguel the Colt.

"How does that one feel?"

"Better."

"Try again. Try and hit a bottle."

Bang.

Miguel's hands shook. "It was loaded."

"And you missed by a mile," Sullivan said.

I adjusted Miguel's stance, positioning his feet shoulder-width apart, and placed the weapon back in his hands.

"Breathe first," I told him. "Feel calm, then aim. Then squeeze—don't pull."

Miguel nodded too quickly. "Breathe. Aim. Squeeze. Got it."

Sullivan pulled a flask from his pocket and took a swig. "Been telling him that for twenty minutes. Kid's got the

257

shakes so bad he'd miss the ocean if he was standing on the beach."

Miguel's face flushed. "I'm trying, damn it," he muttered. "Never shot anyone before."

"You said you could do this," Sullivan muttered.

"And I will."

Sullivan looked at me.

"Try again, Miguel. Breathe, aim, squeeze."

Miguel raised the gun again, this time a bit steadier. He aimed at an empty bottle perched on a crate about fifteen feet away, took a deep breath, and squeezed the trigger.

Nothing happened.

Sullivan looked at the gun. "You clicked on the safety," he said with exaggerated patience. He reached over and flicked a small lever on the left side. "Now try."

Miguel aimed again, breathed, squeezed.

The gun barked, the sound ricocheting off the shed walls. The bottle remained untouched, but a chunk of brick exploded from the wall about two feet to the right.

Sullivan winced. "Jesus, Mary, and Joseph."

Miguel lowered the gun, his face a mask of defeat. "I don't think I can do this."

I looked at the kid—really looked at him. Twenty-two, maybe twenty-three years old. Still had acne scars. Hands soft from desk-bound work. Normally a young man full of confidence and self-belief. But this was different. This required a coldness Miguel didn't have.

"Maybe we're approaching this wrong," I said slowly.

Sullivan raised an eyebrow. "You think? I've seen blind nuns with better aim."

"You can run," I said to Miguel.

"Sure."

I looked around, picked up the chuck of brick that had come off the wall. It was smaller than I'd like, taking up half a palm, but it would do.

"How's your throwing arm."

Miguel's face split into a grin. "Give me a target."

"The middle bottle."

Miguel whipped his arm through the air and the stone flew, clattering a few inches above the target.

I found more chucks of brick and out of three, the second smashed a bottle. The third was just wide.

"Pretty good." I said reaching into Sullivan's canvas bag. My fingers closed around a hand grenade.

I handed it to Miguel, who took it with significantly more confidence than he'd held the gun.

"How does it feel?"

He weighed it in his hand then frowned. "You're thinking I do Quick's job. You want me to be the distraction?"

"Then what would Quick do?" Sullivan asked me. "He's no better with a gun than, Miguel here."

"And I don't think I can run like Quick."

"No," I said, "I was wondering whether he backs you up with the grenades."

"Backs me up?" Sullivan shook his head. "We don't know how many guards we'll be up against. Ash, I'm good but I can't do this with... with someone just lobbing grenades and hoping they take out the shooters. Manners might be able to take on an army, but not me."

We stood looking at one another, hoping for inspiration. Nothing came.

Eventually, Sullivan handed me the sack.

Miguel went to hand me the Colt but I held up a hand. "Keep practising. We'll work something out."

This hadn't been a consideration. We thought we'd covered our assumptions, but neither Patel nor I had considered Miguel wasn't up to it. A good job, Sullivan had tested him.

I had to find Patel and reconsider the plan. He'd think of something I hadn't.

That was my hope, but as I left the dockyard shed, I discovered things were about to get even worse.

Chapter 54

Raj Patel met me outside the shed.

"Your clothes," he said, handing he a top and trousers from a satchel slung over one shoulder.

I almost laughed with relief. They were normal. Of course he wouldn't give me oriental clothes. These looked perfect for the job.

He handed me another set for Quick.

His face continued to show the hidden thoughts I'd detected earlier.

"What aren't you telling me, Raj?"

He cleared his throat. "Is Miguel inside? I've his clothes too."

"What is it?" I challenged.

"Nothing."

"Be honest!"

"It's my wife. She's not well. I…"

"You're worried about her." I gripped his shoulder. "Look, Raj, the same goes for you as for Frankie. You are just a driver. We can do this without you."

His eyes lit up with hope. "But…?"

"Who will drive?" I thought quickly. "We don't need two men outside with a driver. They can charge in and leave the truck. We can block the senator's escape with the truck. I was worried about how you'd deal with it, anyway. This just makes it simpler."

He didn't look convinced.

"We can manage," I said with far more confidence than I felt. The plan was coming apart at the seams. I needed to talk to Manners, the most experienced member of the team. We'd carry on as though this was happening tonight, but if Manners had doubts, we'd call it off and reschedule.

That would be the smart move.

Manners didn't look up when I entered his hotel room, just continued his methodical work.

"Didn't expect you," he said, not breaking his rhythm.

Manners sat cross-legged on a worn bamboo mat, an unfinished glass of whisky at his side. Before him lay an olive-green cloth unfolded like a ceremony, revealing a collection of blades catching amber light from his bedside lamp. His large hands moved with surprising delicacy as he ran a whetstone along the edge of what I recognized as a British commando knife.

The stone made a soft, whispering sound against the blade. Sssshhk. Sssshhk.

There was something almost hypnotic about watching Manners prepare. Unlike Quick's nervous energy or Sullivan's constant chatter, Manners possessed a stillness that reminded me of predators I'd seen in the jungle. Economy of movement. Purpose in every gesture.

He turned the knife over, working the other side. His callused thumb tested the edge, and he frowned slightly. Not satisfied yet.

"We have a problem," I said.

Manners's eyes flickered up to mine for just a moment. "What?"

"Two problems, in fact. Raj's wife is unwell and he's worried about her. So, he's not coming."

"We'll cope."

"And Miguel isn't up to the job."

Manners stopped sharpening and looked at he hard. "What?"

"I've seen him… Spider's trying to teach him to shoot, but it'll take more than a lesson. The kid is more of a liability than support. He can be part of the distraction but we can't reply on him to contain the exterior guards.

Manners cricked his neck and took a slug of whisky.

"Why are we doing this?" The question surprised me. I expected Manners to focus on execution, not question objectives.

He tested another blade, this one small enough to conceal in a boot or sleeve. Its handle was wrapped in dark leather, worn smooth from years of handling. He balanced it on his fingertip.

"We need the evidence," I replied.

He nodded slightly. "Evidence is for courtrooms. We're not exactly officers of the court tonight, are we, Ash?"

I couldn't argue with that.

He said, "We're doing this for Wolfe."

Manners lined up his knives in a precise row, each blade gleaming in the lamplight. There was something almost ritualistic about it, like a priest preparing communion.

He said, "I should have been part of Operation Rimau."

"October '44, Singapore," I said.

He nodded. It had been a re-run of the earlier operation, Jaywick. That one had been successful. From what I knew of Rimau, everyone involved had been killed in battle or executed after capture.

He said, "I didn't go because of an injury. They were failed by equipment first. Later they were betrayed by a local, then by the rescue sub arriving late, and worst of all, betrayed by Command. Australian forces intercepted a Jap coded message about 20 commandos being attacked. They didn't respond because the Japs might have realized their code had been cracked."

I said nothing. Manners had survival guilt. The team had been wiped out, but he'd not been there.

He carefully folded the knives into a cloth and I suspected his mind was elsewhere.

After a long silence, he said, "In Darwin, they taught us that the most dangerous moment in any operation is the one you think is safest," he said. "But there was another lesson. It's not about numbers, it's about strategy. One man can do more damage than ten. We showed that with Operation Jaywick. I wasn't a hero, I just had a task and I executed it. We all did. As long as you aren't failed or betrayed, you will succeed."

Manners tied the bundle and tucked it into his canvas bag. He drained his whisky glass in a single swallow, then stood in one fluid motion.

"I don't need support," he said firmly. "We revise the plan. I'll take the guards outside. You go inside with Spider. He can run faster and pick a lock faster than me anyway."

"There may be too many of them."

He shook his head. "Like I said, it's not about numbers. Miguel can drive the truck, stay with it if necessary. Don't want to have to worry about him. He'll throw grenades and I'll sweep the grounds with a Tommy."

I figured he was talking about a machine gun.

He said, "Are you up for that, mate?"

"I am, but we need to make sure the others know what they're up against. We're two men down."

"Two drivers."

"And Miguel isn't the shooter we thought."

He nodded. "I'll tell them. And if this goes sideways, there's no middle ground. We either all get out, or none of us do."

I'd been military police, not commando, but I recognized the calculation in his eyes. Manners wasn't afraid of dying—he was afraid of failing the mission.

"We'll get what we came for," I said. "Same plan, rendezvous at midnight. If you don't turn up, we'll reschedule another night."

As I left his room, I couldn't shake the feeling that of all men we'd assembled for tonight's operation, Manners was the only one who truly knew what we were walking into.

Chapter 55

Quick was waiting at the rendezvous point when I arrived. I updated him with the changed plan.

I didn't like his facial expression. "What?"

"If John Manners is confident—" he started to say.

"This is not going to be easy, Quick. John made a good point: most dangerous moment in any operation is the one you think is safest. Confidence can get you killed."

"This could get called off," I said as he dressed in the black clothes Patel had provided. "If the others don't turn up, we'll try for tomorrow night."

He shook his head. "I was in the town... buying meat for the dogs... the butcher thought I was on the senator's staff. He talked about the security. There are more people coming because of the party. And they're arriving tomorrow."

That would be an issue. I started to wonder whether we'd have to reconsider Frankie Dee's plan to get us in as musicians. No, getting in and out with the evidence without triggering a firefight seemed impossible. We'd have to delay until after the party.

"But there's good news," Quick said, breaking into my negative thoughts.

"I've dealt with the dogs."

"Already?"

"Needed a plan," he said. "Also I needed to test the route across the field. Covered it in twenty seconds. No problem though the ground is uneven."

I didn't like that the young man had taken the risk, but it sounded like it had paid off. He'd scouted around and broken into the office beside the stables.

"Found horse tranquilizers," he said. "I was just going to give the dogs meat I bought, but now I've drugged it."

I took a calming breath.

"It's worked a treat," he said, happy with himself, unaware of my concern. "Hope I've not given them too much."

"Or too little," I said.

He nodded.

"And you're sure no one saw you?"

"No one. The routine hasn't changed. I've also been to the fence and cut the wire. I found a sack in the shed too, used it to hide under. From the gully, I watched the guards do three patrols of the grounds."

He'd used initiative but could have ruined the whole operation before it got started. He wasn't military trained. No point in being annoyed. And, I reminded myself, he'd prepared. He would be ready to breach the fence and begin the diversion. One contingency Patel had considered was around Quick getting into the grounds. If he hadn't, he'd have been running beyond the perimeter and been restricted by the jungle to the south-east.

Quick told me he'd seen six guards. When on duty there was one at the gate and two in the grounds, like before. They were sticking to the same route. Gate sentry changing every two hours. The patrol guards changing every ninety minutes.

He reported that he'd seen ten civilians. House staff and groundskeepers, he said, now safely tucked away in the ranch.

We needed to keep the fight away from there.

Quick had more good news: the side gate wasn't locked. Nothing to slow us down when we broke cover for the house.

We waited in our secluded spot. Insects created a background hum. Occasionally, larger animals cried out. I leaned against the Jeep and watched the road, hoping a truck would appear.

"The boss once told me that you military police types are all about justice," Quick had said quietly from the Jeep. "We're doing this for justice."

I considered the burned bar, thought about Gillie's body in the river, about Cortez bleeding out in the warehouse. He was right, this was about justice. And something else. Men like Delgado thought they could do anything, hurt anyone, because they had power. Tonight, we would show them they were wrong.

The minute hand on my watch ticked round to midnight. I wondered whether the rest of the team were coming.

Chapter 56

The US Army truck rumbled up the track to the rendezvous point. It was ten past midnight, but they were here. Manners, Sullivan and Miguel, all ready for action.

The truck had a chunky metal grill that seemed solid enough. Apart from the modifications, it looked military. Patel had liked the idea. The gate sentry would undoubtedly hear it approaching but the Army regularly patrolled the district. With luck, he'd not suspect our intentions.

We checked our gear, synchronized watches and went over the plan.

Quick would be our diversion. He carried a canvas bag containing the grenades. He'd go ahead of us, across the paddock, past the ranch house, then along the fence. He'd wait for the right moment. About two fifteen. We'd know because the first grenade would go off.

I checked my Barretta one more time. Fifteen rounds. Sullivan had obtained Manners an American machine gun at short notice. Not a Tommy, but Manners didn't complain. Much.

The two of them also had Colts: seven rounds in the magazine, one in the chamber. Each had two spare magazines. Standard .45 ammunition. The kind that stops a man, no questions asked. Reliable weapons for reliable men.

We hiked up the road. Then, hidden by trees, we watched the entrance.

The guard at the front gate was ex-military. I could tell by his stance. The way he held his weapon. A Philippine Constabulary-issue carbine, Manners whispered. Effective range about two hundred yards. Even if he expected trouble, he didn't know when or where it would start. Surprise. That was our advantage.

In addition to the gateman and guards patrolling the grounds, we located one more outside. He was currently by the garage. Which meant at least two more, either inside the house or above the garage. One of them was Goliath.

Sullivan and I jogged back to the edge of the horse field and circled it until we found the blind spot. Quick had already gone. I couldn't see him but was sure he'd be in position.

We hunkered down, waiting for our moment. We would be going through the side gate with a beeline to the main house.

I could see the kennels along the fence. The dogs were silent—assuming they were inside.

We'd talked timings, but as soon as the shooting started, strict plans would go out of the window. We all knew that. After the initial assault we'd have strategy and contingencies. Plus, Manners assured me, tried and tested whistle signals.

The diversion would start. We would be clear to get to the house. Then the truck would plough into the main gate, Miguel driving fast. The gate guard would come out shooting.

Manners would be there and take him out.

While Manners moved to the garage, Miguel would wait by the gate. His job was to stop anyone leaving, and—we prayed this scenario wouldn't happen—stop anyone arriving in support. He'd chosen the Smith & Wesson in the end, but would rely more on grenades if trouble approached.

Despite his lack of skill or combat experience, he assured us he would shoot, if needed. He seemed calmer now things were about to happen.

Right on schedule, the first explosion lit up the northeastern corner. one hundred yards from the main house. Far enough to be safe. Close enough to demand attention. The nearest guard reacted exactly as trained. He moved toward the threat, weapon raised.

His circuit included keeping watch over the side gate. He was now in the process of leaving it exposed.

The dogs stayed silent.

Thirty seconds later, the second explosion. Eastern perimeter and moving south. Classic misdirection. The rearmost guard hesitated. The other perimeter guard started running towards the explosion. Fifty yards apart, the two men effectively joined forces. Then moved to investigate. Standard response to potential flanking manoeuvres.

"Gate clear," Sullivan whispered, his voice barely audible at two feet.

We went through the gate and crossed forty yards of open ground in twelve seconds. Fast enough to avoid detection. Slow enough to stay silent. The closest guard was now moving back toward Quick's first diversionary location.

A third explosion came right on cue. Quick was leading them in an arc. Away from our direction of approach. Military deception. Patel had assured us; it always works if executed properly. And he was right.

The men changed direction, and both headed for the third location.

We were at the back door. It was locked and Sullivan took only five seconds to have it open. I'd have taken at least twice the time.

The door opened silently. No squeak. No alarm. Professional security. But not professional enough.

We slipped inside, the darkness enveloping us. The house smelled of furniture polish and fear. To our right, a laundry and then a kitchen. To the left, two closed doors, then a living room opened up, full of shadows and hiding spots. Ahead, the lobby and the sweeping staircase I remembered from last time.

The laundry was dark. Pale light through windows made gray shapes of appliances and hanging sheets. Upstairs, I heard light footsteps. House staff, not guards. Civilians. We'd talked about this. Even at this late hour, there might be civilian staff in the house. We didn't want collateral damage.

A shout from outside. I figured the fourth guard I'd seen at the garage had joined the two chasing Quick. Or maybe it was another one. Maybe more. Maybe Goliath was out there now.

Ex-commando Manners was allegedly good, but surely four or five would be too many for him. And they'd spot Quick. It was going to happen. Just a matter of time.

More shots cracked through the night. Hopefully wide. Quick already gone and running. Another shot.

"He'll be fine," Sullivan whispered, reading my concern. "That boy is fast."

Then deliberate confusion as Miguel thundered the truck into the front gate, blasting the horn. And Manners started shooting.

Return fire.

A grenade exploded at the front.

We reached the lobby. Everything was in tones of gray, no lights on anywhere, but I could the wide reception room beyond. The French doors into it were open, and I indicated caution. If they were ready for us, it would be a great place to lie in wait.

More gunfire. Manners again, I guessed.

We saw a guard run past a window then use the garage as cover. Manners would have despatched the man at the gate, now he'd have to handle the one by the garage.

"You sweep left, I'll take right," I whispered. "Watch the corners—ex-military, they'll know all the tricks."

Spider nodded, his face showing the intense focus I'd come to expect. We went to the French doors, my Beretta ready in a two-hand grip. Years of military police training guiding every step.

No sign of trouble.

We moved on, passed two more rooms and then left, down a corridor to the office.

The office was empty.

This had been too easily.

"Blow the safe?" Spider asked.

"They're waiting for us," I breathed. "Or expected us here and will tighten the noose. We go back."

He nodded. The playbook: find the senator first.

Chapter 57

We were back in the lobby, considering the stairs.

Two sharp whistles—Manners's signal. Someone was coming our way. Someone Manners couldn't deal with. Backup, maybe. Or more guards than Quick had spotted.

"One's coming in," Spider reported from his position by the window. "Others still outside."

We took up positions on either side of the entrance hall. Textbook ambush formation.

The man was good. He sensed the trap the instant he entered. He dropped and rolled before we could fire. Then he came up shooting.

I saw Spider's baseball cap fly off as he dived behind a marble pillar. My shot ricocheted and caught the massive chandelier. Crystal exploded.

The guard was shooting again. I couldn't see him, but Spider cursed. Anger more than anguish. I guessed he'd been hit, though nothing serious.

Return fire forced the senator's man back. He knocked over a table. Expensive wood crashed on expensive tile flooring. He'd done it deliberately for cover. Good position. He had control of the main entrance. But he didn't know about Spider Sullivan's training.

Spider fired three shots, spaced exactly half a second apart. Designed to make the target think he knew the shooter's position. The guard returned fire at the pillar. Empty air. Spider had already moved.

I fired too, drawing the guard's attention. Then, one second too late, he realized his mistake. Spider was behind him. Two shots, centre mass.

The sound echoed through the hall. Then silence. Heavy silence. Like the house was holding its breath.

"Clear," Spider called softly.

We could hear gunfire outside again. Manners against the remaining men. How many out there? How many in the house?

A whisper of movement to our right. The laundry or kitchen? Someone else had come in, flanking us. Spider melted that way, his footsteps silent except for the odd crunch of broken glass. I took three steps toward the stairs, then froze as I heard it—the slow, deliberate sound of heavy footsteps above.

The big man. Goliath.

I caught a glimpse of movement at the top of the stairs. Smart. High ground, protection.

The senator would be upstairs, too. In a safe room, probably. Goliath would have been securing him before confronting us. Or maybe the big man saw himself as the last line of defence.

Around me, wall lights suddenly blazed on. It would have been brighter if not for the smashed chandelier. Goliath stood at the top of the stairs. He looked even taller than last time. His bulk appeared to fill the entire width of the staircase, although shadows undoubtedly exaggerated the effect.

In the kitchen, I heard a scuffle start—Manners engaging whoever had come that way.

Goliath's stance told me everything I needed to know—he was ready for a fight, and he wasn't alone. Not the last line of defence. Movement behind him confirmed another guard, this one carrying what looked like a shotgun.

Goliath had hoped to draw me out by making himself a target. Meanwhile, shotgun man would have blasted me.

I ducked beneath the stairs, breathed, checked my gun.

We'd got the numbers wrong. More than six of them. The situation was deteriorating fast. Spider Sullivan was occupied in the kitchen, the sounds of combat growing louder. Manners was signalling movement outside. Maybe warning more were coming in.

He needed to deal with that threat.

I was facing a giant who had the high ground and backup.

I shot two of the six wall lights I could see. Then I bobbed my head out to check my opponents' positions.

Goliath smiled, and it wasn't a pleasant sight. He started down the stairs, each step making the wooden treads groan under his weight. The guard with the shotgun moved to cover him from above.

I heard dogs barking—they'd woken up. Not too much tranquillizer after all. Were they free? Did Manners have to cope with dogs as well as multiple gunmen?

Spider's fight in the kitchen reached a crescendo—something metallic clattered to the floor, followed by a grunt of pain. I couldn't tell if it was Spider or his opponent.

I had seconds to make a decision. Upstairs or kitchen? Goliath or Spider? The night was far from over, and things were about to get very, very messy.

Chapter 58

The decision was made for me when the shotgun blast tore through the banister where my head had been a second earlier. At the same time, the thunder of the big man's footsteps told me he was charging down the stairs. Trying to draw me out again, I figured. He'd be covered by the man with the shotgun.

I could wait, but there was also the man Spider had been fighting. If he came from the other side, I'd be exposed to him.

Fast decision: I darted through the French doors and into the reception room. The shotgun fired again with a splinter shower of wood and plaster.

As I found cover—a heavy leather armchair—I heard Goliath's tread. He was still coming, but now unhurried and confident.

From beyond the lobby came the sound of breaking glass and a heavy thud. I hoped that was Spider fighting again, not beaten after all.

I risked a glance around the chair. Goliath was at the French doors, his massive frame silhouetted against the light. The shotgun guard was also down, moving to a better position, trying to get an angle on me. Behind them, I caught a glimpse of a third man—smaller, quicker—slipping upstairs. Heading for the senator, most likely.

One sharp whistle from outside repeated three times. An urgent warning. More company coming. Thanks Sergeant Manners!

The shotgun guard would soon have a clear shot if I stayed put.

A crash from the kitchen again. Spider was still engaged, which meant I was on my own with Goliath and his friend. With more coming, if Manners couldn't deal with the threat.

Hoping the crash had distracted them, I scrambled for a sofa. There was a side table with a brass lamp and photo in a frame.

The shotgun boomed, and I saw bits fly from the chair I'd been behind.

As I dived for cover, I snatched the photograph. Using it like a poor mirror, I held it out and round the sofa. It worked. I could see the shotgun guard was moving again. He'd lost his line of sight when I went deeper into the room. Goliath was methodically moving furniture, cutting off my escape routes one by one.

Behind me, about ten paces away, were more French doors. The garden would be beyond. But if Manners hadn't neutralized the grounds' guards, then I was now exposed to someone coming that way.

Another blast from the shotgun, this one punched through the wall close by. They were getting impatient.

I had three rounds left in my gun, and rapidly diminishing options. The senator was upstairs, probably being moved to some bolthole or escape route by now. Every second we delayed increased the chances of him slipping away.

One long whistle from Manners. He was checking we were all right. I went to blow my own whistle, call for his assistance, but it wasn't there. I'd dropped it.

"Manners!" I yelled.

Goliath lifted a heavy oak table like it was made of paper, tossing it aside. "Running out of places to hide, Carter," he said, almost gently. "Why don't you come out? Let's make it sporting."

I checked my makeshift mirror again. The shotgun guard had moved—the angle was wrong now; I couldn't see him. But I could hear the creak of the floor as he tried to flank me.

From upstairs came the sound of a door shutting, then rapid footsteps. The senator moving, perhaps.

I had seconds to act. Stay here, pinned down by Goliath and the shotgun, while the senator escapes? Or make a move that would either get me killed or...

Decision time. I grabbed the heavy brass lamp from beside me, took a deep breath, and prepared to move. Sometimes the only way out is through.

I hurled the lamp toward the window, the crash of breaking glass filling the room. In the split second of distraction, I moved. I wasn't fleeing to the garden. Nor was I heading toward Goliath—that's what he might expect. Instead, I rolled right, into the open, firing two quick shots at where I'd heard the shotgun guard's movement.

A cry of pain told me at least one bullet had found its mark. The shotgun clattered to the ground. I was already moving, staying low, using the confusion.

Goliath reacted faster than I expected for a man of his size. He swung or threw something—furniture probably—at the space where I'd been, catching my shoulder as I dived for more cover. The impact sent me sprawling, my gun skittering across the floor. The pain was immediate and intense.

"That's better," he rumbled, advancing on me. "Now it's interesting."

Above us, more fast footsteps. The senator was on the move again, and I was running out of time. I scrambled to my feet, ignoring the screaming pain in my shoulder. Goliath charged, surprisingly quick, but this time I was ready. I used his momentum against him, sidestepping at the last second. He crashed into the wall, giving me precious seconds.

He growled and pointed his gun. But at the same second I expected a bullet, Spider struck. He came in low and fast, catching Goliath on the back of the knees. The giant staggered, and I launched myself forward, driving my shoulder into his midsection despite the pain.

Even with both of us, it was like trying to wrestle a bear. Goliath roared, throwing Spider aside like a rag doll. His massive hands found my throat, lifting me off the ground.

"Now," the giant breathed, "we finish this properly."

Through darkening vision, I saw movement. Was the senator making his escape while Goliath kept us busy? The other guards coming in? Spider was down, Manners was outside, and I was rapidly running out of air.

Stars burst behind my eyes as Goliath's grip tightened. In desperation, I drove my knee up—not toward his groin where he'd be expecting it, but into his elbow. The sudden impact on the joint made his arm buckle. Not much, but enough. As his grip loosened slightly, I got my fingers between his hands and my throat, buying a precious half-inch of space to breathe.

"The senator's getting away," I wheezed. "Is that what they're paying you for?"

His face twisted in rage. He slammed me against the wall, hard enough to rattle pictures off their hooks.

Through the spots in my vision, I saw Spider stirring, blood trickling from a cut above his eye. But he was still incapacitated. No help.

Behind Goliath, I saw the other man again, moving fast. A thought flashed in my head: *The senator's making a break for it!*

Two sharp cracks split the air. Goliath's head turned slightly. A natural reaction to sound, I thought as I used the opportunity. I drove my thumbs into the pressure points at his wrists, simultaneously snapping my head forward into his nose. Pain exploded through my skull, but his grip broke. I dropped, legs buckling, gasping for air.

The giant staggered back, but not from my headbutt. Manners was standing close, bloody commando knife in his hand.

Not another guard. Not the senator escaping. Sergeant John Manners coming to our rescue.

The giant guard hit the ground. Heavy and dead.

"Thanks," I rasped, my throat feeling like it was full of broken glass.

"Outside's clear," Manners said. "Five men dealt with."

"Quick?" I asked.

Manners grinned. "Fine. Now making sure the staff stay put, out of trouble."

"Dogs?" I asked because I'd heard their barks.

"No trouble. Awake but groggy and in their kennels."

Sullivan got up, wiped blood from his eye. He was all right. "If you don't mind, let's skip wrestling any more giants tonight."

I nodded. "The senator must be upstairs."

To Sullivan, Manners said, "Stay here, cover the stairs while I sweep down here."

I pointed to the stairs. "I'm going up."

"Soon as I'm done, I'll join you."

I managed a grim smile. "Let's finish this."

Time to find the senator.

Chapter 59

At the top of the stairs, I paused, straining to hear any sound that might give away the senator's location. I could hear Manners downstairs checking other rooms.

Occasional floorboards creaked. There were no lights on, just shades of gray. The hallway branched in two directions. Fifty-fifty. Doors on either side. No light coming under any of them.

Which way? I listened but heard no sound or sensed movement.

Given a choice, I always go right. It's a left-handed thing, I suppose.

I crept down the corridor, my boots barely making a sound. The doors lining the hall were all closed, and I knew the senator could be hiding behind any one of them. Heart pounding, I approached the first door, the handle cool and smooth beneath my palm.

Slow or fast? Not fifty-fifty. I kicked the first door open.

Crash.

If the senator was on the other side, he'd be waiting. probably armed. Shocking, explosive force was better than easing into the room.

I went in low. The room was dark, the furniture shrouded in shadows. I swept my gaze across the space, searching for any sign of movement, any indication that the senator was here.

Nothing.

Footfall behind me in the corridor and whispered reassurance.

Manners.

At the next door, I went high, Manners low. Once again, the room was empty. I gritted my teeth in frustration, my grip tightening on my weapon.

Where was the senator?

We continued down the hall, kicking open doors. Me high, Manners low.

No sign of the senator. I felt my tension rise with every empty space.

Was he hiding, or did he have an escape route? Miguel was outside waiting in the truck, watching the road. Spider had now gone outside and was sweeping the grounds. He'd go after anyone fleeing. That's why we told the staff to stay put.

I reached the end of the corridor. But it wasn't the end. A thin strip of light was the clue. A set of double doors formed a barrier.

Taking a deep breath, I kicked the one on the right. Hard.

Light spilled out.

Manners and I got in position. Counted down from three. Swung in. Me high, Manners low.

"Don't shoot!" Not the senator. The girl; his young assistant. The smaller figure I'd seen run up the stairs. She stood with her hands raised, fear evident in her eyes. But there was something else there too. Determination.

"He's gone," she said quickly.

My eyes narrowed. This had been a decoy. All that movement up here. We were supposed to think he was upstairs.

"He has a secret escape tunnel from the wine cellar," she said.

She was up against a wall. Not a plaster wall, wood panelling.

Her eyes betrayed her concern at me thinking about the panel behind.

"Move away," I said.

"The senator's not a bad man," she said desperately.

Manners pulled her aside.

I spotted it immediately: a vertical gap. Then I traced the line to a corner. There was a hidden door within the panel.

"They're coming!" she yelled bravely.

There may have been a switch to open it somewhere, but I kicked the panel twice and the door snapped open.

A secret office. Senator Delgado was there, standing behind a desk, a silver revolver in his hand. Despite the fear in his eyes, he still managed to look dignified.

"Drop it!" I said. "It's over."

He hesitated.

"We know everything, Senator. It's over."

He slowly put the gun down.

"He's done nothing!" the girl said, her voice finally betraying her fear.

"This isn't worth killing for, Carter," he said, then must have realized we'd eliminated his guards. The killing had already happened. "It's not worth killing me over," he corrected.

"Too late for that," Manners growled.

The girl began to cry.

I said, "You had Chrisanto Cortez murdered."

"The mayor's assistant?" The senator appeared genuinely surprised.

"Cortez *and* Martin Gillie, the reporter. Both murdered."

"No! You've got it wrong. That wasn't me... I didn't kill anyone. I'm just the money man in the deal."

"So, who did have them killed?"

He looked at me then his assistant. "Lucy, go!"

She choked back sobs. "But..."

"Go!"

She scurried from the room. We didn't stop her although I sensed Manners watch, making sure she wasn't going for a weapon. I heard hurried footsteps fade down the hall and guessed it had been her I'd heard before.

Then Manners called out to Spider, warning him that a civilian was on her way down.

Now that his assistant was out of earshot, the senator took a breath and nodded. "Mayor Lopez is the boss."

"The mayor?" I said.

"Yes. Not me."

"All the company information points to you," I said.

"Yes, but... If anyone arranged murder, it will have been him. My men... I was just keeping an eye on you, finding out what you knew. We could have killed you a number of times."

"We know there is evidence. I want the documents. All of them. The weapons deals, the reports, everything."

"Or what?" His voice was steady. "You'll shoot me? You'll shoot me anyway."

I had one bullet left. I only needed one.

Manners growled. "We'll tear this place apart. Blow every safe we find. We'll get what we came for."

Delgado looked from Manners to me, thinking for a long moment. "Perhaps we can reach a compromise."

"No deals," Manners said.

"Not even for proof of the mayor's involvement? Evidence that would bring down not just me, but an entire corrupt system?"

I said, "In return for what?"

"You let me go."

Manners scoffed.

I kept my weapon trained on the senator, considering. Exposing two corrupt officials would be better than one. And if the senator fled, he could be found later.

"I agree," I said.

"Ash?" Manners questioned.

"If the documents prove what Gillie believed, then it's worth it." *For him and others*, I thought.

To Delgado I said, "Show me."

He shook his head. "I want guarantees."

"You have my word," I said.

"You make sure I get away safely. None of your other men get me. Our deal is their deal."

I suspect he thought we had a whole army out there, not just Spider, a finance man, and a barman who could run like the wind. I nodded.

"And you give me forty-eight hours head start. You don't come after me."

"Twenty-four," Manners said.

"Deal?" I asked Delgado.

He sighed and moved slowly to a painting, swung it aside to reveal a wall safe. The combination clicked softly in the tense silence.

The documents he showed us were contracts and banking records. It all pointed to the company which we knew linked to the senator. He must have seen my doubt.

"The weapons contracts have Mayor Lopez's signature," he said. "They were for the rebels he... *encouraged*."

"There's evidence of deals with the rebels?"

Delgado snorted. "No. There aren't any contracts with the rebels. Lopez ordered the arms and had them shipped here. I had them delivered. But in stages. Guns for each job, which then got them more weapons."

"To force land sales."

He nodded.

"That you snapped up under the guise of Enexacion."

He sighed. "The Mayor had broader agenda. I wasn't comfortable with using the rebels."

"Of course you weren't," Manners said, his voice full of scorn. "All you cared about was the money."

"No one was supposed to get killed."

I shook my head at his weak argument, but we were getting diverted.

I said, "There has to be more... damning evidence of Mayor Lopez's involvement. So far everything points to him buying weapons. I'm sure he can explain that away. I need proof he wanted them to go to the rebels."

"We have a deal?" Delgado confirmed.

"We do," I said. "Providing—"

He fished out a contract.

"This is what you need."

I signalled Manners. He went to a window, opened it and blew his whistle. In return we got Spider's signal whistle—three short bursts. *All clear outside.*

"You can go," I said. "Hurry before I change my mind."

"You're more intelligent than I expected, Carter. You understand that sometimes justice requires... compromise."

He grabbed a bag and I realized he was already prepared for this.

I gathered the documents, and we strode out of the building. The night was eerily still after all the explosions and gunfire.

We regrouped by the garage. Quick was there, out of breath and soaked in sweat.

"Had them running in circles," he said proudly.

Miguel was waiting by the truck. One of the headlights was out and it listed to one side.

"Not driveable," Miguel said. He grinned and hopped from foot to foot, alive with adrenaline.

Spider Sullivan had more than the gash to the head. In the lobby, he'd taken a bullet to the shoulder. He'd ripped his shirt sleeve and created a bandage. I figured until it was cleaned it would look worse than it was.

"Just a scratch," he said.

We abandoned the truck and jogged back to the Jeep. As we left, I saw lights coming on in the staff quarters. Soon, I was sure, the whole place would be swarming with police.

I wondered whether Delgado would have a problem with them. Would he get away from the law? I didn't care. We had what we came for—proof of corruption that went beyond land fraud and weapons deals. Evidence that would bring down not just a senator, but a mayor as well.

Five in the Jeep: me driving with Manners riding shotgun. The others were holding on and undoubtedly uncomfortable, but no one complained.

As we drove back into Manila's darkness, I knew this wasn't over. The senator would run, but the evidence we'd taken would destroy his power base. I was sure I now had everything that would bring the whole crooked house down. The mayor would fall. And the truth about Gillie's murder, about the weapons and the land deals, about all of it—would come out.

But it wasn't over, because having the information didn't finish the job. I figured Hilary and the newspapers would make the information public.

I dropped Sullivan off at the hospital. His wound wasn't bad, but we insisted he get it checked. Quick and Miguel got off at Wolfe's bar and crossed the river to take Manners to the Bayview. I was going to Hilary's apartment, armed with the evidence.

Each farewell accompanied back-slapping and firm grips. We agreed to meet tomorrow morning. We'd reconvene in Frankie's Jazz Club and make plans.

They were excited.

I was excited. That was until I mounted the stairs and entered Hilary's apartment.

Chapter 60

Hilary's rooms were dark. The door was locked, everything in place, but something felt wrong. I found her note on the kitchen table: *Ash, going to speak to SA. Back soon.*

S Acosta, the author of the Oil and Minerals Survey.

"Damn it."

I'd been so focused on revenge, on planning the raid with Wolfe's team, that I'd forgotten the most important thing—keeping Hilary safe. She'd been investigating too, following her own leads while I planned the assault on the senator's ranch.

The note gave me no idea of how long she'd been gone, but my gut said, this was a long time. She hadn't left during the night. This was yesterday's note, and she hadn't come home. Hilary was in trouble.

Unless… I used her phone to ask the concierge to put a call through to Wolfe's bar, just in case she'd gone there.

She hadn't.

I decided to stay in the apartment in case—by some miracle—Hilary returned.

Sleep was impossible. Adrenaline from the raid still coursed through my system, now mixed with growing anxiety about Hilary. I spread the senator's documents across her kitchen table, hoping work would calm my nerves.

I was soon frustrated. The contracts were in Spanish. Hilary could have translated them. I had no hope.

Thirty minutes later, I was rousing Quick from a deep sleep and showing him the papers.

By around six in the morning, we had the complete picture. The weapons shipments, the fake rebel attacks, the land grabs—they were all connected. This was all tied back to the Oil and Minerals Survey. They had bought land with potential. The senator had been the chair of the committee supervising the surveys. He'd learned of the potential then delayed the reports. When the regions were identified as locations for mining and drilling, Enexacion would be ready. They'd sell the rights. The senator and mayor were sitting on land worth millions.

And Mayor Lopez had created a system designed to protect him. The companies led back to the senator. He'd signed a separate agreement with Delgado securing his unofficial assets. Delgado couldn't claim everything for himself. But the senator had been smart. He'd kept a copy for himself, prepared in case he needed to point the accusing finger. And that day had come.

I knew we had the damning evidence. But I'd also given up hope of Hilary's safe return.

She'd gone to meet the author of the surveys. Delaying their publication was critical to the success of Enexacion. Which told me that S Acosta was probably in their pocket. Hilary had undoubtedly walked into a trap.

Quick's initial excitement at us piecing the puzzle together soon vanished when I told him my suspicions. I sent him out to gather as much of last night's team as could make it.

It was 9 AM when I picked up the bar's phone and asked for the City Hall, then the mayor's office.

"Ah, Mr Carter." The mayor's voice was smooth, professional. "Good morning. I was hoping you'd call. Miss Wigglesworth and I have been having a fascinating discussion about journalistic ethics."

I sucked in air, unaware that I'd been holding my breath.

Hilary is alive!

My grip tightened on the receiver. "Let me speak to her."

"She's resting at the moment. Last night's interview became quite... intense."

"If you've harmed her..."

"Not yet, but the future depends entirely on you, Mr Carter. I understand you acquired some interesting documents last night. The senator was most careless with his filing system."

Of course, he knew about the raid already. The senator would have contacted him before fleeing. Or perhaps Lopez had received a police report and guessed the truth.

"I should have you arrested. Breaking into the senator's estate. Killing eight men."

"But you won't," I said.

He said nothing, confident, playing a game.

"What do you want?" I asked though clenched teeth.

"A meeting. Just us. Bring everything you took from Delgado's. Come alone and unarmed." He paused. "I don't need to explain what will happen if you don't comply."

"I don't have it all," I lied.

He said nothing.

After a pause, I added: "I need some time to gather everything. One of my colleagues took a briefcase..."

"Bring it all. How long do you need, Mr Carter? The clock is ticking."

"I'll call you back soon."

I hung up. Hostage negotiation training taught me to take control. By telling him I'd call back and ending the call before he could respond, put me in a stronger position. However, the worry brought bile to my throat.

I was staring at the documents, still trying to get my thoughts in order when Manners and Spider Sullivan arrived. Manners's Colt was stuck in his belt. Sullivan's arm was in a sling and the cut above his eye had been stitched.

"I'm fine," he said to my unasked question. "War wounds are good."

"The mayor has Hilary," I said.

Manners's hand moved instinctively toward his weapon. "We arming up again?"

"As I see it, there are two options," I said. "Go in shooting or try persuasion."

"I vote shooting," Manners said quietly.

I shook my head. "This conspiracy could go deep. No matter how many men we have, they'll probably have more. If I get it wrong, we could be up against the whole damn army."

Quick came back in followed by Patel, who looked fresh, unlike the rest of us who'd been up most of the night.

I checked on his wife and Patel said she was much better this morning. He felt terrible for abandoning us. Then he noticed the faces.

"What's wrong?"

"It's Hilary," Manners said.

"The mayor has her," Sullivan said.

Patel nodded, his face contorted with concern. "So, what's the play?"

We spent the next hour gaming out scenarios.

Finally, I saw the path forward. It was risky, but it was our best chance.

I called the mayor back. "Midday. I'll bring everything. Alone and unarmed, as you asked."

"What took you so long, Carter?"

"My friends didn't like the alone and unarmed part."

"Am I going to have a problem?" His tone was laced with implications. Any trouble and Hilary wouldn't be coming out alive.

"No," I said.

"Wise choice."

"Where?"

"The City Hall. One hour, my office."

"Twelve o'clock," I said, and put the phone down. Not one hour. I was in control, but felt acid in my throat.

I had two hours and needed to act fast.

First things first. I called Chief of Police Santos and then Major General Valdez at the Constabulary headquarters.

The others strained to listen in. I had a script to follow. Strict instructions for both men.

I prayed they'd do as I asked.

I prayed I wasn't wrong in my assumptions.

Chapter 61

Parts of the cathedral were cool and dark. Father Reyes listened to me without interrupting, then agreed immediately to my request.

"Sometimes," he said, "the church must take sides."

My next visit was to the Olympic Boxing Club. The conversation there wasn't as straightforward. The morning session had finished but Coach Happy Jose was still there. He listened to my request, shook his head, then listened some more. Finally, he agreed, though he clearly didn't like it.

"You're sure about this timing?" he asked.

"It has to be exact," I said. "Everything depends on it."

He nodded. "Then we haven't much time."

Thirty minutes to go.

I walked through the park and breathed, going over what I needed to do, how I needed to say it.

At eleven-fifty, I was ready.

Sullivan met me on the City Hall steps. He handed over a briefcase.

"Documents are inside," he said quietly. "You sure about this?"

"No." I took the briefcase. "But it's the only play we've realistically got."

"All right," he said. "I just needed to hear it one more time." He grinned without humour and was gone. He'd fulfilled one job, now there was more to do.

I climbed the steps slowly, feeling the weight of the briefcase in my hand. The mayor's secretary was waiting, ready to escort me up to his office.

This would work, or Hilary would die. Maybe both of us would. But in planning raids with the military police I'd learned that sometimes the best plan is the one your opponent thinks they've already figured out.

I just hoped I'd read this right.

The secretary opened the mayor's office door.

Time to find out.

Chapter 62

Mayor Lopez stood as I entered his office. He was pale and worried. But he puffed out his chest and tried to look confident. To the left of the mayor's desk, stood Chief of Police Santos, his face professionally blank.

We made brief eye contact. I switched my attention to the mayor.

For a long beat, we all stood and waited. Even the air tasted tense.

"Chief Santos," the mayor said smoothly. "This man is attempting blackmail. Please check him for weapons."

Santos's pat-down was thorough and found nothing. As promised, I'd come unarmed. I stood still, letting him work, watching a satisfied smile grow on the mayor's face.

Santos stepped back, his right hand hovering over his holstered gun. Had I got this wrong? I forced unbidden worries from my mind.

I said, "Is Hilary all right?"

"She is," the mayor said.

"Not good enough." I shook my head. "Let me speak to her."

In the scenarios we'd played out, the mayor had denied my request. Because Hilary was dead. As I waited for his response, my pulse thumped in my neck.

The mayor's eyes narrowed before he put me out of my misery. "Of course. I'm not an unreasonable man." He lifted his desk phone, dialled, spoke and waited. Then he said, "Miss Wigglesworth, I have your friend here. He wants reassurance." He handed me the receiver.

"Ash?" Her voice was strained, exhausted. "I'm okay. But listen to me—don't do anything for my sake. Do the right thing!"

"I will," I promised. "The right thing. Nothing else." I listened hard, hoping for background sounds that'd give me a clue to her location. I got nothing.

The mayor took back the phone. "How charming. Now, hand me the briefcase."

"Where is she?" I persisted. "After this, I want to know I can find her."

He thought for a second, then must have decided there was no harm. "Carcer Building. Room 412. Satisfied?"

"Room 412... Carcer Building? I don't know it."

He shook his head. "You'll find it. Now..."

I placed the briefcase on his desk but kept my hand on it. "Before I open this and hand everything over, we talk. I need to understand."

He glanced at the briefcase's locks, clearly considering forcing them open. But curiosity won out. "Talk about what?"

"About greed." From somewhere outside the building, I could hear a distant rumble. "About delaying geological surveys so Enexacion could buy land cheaply. Land that would be worth millions once the oil and mineral rights were public."

"Speculation," the mayor said. "Baseless accusations."

Chief Santos stood by the window, trying to look professionally detached. But I caught him glance at me, probably recalling our conversation this morning.

"Perhaps we could come to an arrangement," I'd said. "Regarding your involvement, Chief Santos. Your involvement is nothing compared to the mayor's."

Time to bring the chief into the conversation.

"Explain something. There was a rebel attack in Palawan."

Santos shifted slightly. "It was a regional police matter. It was handled."

"With new vehicles," I said. "New Volkswagens. Quite an upgrade for a provincial force."

"The funding was justified," Santos said quickly. "Given the circumstances."

"The circumstances being that you wouldn't report the attacks to the military."

The mayor's eyes narrowed. "Chief Santos handled the situation appropriately."

"Did he?" I looked at Santos. "Or did he look the other way while you supplied weapons to specific rebel groups? Pointed them at targets that would drive down land prices?"

"Nonsense," Mayor Lopez said.

"You don't understand," Santos said. "Resources were tight. The mayor... offered solutions."

He was a good actor. On our phone call this morning, I explained that I knew about the bribe of vehicles. I claimed I had the evidence, although it was just an assumption. It was the only piece I could fit to explain what had happened, why the attacks hadn't been reported. Reporting them might have helped funding, but it suited the mayor and senator to keep them quiet. And funding could be addressed in subtler ways.

So we struck a deal. Play his part and that minor infringement would be overlooked. He'd been coerced, he said. I agreed. It was nothing compared to what Mayor Lopez had done.

"Solutions like patrol cars," I said.

The background noise outside was growing.

"The department needed support." Santos was warming to his justification. "When rebels are active in new regions, we require proper equipment to respond."

"Even though you knew they were being armed and directed by the mayor?"

I hadn't mentioned arms on our call. He should have denied it, should have claimed ignorance. He didn't.

"The situation was complex," Santos said quickly. "Sometimes maintaining order requires compromise."

The mayor's face hardened as he caught up with the implications. "That's enough, Chief!"

"Is it?" I pressed. "How many died because of these so-called compromises? How many people were injured while you played along?"

"I had no choice!" Santos's mask cracked. "Do you know what it's like, trying to police these areas with limited resources? The mayor promised us proper funding. Equipment. Support."

"Support to ignore his weapons shipments? To let him arm rebels for his land schemes?"

"Better that than nothing!" Santos was fully committed now. "At least we got something out of it. At least my men got decent vehicles, proper equipment..."

"Chief," the mayor's voice was a shard of ice. "Be quiet!"

But Santos was too far gone, too convinced he was saving himself by playing along with me. He switched his gaze to the mayor. "You orchestrated the whole thing! The weapons, the targets, everything! And now you—"

"Stop, you fool!" the mayor shouted, and Santos finally stopped digging their grave.

"The senator's files prove your involvement," I said to the mayor. "You needed those landowners to sell. People like Rodriguez in Palawan and Flores in Quezon. So, you created rebel activity in peaceful regions. Supplied them with weapons, gave them targets."

"Ridiculous."

I tapped the briefcase. "The evidence is here. Contracts. Bank transfers. The land surveys that you suppressed. All of it." An exaggeration, but he didn't know the extent of what I had.

"I don't own Enexacion." he declared.

"No, you don't," I said. "It's Senator Delgado's name all over that, but he was smart enough to keep your contract. You thought you were protecting your share, but he knew it might give him leverage one day."

The mayor's desk drawer opened. A revolver came up smooth and fast.

"Open the briefcase," he said, pointing the gun at me. "Now!"

I didn't move. Chief Santos drew his gun, although he didn't aim it.

The background noise was louder now. Not a rumble or buzz. It was chanting.

"Chief," I said, "open the window."

Santos hesitated, then complied. The sound flooded in—hundreds of voices chanting in Tagalog, punctuated by a trumpet's clear blasts, whipping them up into a frenzy. I don't know what they were chanting but guessed it was along the lines of, "Down with the mayor".

"It's over," I said, "Everyone knows."

"Shoot him," the mayor suddenly ordered Santos. "Now!"

The police chief didn't move. "No. You're the criminal, Mr Mayor."

"Traitor!" The mayor's face twisted. "After everything I've given you! Backhanders for the vehicle contracts. Promises of more funding. You're complicit in all of this!"

Santos looked at me. "We have a deal, right?"

When I called him earlier, I'd let him think I could be bribed. Patel had felt sure our play would work. Greedy men always assume others are motivated by the same thing. I suspect Santos was ready to play it either way when we started. Now there was clearly only one horse worth backing.

I nodded.

"I'll take you down with me," the mayor said, now swivelling his aim toward the police chief.

Santos laughed mirthlessly. "You have no bullets, Mr Mayor. I removed them while you were getting ready. I, on the other hand, could quiet easily shoot you now. You threatened me with a gun. But"—he paused, savouring the moment—"there's no need. It's two against one here. And you won't say anything against me, anyway. Why? Because you'll be serving time and it'll be my men guarding you. Very easy for you to have an unfortunate accident if you don't behave."

The police chief was enjoying himself, demonstrating how smart he'd played it. He'd chosen his side and was relishing the clear path ahead. Maybe he was also imagining the accolades for bringing down a corrupt mayor.

Mayor Lopez's head dropped. Santos took the gun from his hand, and we exited the office.

Chapter 63

Outside, the crowd filled the square. Father Reyes stood with his congregation, holding signs demanding justice. Happy Jose and a group of young boxers had formed a protective line at the front. Patel's entire staff was there, the women's bright saris like flowers in the sea of protesters.

Frankie Dee's trumpet called out again, and the crowd roared in response. There was a group of hard-faced men that I figured had been recruited from the Army and Navy Club. They'd all come. And more were flooding in. Ordinary people who'd heard the news. Everyone had had enough of local government greed and corruption.

I scanned the throng for Sullivan and Manners but saw no sign. As soon as the mayor had confessed to her location, the two ex-soldiers had raced to find her. At least that had been the plan.

We stood on the steps, Chief Santos had the mayor by the scruff of his neck, an ignominious pose for the proud man.

I spotted Major General Valdez and raised the briefcase. He nodded and started toward us.

"Where are my officers?" Santos asked, looking at the armed men in black uniforms surrounding the square.

Valdez came up the steps, hand extended toward Santos. Not for a handshake—for his weapon.

Realization of my duplicity finally struck him.

"Police!" Santos shouted. "Civil police!"

"They're not coming," Valdez said, enjoying the moment. "My men are holding them."

"This is Manila," Santos protested. "You have no authority here!"

"Oh yes I do," Valdez said. "The mayor's being arrested and he's your boss. The civil police force will cede to my authority. The Constabulary is in charge. And Chief... we heard everything you said."

Santos's eyes bulged. "What do you mean?"

I held up the briefcase again. Alongside the documents was a hidden device. Patel had sourced and fit it, reinforcing my suspicion that he'd been a spy rather than simply military intelligence during his service.

I kept looking for Sullivan and Manners. Where were they? Had they failed?

My stomach twisted in knots.

Valdez said, "We've captured your confession about suppressing reports of rebel activity so that the Constabulary wouldn't investigate. About letting your own men die because the mayor promised you more funding. And about being complicit in a plan to support terrorism."

Santos seemed to shrink, his authority falling away like a discarded coat. Constabulary officers moved in, taking his weapon and badge.

As they led him away, I saw people moving fast through the crowd. Sullivan, Manners... and Hilary.

She's alive!

She bounded up the steps, and I met her halfway, embracing hard. She was unharmed, breathless and crying tears of joy.

Manners and Sullivan strode either side of us.

"Building was barely guarded," Manners said with professional disgust. "They got sloppy."

Sullivan said, "You did it!"

"*We* did it," I said. I noticed that Sullivan wasn't wearing his sling and blood from his shoulder wound had leaked through his shirt.

"I'm fine," he said, noticing my concern.

"How did you know?" Hilary asked softly. "That Santos would talk?"

"Guilt," I said. "He'd been justifying it to himself so long, he just needed someone to rationalize it for him."

She was still holding onto me, and I had no intention of letting go.

Chapter 64

The Crazy Bear was jumping. Frankie's band had the crowd swaying, the brass section punching through the cigarette haze that hung in the air.

After the scene at City Hall, hundreds wanted to help clean up the bar. Too many to help really, but it was now completely restored. Better than before. We had new furniture and my bedroom was, well, a proper bedroom rather than a storage room plus an old bed.

As soon as he was ready, Wolfe let everyone know there would be a relaunch party. It was just over two weeks since the fire.

Behind the bar, Quick and two new employees moved with confidence, pouring drinks. Wolfe was in the crowd trading jokes. Acting like the fire had never happened. Only the occasional catch in his breath—which he stubbornly denied—gave any hint of what he'd been through.

I nursed a Coke, watching his old friends cluster around him. They were full of apologies for their absence over the past year, but Wolfe waved them off.

"I wasn't exactly pleasant company," he admitted, his voice carrying over the music. "Sometimes a man needs to hit rock bottom before he can start climbing back up."

The crowd had spilled out onto the street, the warm Manila night alive with laughter and music. Jasmine, the editor's assistant from *the Times,* stood near the bar, looking elegant in a blue dress that caught the light. I'd introduced them. She'd been stealing glances at Wolfe all evening, and he was noticing. A definite step up from his usual companions, though I kept that thought to myself.

"Quite a turn-out," Hilary said, sliding onto the barstool next to me. She'd rejected an offer from *the Chronical* and written series of articles for *the Times*. They had caused quite a stir—the conspiracy to suppress the mineral surveys, the land grabs, the police chief's involvement, the senator acting as middleman with the rebels. The evidence might not all hold up in the legal court, but the court of public opinion had already rendered its verdict.

Hilary had been careful to credit Martin Gillie's groundwork and Cortez's courage in coming forward. They were the heroes. I was mentioned as Hilary's investigator although she avoided any mention of the shootout at the senator's estate.

As for Senator Delgado, there had been no sightings of him. The new police chief made sure the senator became a *Wanted* man. *Dead or Alive* was the usual heading with an eye-wateringly large reward. I figured Delgado would be found dead.

Sebastian Agosta, author of the survey report had been arrested and confessed to taking bribes. In return for a promised reduced sentence, he pointed at a couple of senior executives within the survey business who were also complicit.

A few minor people, including police officers, had been arrested but conspiracies always had hidden layers. I suspected there were other senior players who'd prefer Delgado didn't give evidence.

Wolfe had asked if I'd go after the senator. I hadn't decided yet. Possibly, but I had something more pressing to resolve first.

"Penny for them," Hilary said.

"What have you decided?" I asked, diverting.

"About?"

"Hong Kong." Since the first article, Hilary had been flooded with job offers, including from Edwards at *the Times*. But the biggest had come two days ago from Hong Kong. Senior Investigative Reporter at *the Telegraph*. Double the money she'd been earning before.

She looked uncomfortable. "It's a good opportunity..."

"It's an amazing opportunity."

"But..."

"Take it," I said, meaning it. "You've earned it, Wiggles."

She laughed, her face full of relief. "You're sure?"

"Everything is temporary," I said, using the line she'd used on me. "We just have to make the most of the time we have."

She hugged me. "We'll stay in touch. You could visit me."

"Of course."

"And I don't need to leave for a few more days."

I figured she'd already made plans to leave and bought the ticket. Which was fine.

"Good." We embraced and danced. Now that the decision was made and in the open, she relaxed and enjoyed the evening.

We circulated and chatted. After Wolfe had been with us for ten minutes then left, Hilary said, "He seems better."

"More like the old Bill Wolfe," I agreed. "Still grumpy. Especially that we got revenge for the fire without him."

"He was in hospital."

"Exactly!" I said. "He's still a grouch, but at least there's a sense of hope."

"We all need hope."

"Tomorrow Margarita Galizina returns to work," I said. She'd have a job, cleaning up after this massive party "That's the final piece falling back into place."

Well, almost final. Hilary must have seen something in my expression because she leaned closer. "You're not finished, are you?"

I shook my head. "There's still the matter of who took Margarita's baby. That thread leads somewhere, and I mean to pull it until something unravels."

The music swelled, Frankie's trumpet soaring over the crowd. Wolfe was laughing at something the pretty *Times'* assistant had said, looking younger than he had in months. The Crazy Bear was alive again.

But somewhere out there, someone knew what had happened to baby Isa Galizina. Why she'd been kidnapped and murdered. And they were about to learn that for Ash Carter, debts don't go unpaid.

But tomorrow would come soon enough. Tonight was for celebrating how far we'd come, and for watching old friends find their way back to themselves.

Frankie caught my eye from the bandstand and nodded. The next number was slower, softer. Perfect for Wolfe to ask Jasmine to dance, which he did. I smiled, remembering a conversation about timing. Sometimes things happen when they're meant to, not before.

Just like justice.

Just one more thing to resolve...

Chapter 65

I waved farewell to Hilary, bound for Hong Kong with promises and hopes. Before she left, I handed her a telegram from the War Office in London.

After she'd told me the story of her father, I'd contacted mine. He and I didn't get along, but I knew he'd help. He had contacts and access to information few would ever know or see.

She read the message. Captain Charles Wigglesworth, her father, had been recorded as boarding *HMAS Perth* when the Australian 3rd Field Regiment fled with others from Java. But he hadn't drowned or been captured by the Japanese. He never made it to the ship.

"There's a memorial in Anyer," I said. "He's buried there."

She cried and thanked me and then cried some more with relief. Then she said she'd visit Java as soon as she could. Closure.

I was sad to wave her off, but it was time to move on. For both of us.

I was ready to address the problem that had troubled me since I'd arrived less than six weeks ago.

Bill Wolfe also needed closure.

On the surface, he seemed like the old Wolfe, but he wasn't. I wished he'd been well enough to join us raiding the senator's estate. That might have prepared him better for this.

Wolfe had dealt with criminals in the Philippines, but not the kind of gangs we were looking for. Someone had kidnapped baby Isa Galizina, slit her throat and dumped the body.

It wasn't likely to be a big organization because they had made a mistake. Margarita Galizina wasn't rich. Her parents used to have money from a business, but they'd fallen on hard times. The ransom money wasn't realistic.

I figured the gang hadn't done their research or it had been opportunistic.

Fourteen months later, the trail was cold. Maybe it had been cold since day one—after Wolfe's trap had failed and the baby was murdered. The thought made my stomach churn. Life was too damn cheap.

My strategy was simple. Charge around, stirring up the hornet's nest. The activity would fire up Wolfe and with luck, we'd pick up a trail. We'd find one gang who would point at another and then another and eventually we'd run out of culprits... which also meant we'd have found the kidnappers.

Four days after the launch party, Bill Wolfe and I followed yet another lead down a tributary to the Pasig River. It was polluted here. The labyrinth of slums reeked of stinking fish and raw sewage.

I grabbed a wiry teenager by his frayed tank top as we passed an alley, ignoring his spew of Tagalog curses. "The Black Flags," I barked at him. "Where's their base?"

He tried squirming from my grip. "I don't know nothing, mister! Let me go!"

"Their base..." I repeated. "Where is it?"

"Down that way, three blocks," the teen eventually whimpered, pointing toward the docks. "By the fish market with the green awning. But..."

"But what?"

"You know the boss?"

I looked at Wolfe who shrugged his heavy shoulders. He'd given me the name of the local gang but nothing more. Again, I got the message that this wasn't the Bill Wolfe I used to know. In Israel, and Mandatory Palestine before that, he'd had a reputation for gaining information—the hard way. He'd use his fists first and ask questions later. Now, I read his expression. He hadn't held back on information; he really knew nothing more about Black Flags than he'd told me.

"Who's the boss?" I asked the kid.

He held out a dirty hand and I placed some notes in his palm.

He said a name in Tagalog, then translated it. "Junkyard Dog," he said. "And there will be an armed bodyguard on the door."

The hideout was obvious—men with dragon neck tattoos loitering outside a warehouse with blacked-out windows. The men were kids really. I saw no guns, and no one looked like the bodyguard we'd been warned about.

We entered in a rush, and I grabbed the nearest kid, shoving my Beretta under his jaw before his friends could react.

Wolfe aimed his gun at the mass of concerned kids. They weren't going to do anything.

"Kidnapping... About a year ago..." I barked. "Which of you scumbags was involved?"

My captive stammered that they didn't do kidnappings. I cocked my pistol's hammer and asked where I'd find Junkyard Dog. The kid squealed out directions to another gang flophouse. I dropped him and swept out, Wolfe following two paces behind.

"This is a waste of time," he grumbled.

I ignored his complaint.

Over the past few days, Wolfe's spirits had been high. His bar was buzzing, his friends were back.

Now that we were investigating his old case, he appeared to be sliding into his previous malaise. I had a gnawing sensation in my gut that told me I should have just gone with what I had. We'd made progress with his mood and maybe that had been enough.

Junkyard Dog's real den was crammed with what Americans call hookers and hopheads. I kicked open the door and punched the armed bodyguard before he finished blinking. Lights out.

Wolfe disarmed a hatchet man as screams erupted. I darted forward and pressed my gun's muzzle to the temple of the scrawny figure. He was lounging on a tacky throne surrounded by white powder and cash.

"The kidnapped baby..." My voice was like black ice. "Who did it?"

Junkyard Dog shook his head wildly. "What? Mister, the Flags didn't snatch nobody! We just run girls and powder! Please!"

My eyes blazed. "Then who did?"

I didn't think he'd talk, but after a moment's thought, he squealed out the name of a notorious thug called El Ciego—The Blind Man.

"Don't give me that! He's a fuckin' ghost," Wolfe growled.

The Blind Man wasn't supposed to be real, but Junkyard Dog had a look in his eyes that told me he was telling the truth.

Junkyard said, "He's Chinese. Part of an international gang."

"Where?" I asked. "Where do we find him?"

The bodyguard stirred but showed no sign of defending his boss.

Junkyard shook his head as he gave us a location.

"You're loco," he added.

"Probably," I said as we backed out, covering the mob in case they tried something foolish. They didn't. They just watched us with bemused eyes.

Bursting back into humid daylight we hailed a taxi and provided the address.

"We're wasting our time," Wolfe said. "He's a myth."

311

"We've found myths before," I said, referring to an old case.

He shook his head dismissively.

A short drive across the slums and we were staring at a crumbling Spanish-era mansion. It crawled with armed guards. Iron bars blocked windows. Brown marks—undoubtedly blood—stained a dirt courtyard. This was the lair of El Ciego. If Junkyard was telling the truth. If El Ciego really existed.

Whomever, we'd worked our way up the gang hierarchy, I reckoned.

"All right, assuming we find someone here," Wolfe asked as we got out, "what's the plan?"

"Follow me."

I brazenly strode through the front gate with dead eyes.

Men came out of shadows.

Sawn-off shotguns levelled at me. Bill raised his hands, but I brushed past. The men rushed in and I was immediately surrounded by a dozen guards, armed, safeties clicking off.

Before I could react, my Beretta was snatched away. The way they'd crowded around Wolfe, suggested they'd disarmed him too.

He grumbled something about the plan. I couldn't blame him.

Encircled, I saw evil-looking machetes and knives as well as guns.

A figure emerged from the dark mansion doorway. It was huge and formed into a man of equal stature—not particularly tall, but wide with rolls of fat. He had a shaved head, a neck thicker than my thigh, and a jagged scar where one of his eyes should have been.

"So, you aren't really blind," I said with mock surprise.

"Who the hell are you two monkeys?" he rasped, his voice full of phlegm and threat. "How d'you find me?"

"Junkyard Dog, gave us the address."

The bald, fat man spat.

I said, "Are you the one known as El Ciego? The Blind Man?"

"What if I am?"

"We need to talk."

The Blind Man grunted and started to walk away. "Waste them."

I turned to my friend. "Sorry, Bill."

Wolfe shook his head at me. I saw him ball his fists and tense his jaw. He was ready to fight and would do so to the death. I'd told him we could do this. He'd believed in me, and I'd charged right in, reckless as usual, and gotten us into a mess.

One hell of a deadly mess.

Chapter 66

"Wait!" I shouted.

The big gangster turned back and raised a hand. Hopefully, that told his goons to hold off chopping us into little pieces.

"I have something you'll want to see."

The Blind Man stepped towards me, intrigued.

Wolfe muttered under his breath. "This had better be good."

From my pocket, I pulled out an engraved gold token. "Recognize this?"

The Blind Man leaned in close. He reached for it but then changed his mind. He recognized it, all right. It was the secret symbol of the largest Chinese secret society in Singapore. An icon representing Andrew Yipp, a much bigger crime boss than the Blind Man. His reach went far beyond Singapore and I had no doubt, Yipp had dealings and friends in Manila.

That was the message. A symbol of power and threat.

A sign that I was protected.

But the truth was totally different, and I only used the token as a desperate measure. Use it once too often and Yipp would find out. Then the token wouldn't protect me, it would reflect a price on my head.

Because Yipp hadn't given it to me. His ward and mistress—my occasional lover—had. I'd found it among my things when I'd unpacked aboard the steamer. There had been a letter too, explaining why she hadn't escaped with me as planned.

At that moment, I'd wanted to charge straight back to Singapore to rescue her. But that would have been pointless as well as foolhardy.

I knew I was prone to reckless acts, especially when I thought women or children were at risk. But this was different. Su Ling could have fled with me already but had chosen to stay—because she had a son and because the Yipp empire would come after them both.

Despite all my assurances, I couldn't protect Su Ling and her son.

So, I held out the token as a bluff. And despite only having one eye, I could see that the Blind Man recognized its significance.

I held my breath, unable to suppress the rising concern that Yipp was already after me. Had I just hastened my death sentence?

The fat man straightened, rolled his shoulders and grunted.

I breathed out. The Blind Man knew nothing of my betrayal.

"What do you want to talk about?" he said.

I asked him about the kidnapping of a baby. It had gone wrong. The baby had died.

As I spoke, the big man shook his head. "I don't do such things. And why would my brother in Singapore—?"

I held up my hand. "I can't provide details. I just need to know who did it."

Again, the big man shook his head. I was starting to wish he wouldn't. The fat in his neck rippled with the movement and made me feel nauseous.

"Who?" I prompted. "Tell me and we'll never bother you again."

"Not one of the main gangs." I could see him thinking. His one eye looked up as though searching his fat cranium. "Small... Maybe..." Then he gave us a name—Rojas—and a location in the City of Cavite.

In the taxi, Wolfe blew out a long stream of air. "You could have fuckin' told me! What is that coin? Some cloak of immunity?"

"No," I said, "just a one-time throw of a dice to get what we need."

He looked at me as though I was talking in riddles. Maybe I was, but I still wasn't ready to explain my entanglement with the Singapore mob—or my disastrous love-life. And perhaps I wasn't willing to embroil Wolfe in that too. He had enough on his plate without looking over his shoulder for Chinese assassins.

We found Rojas and three young men holed up behind a seedy gambling den. No posted guards, no perimeter checks. Not a proper gang, just kids.

We caught them completely by surprise mid-dice game. They tried to scramble away, but we had them subdued in seconds. Rojas shouted curses from underneath Wolfe's boot. I leaned down to mutter in his ear.

"The kidnapping. Talk!"

"What kidnapping?"

"A baby from Quiapo just over a year ago."

"You're crazy, man! I run bets, not snatch jobs!"

I looked at Wolfe. We thought we'd made progress. We'd gone up the chain, reaching The Blind Man. Now we'd come back down and found Rojas. He denied it, and I believed him.

No progress at all.

Wolfe picked Rojas up by the neck.

"Why did you take and kill the baby?" he asked, low and threatening.

Rojas paled, shaking his head frantically.

"I got morals, man! I wouldn't mess with no babies— that's sick!"

I believed him. Wolfe didn't.

He squeezed Rojas's throat until the kid's eyes bulged, then Wolfe let go. Rojas crumpled.

"Bill…" I said.

Wolfe kicked him.

Rojas tried to speak through blooded teeth.

"I think I know who might have," he managed to splutter.

"Who?" Wolfe growled, picking Rojas up by the throat again.

"I didn't snatch a baby!"

"Who?" Wolfe shook him until Rojas tried to speak again.

"A nasty kid…" Rojas gasped for air. "It would be his thing…"

"A name!" Wolfe said. "And by God—"

"Cezar," Rojas sucked in air again as my world started spinning. "He goes by the name of Cezar."

Chapter 67

The address Rojas provided was a warehouse, halfway back around the bay to Manila. The air was thick with dust and the lingering smell of fish. Moonlight filtered through broken windows, casting long shadows across empty crates and abandoned machinery. Our footsteps echoed on the concrete floor as we searched for signs of Cezar.

"Nothing," Wolfe growled, his voice tight with frustration. "If that stinking Rojas kid was making it up. If this Cezar's not real…"

"Remember my boxing match… the one I lost?" I said. "He beat me by fighting dirty, then didn't like it when I won the rematch."

"That was him?"

I nodded. "Cezar is real."

A sound from above made us both freeze. Metal creaked, followed by footsteps on the walkway. I gestured to Wolfe, and we split up, moving towards the stairs, checking above and around.

"Looking for someone?" The voice was familiar. Too familiar.

Cezar emerged from the shadows above, his shaved head gleaming in the moonlight. He wasn't alone; two of lads stepped out beneath the walkway, by the stairs. One had a metal bar, the other a chain swinging from his tight fist.

"You're a long way from the boxing gym," I said, keeping my voice steady.

Cezar's laugh echoed off the metal walls. "But not far from my territory. You should have asked around—Rojas answers to me these days."

My mind raced. Cezar was the leader. This had been a setup. Rojas had warned him, and we'd walked into a trap.

"How's the bar doing?" Cezar asked, a cruel smile playing across his face. "I heard it went up in flames pretty quickly. Old buildings, you know? All that wood..."

Beside me, Wolfe went very still. We'd both assumed it had been Mayor Lopez's assassins doing or maybe he'd told Chief Santos to arrange it and scare me off. We'd heard that Santos had arranged for a big fight in the bar, but no one had admitted to the fire.

"You?" Wolfe said, his voice barely a whisper. "You burned my bar?"

"Your friend here," Cezar jerked his chin at me, "needed a lesson in respect. Nothing personal against you and your Crazy Bear bar. Just business."

"Business?" Wolfe's voice had dropped an octave, thick with rage. "That was my fuckin' home!"

"Should have picked better friends."

Wolfe moved so fast I barely saw him. He charged towards the stairs. The two gang members in front of us moved to intercept him. They might as well have been trying to stop a freight train.

Wolfe crashed into the first man like a battering ram, sending him sprawling. The other swung his chain but Wolfe caught it, yanked the man off his feet, and threw him onto the first man. They were down in a tangle of limbs and curses.

Wolfe continued, up the metal stairs, the whole structure shaking with each step.

Cezar hadn't moved, that arrogant smile still on his face. Only now, as Wolfe reached the catwalk, did he step back.

"You want to dance, old man? Let's dance."

Below, I was dealing with my own problems. Two of more of Cezar's men had approached from behind. I backed up, so that I could see all four, holding them at bay with my gun.

"Don't get involved," I warned. "Let them deal with this one on one." They seemed to buy the suggestion... for now.

Above, the fight had begun in earnest.

Cezar struck first, a lightning-fast kick that caught Wolfe in the ribs. He followed with another to the thigh, showing kickboxing skills I'd suspected from our boxing matches. Wolfe grunted but didn't slow, pressing, trying to close the distance.

Another kick came in, but this time Wolfe was ready. He caught Cezar's leg and drove forward, slamming him into the railing. The whole walkway shuddered.

Cezar broke free with an elbow strike that opened a cut above Wolfe's eye. Blood trickled down his face, but he didn't seem to notice. His eyes were fixed on Cezar with a predator's intensity.

"Is that all you got?" Wolfe's voice was a growl. "Fuckin' parlour tricks?"

Cezar's face darkened. He launched into a combination of strikes—kicks, punches, and elbows flowing together. Some connected, most didn't. Wolfe kept going forward, absorbing the shots, getting closer.

Finally, he got what he wanted. As Cezar threw another kick, Wolfe stepped inside his guard and grabbed him. They crashed through a wooden office partition, splintering the wall.

I heard the impact from below, where I was still dealing with Cezar's men. All four were now spaced out. Two with iron bars, one with the chain and another had pulled a knife.

I sensed they were no longer happy to watch and wait. Which complicated things. I grabbed a piece of broken pallet and backed toward the stairs. If I could get up there...

The sound of breaking furniture drew my attention back to the fight above. Wolfe and Cezar had emerged from the broken partition, grappling furiously. Cezar tried to break free, but Wolfe's grip was like iron. They slammed into something wooden, smashing it.

Cezar's kicks were useless now. This was Wolfe's kind of fight—close and brutal. He drove his knee into Cezar's ribs repeatedly, each impact punctuated by a grunt of pain. When Cezar tried to headbutt him, Wolfe responded by picking him up and driving him through another partition.

They emerged again, covered in dust and splinters, Cezar's face showing fear now. He tried to punch, but Wolfe caught his arm and twisted. The crack of breaking bone was followed by a scream of pain.

The four gang members took a step toward me and I swept my aim across them.

"Not another step!"

Above us, Wolfe was growling. "My bar." His fist drove into Cezar's face. "My fucking home." Another punch. Cezar staggered back, blood streaming from his nose. "People... me... I could've been killed." A third punch sent Cezar to his knees.

"Please," Cezar gasped, holding up his good hand. "Stop..."

Wolfe grabbed him by the throat, lifting him off his feet. "Give me one reason."

"I'll pay... I'll make it right..."

"Not good enough." Wolfe drew back his fist.

"Bill." I'd made it to the stairs. "That's enough. Remember why we're here!"

For a moment, I thought he wouldn't listen. His whole body trembled with rage, his fist still cocked back. Then, slowly, he lowered Cezar to the ground.

I looked at Cezar's men, but they were backing away. Their leader had been defeated and this was not their fight after all, it seemed.

I bounded up the ladder.

"We want answers," I said, reaching Cezar.

He looked up at me, cradling his broken arm. All the fight gone out of him.

I pressed on: "Did you kidnap the baby... Isa Galizina?"

His eyes didn't deny it. No surprise at my question.

"Why? Why do it?"

"For money."

"They weren't rich."

"*They* didn't pay. And no, I didn't kill the baby."

I asked what he meant by 'they didn't pay'. He wasn't referring to the ransom although he'd hoped to get it. He'd been paid to take the baby.

Gradually, it all came out. And it made sense of a senseless crime.

Wolfe turned away, his face a mask of barely contained fury. He walked past me without a word, his footsteps heavy on the metal stairs. I followed, leaving Cezar to lick his wounds.

Outside, the night air was cool and clean after the dusty warehouse. Wolfe stood with his hands braced against a wall, his shoulders heaving with each breath. Blood dripped from his knuckles, leaving dark spots on the pavement.

Chapter 68

Baby Isa had been kidnapped on demand. The ransom was a smoke screen. The body? Well, it wasn't Isa Galizina's. I prayed to God that the dead child had already been dead and just used for the purposes of a convincing story. Without the body, Wolfe would have continued to search.

The mother would never have given up either. Human instinct, to hope for the best, believe the child is still alive somewhere.

So, the people who'd arranged this had arranged for a body. Evidence that she was dead.

Pablo, the father, had identified the body as Isa. Although he hadn't. He'd told me that the body was almost too awful to look at and her necklace had confirmed it.

I'd been troubled by his confession. There was no need to tell me about the necklace. Pablo Galizina had been crying. He couldn't make eye contact with me. I'd bought his story, but it had been a lie.

Now that I cast my mind back, I remembered how afraid he'd been when I first turned up. He thought I was the police. He probably thought I'd guessed what he'd done.

Cezar didn't know who had paid him for the job. And even if he did, it would have been a middleman. Maybe a whole string of intermediaries to protect the man at the top.

We had a good sense of what had really happened, but I needed Pablo to confirm it before we acted. Because if we were wrong, this could be even more painful for everyone, but most of all for Margarita.

When he saw me outside his café, Pablo Galizina ran again. This time he was in for a shock. Wolfe was at the backdoor waiting for him.

We met inside, Galizina pinned at the neck by Wolfe's grip. The father was forced into a chair and looked up at us like we were demons, ready to claim his soul. If he had one.

Maybe we were.

I said, "Do I need to explain why we're here?"

He stared at me, eyes wide, body trembling.

"Fine," I said. "Over two years ago you lost your job. You turned to drink. You gambled. You were, in some people's eyes, a good-for-nothing. And you made your hard-working wife, Margarita, work more hours. Then she became pregnant. A beautiful baby girl was born 20 months ago. Isa." I didn't need confirmation. These were the facts. I continued: "A couple of months later, you left home."

"She forced me out. It was—"

"Shut up!" Wolfe snarled.

"Margarita worked right up to the birth and returned to work within a month. Did she take baby Isa with her sometimes... to work?"

Galizina said nothing.

"That's a question!" Wolfe said. "Talk now."

"Yes," he said quietly. "A few times."

"But, then tragedy struck... the first one... Margarita was dismissed, accused of stealing silver. A candlestick. And despite a lack of evidence, Margarita was suddenly without her main livelihood, working for Señor Martinez."

I saw the reaction. A slight wince as I said her boss's name.

"And then the second... bigger tragedy... Isa was kidnapped and murdered." I paused. "Kidnapped and *allegedly* murdered."

"We found the kidnapper," Wolfe said. "A scumbag thug called Cezar."

"I don't know his name," Galizina said hoarsely, clinging to a truth.

"It wasn't a kidnapping for ransom," Wolfe said. "The man was paid to take your baby."

"Not me! I didn't pay—" The denial had no force in it.

"No," I said. "At that point you had no money, but then you did, suddenly. Miraculously. Not a new job. You set up this café with the proceeds. Cezar was paid and *you* were paid. Your job was to identify the wrong body. Your job was probably to ensure Margarita believed the lie. Why? Because there is no way she would have accepted payment for her baby."

"We think we know where Isa is. And we'd like you to tell us."

"What will happen to me?" he asked. "If I talk?"

"I don't know," I said.

"But if you don't..." Wolfe took out his gun.

We'd discussed this. I didn't want Galizina to fear anything but the truth. I didn't want threats because they can lead to more lies.

However, I needn't have worried. Pablo Galizina told us what we had expected.

Señora Martinez smiled as she met us in her entrance hall. She dismissed the girl who had answered the front door, asking her to check on 'Little Maria'.

A nanny, I thought.

Señora Martinez had an elegant dress hugging a fine figure. She was a Filipina and I placed her at late thirties, possibly older, and in good condition. The family were well-off.

"How can I help you gentlemen?"

325

"Could we sit?" I asked.

"Of course."

We were shown into a sumptuous sitting room. As we took chairs, she asked if we'd like a drink. We declined.

There was a painting on the wall. The Martinez couple, a few years earlier. He was an attractive man, dark hair, not graying or balding. His skin was the same as ours.

"Your husband's not from the Philippines?"

She frowned, then smiled again. "No. He was born in Spain. Is this about my husband?"

"No. It's about Little Maria," I said.

She froze and swallowed.

We waited.

Her eyes first flicked between us. She sat straighter, her jaw tense.

"What about my daughter?"

"You know," Wolfe said.

She swallowed.

"Why?" I said. "Why take another woman's child?"

Thoughts flashed behind her eyes. Maybe she considered denying the truth. But then she took a ragged breath. "Because I..." she choked up, wiped an unbidden tear from her cheek. "I can't have one."

"You could have adopted."

She nodded. "Isa was so perfect. Her skin was fair. Her father was a drunk. Her mother couldn't afford to raise her. It was better for the child. She'd grow up loved and wanting for nothing. I know it was wrong, but I became obsessed. I wanted her. It seemed to be a message from God. She was my Maria. Mine."

"She wasn't yours," I said quietly.

Her frame trembled as she breathed in. "Davide... my husband arranged it. He said Margarita couldn't look after her baby... and her husband didn't want to know. Davide sorted it and my Maria was here. I had her." Tears flowed freely now. "I couldn't let her go."

Señor Martinez was a director of an insurance firm. The police arrested him at his office a few hours later. They also arrested his wife and Pablo Galizina.

Isa and Margarita were reunited. Wolfe paid for the nanny from the Martinez household to help with the transition. She turned out to be delightful, so much so that after the month Wolfe paid for, the girl continued to visit and help Margarita without charge.

The kidnapper, Cezar, was never found although there were rumours that a big white man had 'dealt' with him and disposed of the body.

I suspected Wolfe had done something. He disappeared for two days and came back looking tired but satisfied.

Later, I questioned if it had been him.

He denied it.

I'd found my old colleague, and he'd rediscovered himself. My job was done.

I thought about resuming my journey to Hong Kong. Hilary would be there. She could have asked me to go with her but hadn't. And, I already liked life here in the Philippines. Why start somewhere new when I had a ready-made group of friends and an office? Granted, it was a bar called Crazy Bear with an old Juke Box and a stuffed, singed grizzly.

Wolfe might not want to be a private detective, but I figured there was plenty of work here for me.

THE END

Also by Murray Bailey

Ash Carter Singapore series:
Singapore 52, Singapore Girl,
Singapore Boxer, Singapore Ghost,
Singapore Killer, Singapore Fire.
Singapore Rain, Singapore Worlds,
Singapore Blood

Ash Carter Near-East series:
Cyprus Kiss, The Killing Crew,
Troodos Secret, The Prisoner of Acre,
Dead Man's Run
Wolfe's Gambit, Wolfe's Shadows,
Wolfe's Traitor

Philippines series
No Safe Place to Hide

Blackjack series:
Once A Killer, Second To Sin,
A Third Is Darkness

Egyptian Stones series:
The Heretic Cypher, The Mark of Eternity,
Codex of the Gods

Yanhamu stories
Scorpion and the Tomb, The Second Truth
The Lost Pharaoh

Anthologies
Singapore and Other Stories Vol. 1
Singapore and Other Stories Vol. 2
Singapore and Other Stories Vol. 3

Other
Black Creek White Lies

Printed in Dunstable, United Kingdom